doghornpublishing.com

Editor: Deb Hoag
Cover art by Ashlyn Fenton
Design and typesetting by Adam Lowe

Published by Dog Horn Publishing, 2014

First published in the United Kingdom in 2014 by
Dog Horn Publishing
45 Monk Ings
Birstall
Batley
WF17 9HU

doghornpublishing.com

British Library Cataloguing-in-Publication Data
A cataloguing record for this book is available on request from the
British Library

ISBN: 978-1-907133-44-2
Printed and bound in the UK.

In memory of Janett L. Grady

ABOUT THE COVER ARTIST, ASHLYN FENTON

Ashlyn Alexandra Fenton is a part-time recluse, part-time wandering artist based in western Canada. She has won the Dorothy Gardner Award (three consecutive years) and Mixed Media Award from the Alberta Community Arts Club Association, participated in various art shows and does graphic design and fine art, both personally and as a freelancer. Ashlyn has a love for all things dramatic, outlandish and twisted. Her central belief is that reality always needs a healthy dose of the fantastical and thus she's often busy escaping to other times and worlds through movies, visual art, music and the written word. Her passions include playing dress-up, drinking ludicrous amounts of coffee, flirting shamelessly with boys, researching medicine and biology and trying to entertain her friends and family. For more of her work visit **lushlynx.deviantart.com.**

"The title *Dreadful Daughters* was such a wonderful concept to keep in mind while working on this cover," Ashlyn says. "It carries on the beautiful and terrible feminine themes from the first *Women Writing the Weird*, but 'daughters' in turn evokes the idea of one creative female force birthing another into existence. It was so poetic for me because, as I had the pleasure of reading through some of these brilliant stories, I could feel the images and ideas in them immediately begin to gestate in my mind, sparking my own creation. Alex Dally MacFarlane's character, Za, became so vivid in my imagination that I wanted to add yet another dimension to her existence. As a mother bears a daughter and a story inspires a work of art; the everlasting cycle of creativity."

We originally found Ashlyn quite by accident. Shortly after acquiring "Catfish Gal Blues" from Nancy Collins for the first *Women Writing the Weird*, Nancy posted a piece of art on her Facebook page that caught my attention. Murky and luminous, lovely and hideous at the same time, I spent the next two months trying to track down the artist – all I had to go on was her deviantart name, lushlynx.

Eventually we tracked her down and inveigled her into our weirdness. The result is the eerie, stunning, controversial cover of the original *Women Writing the Weird*: "Catfish Gal". Is it any wonder that I went straight to Ashlyn for our second cover?

It's a gorgeous illustration, based on "Fox Bones. Many Uses" by Alex Dally MacFarlane – completely different from the dreamy decay of "Catfish Gal", with its precise lines and noirish flourishes. And it perfectly sets the tone for the strong, strange and dreadful characters you'll find waiting for you in *Women Writing the Weird II: Dreadful Daughters*.

INDEX OF STORIES

INTRODUCTION

Welcome back for the follow-up to *Women Writing the Weird*. This time, we decided to narrow the focus a smidge, and chose a topic: *Dreadful Daughters*. I have to admit, when we first broached the theme, I envisioned receiving a ream of neo-gothic bad seed stories.

What I got is so much more.

Inside, you'll find a wealth of short stories featuring iron-willed heroines, soul-shredding monsters and hilariously misguided buffoons. Despite the vast differences in plot, circumstance and voice, our main characters all share one feature: they are women – mothers and daughters, sisters, midwives and waitresses, heroines and traitors, cold-hearted huntswomen and decadent goddesses.

I hope you enjoy this cornucopia of fiction as much as I did. I hope you feel as terrified, enthralled, uplifted and debauched while you read it, and that the stories linger in your mind for a long, unsettling time. And that the next time you see the woman in your life, be it lover, mother or daughter, you pause and check for the hidden blade before she envelops you in her loving, familiar arms.

– Deb Hoag, Series Editor

HUNTSWOMAN
by Merrie Haskell

EDITOR'S NOTE

Merrie Haskell grew up half in North Carolina, half in Michigan. She wrote her first story at age seven, and now works in a library with over 7.5 million bound volumes. Along the way from here to there, she picked up a degree in biological anthropology. Her first book, the Middle Grade historical fantasy The Princess Curse, *was a Junior Library Guild selection and a finalist for the Mythopoeic Fantasy Award for Children's Literature. Her next two books are* Handbook for Dragon Slayers *and* The Castle Behind Thorns. *Her short fiction appears in* Nature, Asimov's, *and various anthologies.*

About this story, Merrie says, "The Huntswoman herself came to me in a blinding flash; it was after a long day of work processing course reserves at the library, which is tediously cross-eying work even as you are getting glimpses of fascinating feminist theory and literary criticism and a host of other subjects – but that day it was all Women's Studies courses. Instead of packing up and going home, I sat down and wrote a thousand words of the Huntswoman wandering her narrowing world. I picked it back up at a writing date later that night; the story unspooled like it had been meant for me to unwind. (This almost never happens.) I sat with it a week, heard some critiques that I should take out the bard, took out a wizard character instead, and realized I'd harvested something that had been planted in me long ago, when I first read Tanith Lee's Red as Blood *and Angela Carter's* The Bloody Chamber. *Whether this is the true harvest, I do not know."*

Well, yes, Merrie, I rather think it is.

In the morning, the huntswoman's gloves were clean again, and her boots creaseless once more.

The huntswoman left her darkening room in a corner of the castle and strode through the halls to the solarium, to find the queen sitting in a puddle of sunshine, pouring tea.

"Good morning!" said the queen.

"I suppose," the huntswoman said. She was cautious, and prefaced her decision as to the goodness of the morning with a glance through the wide windows of the solarium. She noted that the forest was still dead with winter, and brown of leaf. She noted the patterns of the birds in the icy blue sky, and nodded to herself. "It certainly has a look of promise about it."

"Tea?" the queen asked, hoisting the pot aloft suggestively.

"I suppose," the huntswoman said, and took a delicate bone china cup from the table. Held in her leather gloves, china became solid stoneware, and tea became milk. The queen raised an eyebrow but said nothing. The two sipped, one sitting and one standing.

The king hurried into the room, distracted and muttering. "Good morning, my queen, my huntswoman," he said, and took up a teacup at his wife's urging. It did not change in his hand.

He turned to the huntswoman with glittering, glassy eyes. "Did you find her?" he asked the huntswoman. "Did you find my girl?"

"No, sire," the huntswoman said, and bowed her head. Her daily defeat preyed on her.

The king's eyes shifted, and he looked both lost and angry. He slammed down his teacup without saying anything. It shattered. He left.

The queen picked up the fragments of china; in her hands they became whole again. The china pieces, coming back together, looked like the small fluttering of a bird. The queen looked up from her work, cradling the cup.

"No matter what anyone else tells you," the queen said, capturing the huntswoman's eyes with her own, "remember that you will be best rewarded by me. Just bring me the princess's heart, and her hands."

"Yes, my queen," the huntswoman said, and bowed her way from the solarium.

In the hallway, the bard appeared.

"Huntswoman!" He puffed from running to catch up to her. She waited for him.

"Huntswoman," he gasped, and leaned forward, propping his hands on his knees, trying to find his breath. "Phew. Huntswoman.

Have you had any luck with your quarry?"

"I report to the king and queen," she reminded him.

He looked at her shrewdly. "You report to the king, I thought; the queen is only the stepmother."

The huntswoman knew she had made a gaffe, but there was nothing to do but shrug one shoulder as though it did not matter.

"Let me ask you this: did you dream last night?"

She unslung her bow and rested its butt on the floor to lean against. "I don't know."

"You know," the bard said firmly, pulling an inky quill from behind his ear and a pot from his pocket. "There is no way you cannot know. Now, tell me. It's for posterity. When you rescue the princess, when you bring her back from the dark forest, it will be a grand climactic ending to my story, to be sure; but people are going to want to understand your motivations."

She closed her eyes and concentrated, trying to remember her dreams.

"I dreamed of my mother," she said at last. "I dreamed she came into my room and woke me and said, 'Your father is dead.' And instead of weeping, my heart opened up and a summer garden grew from it."

The bard was writing, struggling to flatten a scroll against his knee. "Yes. Yes, very good. What else?"

"Nothing else," she said.

"Oh," the bard said, disappointed. "Well, I'd like to interview your mother and father for this project. What are their names?"

"They have no names," the huntswoman said. "I am an orphan."

The good morning and all its promise quickly became an ordinary day without much pleasure. The huntswoman followed the game trails, but found no human footprint. She found loose feathers, and tufts of deer fur, and the white skeleton of a raccoon, but never a blood-red ribbon nor a shred of bright, snowy cloth nor a raven-colored hair from a little girl's head.

"She can't have gone far," the huntswoman told herself. "She only had slippers, and they were not very sturdy." She stared down at her boots, seeing how worn they were once again. "These days last for years," she told the boots.

They said nothing.

The sun retreated from the forest. The huntswoman returned to the castle for the night, where her bed would be harder and her window narrower than she had left them in the morning.

In the morning, the window had become an arrow slit, the table by her bed had become a tray, and the bed had become a cot. Almost no light crept in the tiny window to show her that though her gloves were clean once more, her boots now held a permanent crease at each ankle.

The huntswoman descended the many stairs to the solarium, where the queen sat bathed in gray light, staring at tiny rivers running down the windowpanes.

"Rainy morning," the queen said.

"I suppose," the huntswoman said. She looked out the wide windows of the solarium, at the drear winter-dead forest and the pattern of the clouds above it. "It certainly has a look of wet about it."

"Scone?" the queen asked, holding out a plate.

"I suppose," the huntswoman said, taking a scone. In her gloved hand, the scone became a crusty piece of bread. The queen raised an eyebrow.

The king came in, and took up a scone when offered by the queen. It did not change in his hand. "Did you find the princess?" he asked the huntswoman. "Did you find my girl?"

"No, sire," the huntswoman said, and bowed her head.

The king crumbled the scone and threw the pieces on the table, and swept from the room.

The queen picked up the crumbs, and in her hands they became a whole again. The pastry, coming back together, rustled like a mouse. The queen looked up from her work, cradling the scone.

"Remember," the queen said. "You will be best rewarded by me, if you bring me the princess's heart and hands."

"Yes, my queen," the huntswoman said, and bowed her way from the solarium.

*

The bard found the huntswoman in the courtyard.

"Where do you go today?" he asked.

She gestured with her bow out toward the dark, dreary forest. "As ever."

He peered myopically past the leafless briars that surrounded the castle, and shivered.

"What did you dream last night?" he asked.

"I think if you want to know what I dream at night, you should come into the forest with me during the day."

The bard looked at the dark forest again; the huntswoman held out a hand to him.

He turned away from her. She dropped her hand.

"Maybe you can answer a question for me," she said.

The bard half-turned, twisting his scroll in his hands. "What question, Huntswoman?"

"Why did the princess leave the castle?" she asked.

The bard shuddered, and moved close to whisper. "The queen watches all of us, in her mirror."

The huntswoman considered this. "So, the queen knows why the princess left?"

"We all know," the bard said, and his eyes slid away from hers. "The queen was jealous ..."

The huntswoman frowned. "Was there a fight? An argument, perhaps?"

"Many," the bard said. "They always ended with the princess screaming."

"Did she – "

"I've said too much." The bard scuttled away, sideways, into the shadows. "You shouldn't ask these questions," he said, disappearing.

The huntswoman strode off, through the gates of the castle, and tried to remember her dreams of the night before.

She had finally dreamed of the princess, for the first time since she had come to the castle and been named the huntswoman. She had dreamed of a little girl tearing blood-red ribbons from her snow-white skirts as she ran down a broad and sunlit path in the forest. In the dream, the huntswoman had been the little girl; in the dream, she had felt every stone in the path through the frail slippers, and had hated the dragging hem of her white dress.

In the dream, the huntswoman had stopped running while the princess ran on, sloughing the huntswoman like a cicada sloughs its skin. The dream-huntswoman had watched the little white figure disappear down the sunlit path.

Here in the waking, rain-dark forest, the huntswoman stared down the path ahead. This was the same path from the dream. She followed it cautiously, not daring to believe it was the same, and perhaps it was not; the dream path had been wide and flat, but this was no more than a rabbit's trail. The huntswoman's boots protected her from the stones of the path, and her vest and gloves protected her skin; nothing in the forest could touch her.

The huntswoman studied the ground for any sign of the girl's passage, following the dream's path from desperation. She had no choice; the king and queen would employ her until they died or she died. And though she was young, the huntswoman believed she would die soon; her boots would wear through and betray her in the forest, perhaps, or more likely, the window in her room would shrink to nothing and she would suffocate in her sleep.

The huntswoman broke from the cover of the forest and found a river she had never seen before. The sun broke through the rainclouds as well, and shone down on a mown, green bank. A clear path, strewn with pine needles, led upstream. The huntswoman followed the new path, and shortly came to a small cottage, with a door only half her height.

The huntswoman found a shadow beneath the trees and lurked there, waiting for sign of activity in the cottage; seeing none, she pulled her dagger out and moved cautiously to the front gate.

The gate was missing a hinge; the garden out front was overgrown, but verdant with unopened buds. She slipped the latch and went inside, where seven little beds, neatly made, lay beneath a veil of dust.

She came back out into the sunlight, blinking. A little man stood at the garden gate, staring sorrowfully at her, twisting a pointed red hat in one hand.

"This way," he said. "This way to see the princess."

The huntswoman was surprised. After all these years, that the object of her long hunt should be spoken of so casually by a forest gnome, yes, that was unexpected. She followed along, dagger in hand.

The little man led her upstream and across a bridge, to a meadow surrounded by cherry trees fragrant with pink blossoms.

On a platform lay a crystal casket, and in the casket lay a girl with raven skin and raven hair, wearing a snow-white dress with red ribbons. The dress was far too small: the bodice was tight across the breasts, and the legs stuck out from the skirt like hairy sticks.

"Here lies the princess," the little man said. "She came to us long ago, fleeing for her life. A curse caught her, and she fell into sleep like death."

"Us?"

"My six brothers and I. But they have all passed beyond; I am the last guardian."

The huntswoman stared at the perfectly preserved princess. "You knew she was the princess. Why did you not come to the castle for help?"

"The castle!" the little man said. "But the castle is where the curse came from."

"Indeed," the huntswoman said.

"Please," the little man said, and his red hat was a rag in his hands now. "Please, kiss her, and she will awaken."

The huntswoman stared down her nose at him. Her hunting leathers made her flat-chested, true, but she knew her features were feminine enough, and there was no denying the narrowness of her waist.

"I'm no man," she said. "And no prince, to break enchantments through the unbidden application of my lips."

The little man buried his face in his ruined red hat and wept.

The huntswoman lifted her booted foot and kicked back the lid of the casket. The crystal shattered into a thousand pieces.

The huntswoman took her dagger, and buried it to the hilt into the princess's chest.

The little man shrieked. "What! What are you doing?" He launched himself at the huntswoman, but she put out an arm and shoved him back. He fell to the ground.

The huntswoman slid the knife down, creating an opening. She reached in with both hands and pulled the chest of the girl apart, and took out the heart. She put it in her game pouch, as she would have with a pheasant brought down by her arrow.

"You work for the queen! You are the queen's huntswoman!" the little man cried, and attacked her again.

"I am not!" the huntswoman said.

"The huntswoman took the princess into the forest; only the huntswoman returned to the castle. You tried to kill her then, as you are killing her now!" This time the gnome knocked her over when he leapt onto her, punching and kicking.

She reached up and pushed him hard into a tree. He fell with a thud, and did not get up right away. The huntswoman stood slowly, trying to catch her breath; and then she knelt, and cut away the hands of the sleeping princess.

"No! No, no, no!" the little man shouted, but he did not come near, fearing her now, and knowing also that he was too late.

The huntswoman secured the hands in her game pouch as well. She sheathed her dagger and took up her bow. She left the clearing, left the crying man, and left the princess who had now neither heart nor hands.

The huntswoman strode through the forest toward the castle.

The briars grew thicker and crowded the path to the gate, and as she got closer to the castle, they tried to block her way. She pulled out her dagger and cut through them. They were fierce, piercing her gloves and lodging in the leather, so that with every movement she felt the thorns pricking her. But she hacked away until she reached the gate.

In the courtyard, the bard waited for her.

"It's over now," he said, staring into the forest. "You've brought the queen what she wants. Look at the noose she's pulled around the castle." He put a finger through the gate to touch the briars, which reached for him like yearning hands. He drew back his finger with a drop of blood on it.

"Those are not the queen's briars," the huntswoman said. "They tried to keep me from returning."

"But whose briars would they be, if not the queen's?" the bard asked.

"You are the watcher here, the recorder of events. You are more suited to interpret than me."

The bard fixed his eyes on her game pouch. He reached forth his bloodstained finger to point at the slight bulge. "There," he cried, poking the leather. "There lies the innocent's heart."

The huntswoman twisted away from the bard, but his blood remained, a smeared fingerprint on the pouch. "It was barely beating," she said. "Why do you not run and tell your master I have returned from a successful hunt?"

Before he could answer, the castle rumbled slightly, and all the doors and windows contracted a few inches.

"It's happening again," the bard said, looking fearfully up at the tower as though afraid it would fall on him.

"It happens every night in my room," the huntswoman said, and turned to walk away.

"Not like this," the bard said. "This – this is the end of all things."

He made a weak grasping motion toward the pouch. She sidestepped him, ready in case he should attack her as the gnome had. But when he could not reach her, he simply turned aside, shoulders slumping in defeat.

"I bear witness," the bard murmured. "I bear witness." He wandered away like lonely woodsmoke.

The huntswoman entered the castle.

The queen was not in the solarium, but the king was. He was hunched and silent, and did not seem to notice the huntswoman when she came into the room. She turned to leave.

"Huntswoman," he grated, and she saw that he held two pieces of a dinner plate in his hands. "Have you found her? Have you found my girl?"

The huntswoman watched him as he tried to push the pieces of the dinner plate back together, over and over again, the edges of the china grating against each other.

"She was never your girl," she said, and left.

The queen was not in the great hall. The queen was not in the kitchen; nor was she in the high tower, nor the low dungeon.

The huntswoman searched the rest of the castle and found nothing. Finally, she returned to her own room, and there was the queen, peering out the tiny crack in the wall where once a window had been.

"You were almost too late," the queen said, only half-turning. The queen held a finger in the crack, and a keen breeze whistled there, and a pale beam of light shone through.

"You know that I found her?"

"Of course," the queen said, and a silver mirror slipped from under her cloak and hit the floor, shattering like the crystal coffin had shattered in the spring orchard.

"Your mirror!" the huntswoman said, starting forward, far too late to catch it.

"Let it go. We've no need for such glass any longer." The queen's smile was serene, as always, though the crack in the wall grew smaller around her fingers, cutting into her flesh.

"The window – " the huntswoman said.

"Quickly! Let me see her. Let me see the hands and the heart of the princess," the queen urged.

The huntswoman opened her game pouch, but paused as she touched the flesh within. "How will you know they are hers? How do you know I haven't tricked you?"

"There was nothing else out there for you to find."

The huntswoman gave the heart to the queen. The queen cradled it in her free hand, and the heart began to beat. The huntswoman stared.

"The hands," the queen said. "Take them out, and put them on, over your gloves."

The huntswoman hesitated, unable to see how this could be done; but at the queen's urging, she took the right hand from her game pouch and slid the tips of her gloved fingers into the ragged flesh at the wrists without resistance. The hand slid onto hers, up and over the heel of her palm until wrist met wrist, melding flesh to glove and glove to flesh. In a moment, there was no visible sign that the hand was not her own, and it moved as though it were her own right hand; even faster, the same magic was performed with the left hand.

"Now, take the heart from me; place it in your chest."

The huntswoman, entranced, lifted the heart and pushed it through her hunting leathers, through her skin and bones. It continued to beat there, inside her chest, long after the flesh closed up around it.

In that moment, the huntswoman awakened, as she had not when a thousand princes kissed her.

A sudden brightness of light blinded her: the crack in the wall had blossomed into a window. In the corner, the narrow pallet had grown into a bed fit for the getting and bearing of royal children. By the bed, the wooden plank had turned into a writing desk suitable for the creation of both treaties and decrees.

The huntswoman blinked, looking down at her now creaseless boots and her dark, lovely hands. "What enchantment is this?"

"It is but the work of time," the queen said.

The huntswoman shook her head, bewildered. "I am ... lost."

"You were lost, perhaps, but you have found yourself again. Look through the window, my dear," the queen said, and the huntswoman stared out at the countryside through the wide window. She lifted her face to the summer breeze and smelled the air, and looked with wonder at the trees in leaf.

"It's beautiful, stepmother," the huntswoman said, clutching her new hands to her chest, feeling her new heart beat beneath her skin and her vest. "It's so beautiful."

The queen's eyes glowed. "As are you, princess, daughter."

GOING DOWN
by J.S. Breukelaar

EDITOR'S NOTE

J.S. Breukelaar is the author of American Monster *(Lazy Fascist Books, 2014). Her work has been nominated for the David O Campbell Award, the Million Writers Award and others, and has appeared in* Juked, Prick of the Spindle, Fantasy Magazine, Go(b)et Magazine, New Dead Families, *and* Opium Magazine; *and in anthologies such as* Women Writing the Weird, *among others. You can also find her at thelivingsuitcase.com.*

You may remember her from the first edition of Women Writing the Weird. *Her story was horrifying and relentless and I thoroughly enjoyed it. I couldn't wait to recruit her for* Dreadful Daughters.

When I asked her what led her to write this story, she replied, "Going Down is one of my earliest stories. I wrote it during a very lonely time, in 2007, when I had just returned to Sydney and knew nobody and had no friends. The story was originally called 'Sex and Death', inspired in part by a crazy party I went to in the 90s, and that very materialistic time over a decade later when no one seemed to have learnt anything. I submitted the story in 2008 to an anthology I was co-editing at the time. The editors could contribute because it was a blind selection process and four out of the five other editors hated my story – I mean they really hated it – and the fifth editor loved it. I wrote about the surreal experience of having your work chewed up and spat out in front of you in an article for The Nervous Breakdown *called 'The Fifth Editor'. I came out of that experience with an unpublished story and a lifelong friend."*

You can read that article at: thenervousbreakdown.com/jbreukelaar/2010/10/the-fifth-editor.

This is an interesting story on many levels, not the least of which is in figuring out who's really the monster here – there are so many to choose from.

By the time Nora starts flashing at the guests, the party's all by over.

Done and dusted. I'm no stranger to Nora's front bottom. None of us are, remember? Hadn't Isabel smiled just before in the kitchen, her unsmiling eyes flicking to me, to the guests and back to the plate of olives and dip, anywhere but at the wisp of black silk panties going down into the InSinkerator?

Isabel's twin brother Nick hugs the rail out on the balcony. Nora is his wife. She is sitting on a chair with her back to him so from where I'm sitting, it looks as if he has two heads, each facing in the opposite direction. The Balinese fish pond hums, Nick's knee balanced on its edge. His teeth clamp around a totemic cigar and in his hand he holds a glass of St. Germain, loosely, carelessly. His hair ruffles in the wind and the glass of golden liqueur blazes in his grip like a meteor. Six stories down, waves crash mutely on the rocks. I look away and text for a cab.

Rain, says Nora, I can smell it.

Her knees fan open and shut. Nick shudders. The ash clings to his cigar like a Pompeii cock. I rip its head off with my gaze and Nick looks at it for a moment, shrugs, and then drops it into the fish bowl where it disappears with a hiss. The breeze plucks at his shirt sleeve as he lifts his glass to his mouth. On his fine-boned wrist is a bulky watch, bristling with knobs and probably worth more than my house. If I had a house. He looks askance at his wife as if she were responsible for ruining his cigar. She pokes her tongue out at him and he turns back to the sea.

None of us know what Nick sees in Nora with her new money and old scars (her ex was in gyms) and it doesn't matter. She could flash her fanny all she wanted. In the end it is always the Nickabel story and always will be. Nick and Isabel Leontis, dizygotic twins, whose family had started off in elevators and are now major players in the people moving industry, or would be if it wasn't for the recession – Nick should be in risers, Nora would quip sourly. Nick and Isabel, united utterly, so that what one of them starts, the other finishes: sentences, jokes, gossip. A thought in the mind of one finds its expression in the words of the other. Nick takes a lesser human under his wing, like me, and Isabel finds a way to love them (or at least to use them, said Nora once, not meeting my eyes). Isabel feels the sting of a late summer mosquito, and it is Nick who is woken up by an allergic welt on his ankle at dawn. If Nick strikes out at a vindictive journalist who calls the Leontis family Caligula to the power of two, it is Isabel who makes penance by doing overtime at the rehab clinic in Old town, junkies being the guardian spirits of forbidden things.

The dim light of an oil tanker cuts into a violet horizon. On the balcony, candles splutter and talk dwindles to those sodden phrases about life and art you hear from people genuinely involved with neither. Bottles of Bollinger float in starlit slush. I look from between my bangs at Madame Snatch peeking out sly as a ferret beneath Nora's vintage Prada and I can hear it, like an echo, the morning after talk on the Esplanade, sun glinting off smart phones and shellacked fingernails, and Nora swearing that she'd blacked out, oh my god, couldn't remember a thing, like not even at what point in the night she'd decided to spill Victoria's secret and give her vejayjay some air.

You had to be there, we will say. But you'd wish you weren't.

Isabel has spent most of the night in the kitchen. Her husband, whose last name I can't remember, is at his telescope in a man cave somewhere in the loft, safe in the knowledge that Isabel's money will keep him in stars and mistresses forever. Her figure, sheathed in vintage Chloe makes a slim shadow in the kitchen. This is the year we are all wearing vintage. It is the year the Columbia explodes on reentry; Iraq falls and female bombers will self-destruct in Chechnya. Johnny Cash died last month. Sub-prime lending across the country will hit twenty percent of all mortgages before the Argentinian artist will finish laying out his second line on the glass top of the balcony table. I stare at the line until it bursts from the glass in a cloud of crystalline smoke and disappears.

Fuck, says the Argentinian artist.

Nick places his glass of liqueur on the edge of the rail with an exaggerated precision and I watch Isabel turn around from the shadows of the kitchen. Choosing one mind to live in, their bodies form a parentheses; one sentence to inhabit, they punctuate each other's waking dreams. There were rumors of a child somewhere raised by a relative in Greece. It was all so ethereally hip, gushed a gossip columnist, their parties attended ex Cathedra like a summons from the gods.

I pry myself out of a chair that looks like a post-apocalyptic bird's nest and weave across the balcony, tripping over the threshold in my cowboy boots. The darkness inside the loft is as absolute as an ice bath, and I gasp. Isabel is vaguely silhouetted in the LED glow from the kitchen and I make my way toward her. She has her back to me, and as my eyes adjust they fix on the two perfect mounds of her ass beneath the silk of her dress. My Cuban heels hammer across the slate floor and she turns at my approach, stares at me over the lip of a champagne flute without appearing to recognize me. I'm used to this. Ever since Nick introduced us at college, and she's always looked at me like that. I stand taller than I need to in my cowboy boots, but I'm sweating beneath the cheap material of my department store dress. It had been such a long and troubled summer, the year we are all in vintage. I'd read Steampunk and tried to write it, my own sense of arrival just out of reach, and I couldn't stop, although I wanted to, before I got there. I watched Saddam's statue topple and marines bristling with metal, veiled grandmothers gibbering over cardboard coffins. A confused and mournful season with Nora's muff blinking on and off like a broken traffic light, and that's when I learned I could make things move.

Without touching them. With my mind.

It had happened on a shopping trip of course. Not with my money. Of course. Isabel had summoned me to the loft, given me five hundred dollars to buy baby clothes at Nordstroms. And a toy, she said. Throw in a toy, something fun. But no dolls. I was to have the stuff wrapped and take it myself to the post office. She'd scrawled an island address in Greece, as if it were the first time. As if she'd never asked me to do this before. Like she couldn't remember.

It's me, Issy, I'd said. Okay?

She looked at me blankly before she remembered to smile.

Oh, she'd said, smiling. *Koritsi mou*. Of course it's you?

She had me at *koritsi mou*. Who doesn't like a bit of foreign tongue?

Oh, she'd said. What would I do without you?

She could have bought the stuff online of course, but Isabel never shopped online. Designers sent her things, which pleased her, but she thought shopping online was a stress. She liked people fussing over her, she laughed, in that jumpy way people have of covering their tracks. But not this time. This time she didn't want any fuss. No tracks.

Standing in the line at the mail store I'd noticed a rack of reading glasses in a wire display unit and I stared at a pair and made them fall to the ground. The floor was carpeted so no one heard, but there they were on the rack one minute and on the floor in the next. I looked around but everyone was on their phones or addressing their packages so I stared at the readers again and made them move back to their place on the rack. Black frames with a zebra stripe, I thought, wild. Did they have zebras in Greece? I took the readers off their hook and paid for them. The clerk put them into a slim case that looked a little like a kaleidoscope, and I untaped a corner of the parcel going to Greece, tucked the readers deep into the folded clothes and closed up the parcel again.

The inside of the loft is like a purple cave. I wonder where the maid is. Isabel wears a huge watch that matches her brother's – gifts they'd exchanged on graduation – but on her tiny wrist it looks like a hand cuff. I try not to think about her all over tan.

"Look," she says. "Nora's killing him."

Outside on the balcony, Nora is rocking back and forth on the chair and laughing at some joke that seems directed at Nick. Around her neck glitters a diamond and emerald pendant, her augmented breasts straining against the straps of her dress. Someone raises their hands in astonishment or supplication, a strobe moment, the whole thing caught in the candlelight like a *Tableau Vivant*.

"Her spending?" I say, turning back to Isabel. Nora's?

"It's finished him," she says and burps. "The clothes, the surgery, the parties."

Nick runs a hand through his hair and he looks around with a naked smile, like someone who's just spotted a whale, his lips forming a word I can read from here: Isabel. His eyes search for his sister;

unable to find her, he turns back to his fevered vigil. Isabel swallows a sob and reaches for her glass, sticky with gloss and half way to her lips, lets if fall to the floor with a priceless tinkle. A spreading pool of booze inches toward her bare feet. I make it move until it laps at her tiny toes, a tight sly lick I feel deep in my belly. All the light in the room seems concentrated on a diamond cuff on her forth toe, my own size nines planted firmly on the tiles. Nora had given me a pair of Kendo slippers last year – they were too big for her, she said, knowing they'd be too small for me.

A hollow roar bursts from the guests. They sprawl around the artfully corroded table. Sinking lower in their chairs, their bodies twisted like pole dancers, they'll wake up tomorrow with bruises they can't explain. We all will. Nora's hands ride higher on her thighs.

"Where will it all end?" asks the Argentinian artist, waving one hand feebly in the air. "The downturn ..."

In the awkward silence I watch Nick lift his other leg onto the fishbowl and crouch there like a gargoyle, his eyes fixed on the faraway tanker. Unseen wind chimes sing.

Someone says something about higher military spending and the trade deficit and Nora snorts. Her slip bunched at her crotch. The Japanese film maker, with whom Nick had tried to set me up, reaches across and inserts a joint into her trembling lips. Her false lashes flutter and her eyes narrow behind the smoke. I feel invisible in the kitchen, as if behind a one way mirror, but somehow she finds me through the glass, and gives a little wave. I wave back and send a glass of half drunk burgundy onto her bare thighs. She gasps, giggles. Nick stands unsteadily on the fish bowl, one foot on its lip, the other against the edge of the rail for balance, his shirt whipping in the breeze. An Australian actor is on the phone with his agent. Beyond the balcony, the ocean yawns as wide as a frog's mouth. Nora's rocking back on her chair, pushing with her feet against the table leg, pulling her slip higher and higher. I stare at the chair, at the bruises on the inside of her thighs exposed to the massed clouds, and I give the chair a little push. Alcohol and gravity do the rest, the back of the chair catching the edge of the fishbowl, not a heavy blow, but enough with Nora's weight to make Nick lose his balance, his arms raised like wings and the fiery flash of his shirt born on the wind.

The way they finally untangle their bodies and sit up in their chairs and their smiles freeze like throats cut, Nora's red fingernails sunk into the narrow strip of pale fuzz. Isabel howls.

"Nick!"

Someone bumps the table and Bollinger streams onto the floor like horse piss. Isabel's husband comes running, slips on the puddle of champagne and broken glass in the kitchen and knocks Isabel to the ground, her bare legs arms webbed with blood. She flounders like someone drowning, swimming first toward the empty space on the balcony where her brother was, and then paddling away from it, toward the elevator, down to where she thinks she can find him, or follow him. But she can't follow. And she won't find him, I try to tell her in the elevator, her hair and dress ruined.

No one will find the body, I say, holding her bunched fists, slick and salty, in my hands. They will think it's because he was washed away on the rocks, but that's not it. Nick didn't fall, I try to explain on the way down and again in the cab on the way to my place. He just took off.

I think she finally believes me, now that her daughter, who is also her niece, has come back from Greece to live with us. I still move things around sometimes, but what's hard is knowing how to move people, really move them, with your heart instead of your mind. I look up from the desk at my girls curled up together on the couch like a question mark, the zebra reading glasses looking wild on Issy, as I always hoped they would.

NON EVIDENS
by Nicole Cushing

EDITOR'S NOTE
Nicole Cushing is the author of the acclaimed novella Children of No One *(DarkFuse, 2013) and over twenty short stories published in the US and UK. Her work has drawn praise from Jack Ketchum, Thomas Ligotti, Gary A. Braunbeck, John Skipp,* Black Static *and* Famous Monsters of Filmland. *She lives with her husband in Indiana. She invites contact with readers via Facebook, Twitter, or (if one must be old fashioned about it) email (nicolecushingwriter@gmail.com). You can also visit her online home,* Laughing at the Abyss *(nicolecushing.com).*

Nicole says the following about the origins of "Non Evidens": "Non Evidens was written shortly before a visit to my parents, and gushed out of me quite easily. Like many people, I've never felt my mother has ever seen me for who I am. I've felt that – from birth – she never really 'got' me. Non Evidens simply takes that idea and renders it literally."

I loved this story, and the way it sucks the reader right in. Once you accept the initial premise, there's nothing to do but belt in and enjoy the ride.

When they did the sonogram and there wasn't even the vaguest fetal blob to show for it, Janet assumed the doctor had been mistaken. The missed period, the tenderness in her breasts – perhaps they were psychosomatic. Perhaps her body knew that her mind wanted a baby, and so tried to go through the motions.

"No," the doctor said, pointing to a grainy black-and-white image on his computer, "if you look right there, you'll see the umbilical cord. Your mind can't conjure that out of nothing! I suspect this is merely a case of *fetus non evidens*. Extremely rare, of course, but more likely in women like you, that is, approaching forty."

"*Non evidens?*"

"You're carrying an invisible baby. This means we'll need more frequent prenatal visits, of course. We'll have to do certain tests that will take a gander at the little tyke indirectly, through studying the movement of the amniotic fluid *around* the fetus. But it's nothing to be alarmed about."

"Nothing to be alarmed about?!"

"Mrs. Pruitt, let me assure you that hundreds of mothers in the United States, alone, are raising *non evidens* kids. There are support groups, there are – "

But she couldn't listen to it. Tears welled up. She felt a lump in her throat. She wanted to break down and sob, but she wouldn't permit herself to do so in public. What would the doctor think of her if she had a breakdown right then and there? What would all the young, radiant women in the waiting room think? Janet thought they'd think something like this: *That poor, older lady must have just been told about a birth defect.*

Janet spent a lot of time guessing what other people thought (not just there at the doctor's office, but at the grocery store, the gas station, and at her cubicle.) She suspected *lots* of people all across town looked down their noses at her, but that didn't make it any easier to bear the *particular* criticism of those who had a better knack than she for this pregnancy stuff. So she walked briskly out of the doctor's office without saying a word, ignoring his calls after her. Her shoes clip-clopped down the shiny linoleum tile of the hallway, into the lobby, and out the door. She kept her glance downward the entire time to avoid eye contact with everyone in the waiting room.

It wasn't until she shut the car door that she allowed herself to mourn the loss of visible offspring. "A freak..." she muttered to herself mid-crying-jag. "They'll stare at us!" She dreaded the oddity of the prospect. She'd be pushing a stroller that would – to all outside appearances – look empty except for a onesie and some blankets and people would still, no doubt, *stare* (even though there would be literally nothing at which *to* stare).

She let herself give in to the emotions for about five minutes, then dried her eyes before driving home. The word *freak* still echoed through the nooks and crannies of her brain. It took on a life of its own up there.

She waited until Greg was reading in bed to tell him the bad news. He was perusing the catalog for a company that sold model trains and accessories. He had a small set down in their basement, which he always wanted to expand (but could never afford to).

"I went to the doctor today," Janet finally blurted out. "He says I'm pregnant with a monster."

Janet's husband's mouth dropped open. Words eventually skittered out. "Honey, you mean we did it? We're really preg –"

"What part of 'with a monster' did you not understand?"

He placed his hand on her belly. He grimaced. "No. You mean something's wrong?"

"The baby ... well ... it didn't show up on the sonogram."

He shook his head, pursed his lips. "Hrmm?"

"I'm carrying a *fetus non evidens*."

"What in blazes does that mean?"

"An invisible baby, that's what. A monster, straight from an old horror movie. A zygote-Claude-Rains."

"You're assuming it's a boy," Greg said. The corners of his mouth crinkled in a little smile. "It could always be a little girl. I was sort of imagining we'd have a girl, for some reason. Anyway ... wow. Just. Wow."

"I know we've been trying so hard, honey. But do you think this is worth, well, *continuing*?"

"How far along did the doc say you were?"

"Eight weeks."

"Wow," Greg said. "Just ... *wow*."

"I just want the best, you know. And invisible isn't the best."

"But what if we try again and invisible is *our* best. I mean, I'm not saying I **want** an invisible baby, but if that's what we end up with, well, I could certainly love the child."

Janet cringed, as all the implications became more apparent to her. "We wouldn't have baby pictures. We couldn't watch over it at night to make sure it was still breathing. And what if it gets the measles some day? There'd be no way to tell."

Greg sighed. "I don't know what to say, baby. Except that I love you and I want us to have a family together. But I don't want you to carry a pregnancy you're not one hundred percent happy with. Why not take some time to think it over? Maybe go to a therapist and talk over the pros and cons. We can go together, if you want. I'll even call to make the first appointment."

Janet mulled it over for a moment. *Yes,* she thought, *let Greg go about doing that. That'll keep him busy.*

Then, the next morning, instead of going to work she went to the nearest abortion clinic. She felt bad for misleading her husband, but felt even worse when she saw the protesters outside. Did she recognize one of them? Was that the lady from two doors down? The one who sold her Avon? She decided to drive past. She even honked her car horn, as requested by their signs, pantomiming support for their cause. She tried to make eye contact with the lady who might be her neighbor, to make sure the gesture hadn't been in vain. Perhaps then her neighbor would recognize her. Think well of her. It was about time *someone* did.

That night after dinner, Greg presented her with a scrap of paper bearing the name of a marriage counselor and the date and time of their first appointment. "We'll talk it over, baby. We'll think this through real good to make the right decision."

So they went to marriage counseling. The counselor tried to focus their attention on what having a family really *meant* to them. All abstractions, never getting down to brass tacks. She went to the sessions every Wednesday at 5:30 pm. and stayed awake until 11:00 to check the news to see if the clinic was still being protested. Yes, the newscast verified. In fact, the matter had escalated and out-of-state groups from both sides of the argument marshaled forces in what seemed to be a siege to rival that of Leningrad. The rare woman who made it through the ring of protesters had to be accompanied by a gang of counter-protesters. So much for privacy. At the very least, she'd be exposed to her Avon-selling neighbor (if that *was* her neighbor). She *might* be exposed in front of the whole city on TV. This wouldn't do. No, not at all.

Coincidentally, it wasn't long at all into therapy (maybe just the third or fourth week) that she "had a breakthrough" in which she agreed to have the child. "Wow," Greg said. "I never doubted that you'd come around, I just thought it'd take longer. Um, *wow.*"

Once they stopped going to counseling, she avoided the subject as much as possible. Eventually (at Greg's prompting) she did return to see her doctor, and he had her undergo another sonogram at twenty weeks. It just confirmed the diagnosis: *fetus non evidens.*

She endeavored to keep the news of the baby's birth defect quiet for as long as possible. It wasn't as though she had many friends to confide in, anyway. But the women in the cubicles surrounding hers felt it necessary to hold her a baby shower, and she indulged them.

One asked her about sonogram pictures. She mumbled something about misplacing them. That certainly caused a stir, and it took some doing to convince them that, really, she was okay waiting until the baby's birth to see it again. "I'm sure if you call the doctor's office," one of her co-workers said, "they'll print another out for you."

Janet nodded. Shrugged. She didn't want to seem anything besides a jubilant expectant mother, but she could only stretch the act so far. The other ladies in the office would gossip about her all-too-apparent lack of enthusiasm, of that she was sure. But what of it? Nothing positive could come from talking about sonograms.

But moments like these were few and far between. For much of her pregnancy, she found it possible to ignore the problem altogether; to pretend that she was just like any other expectant mother. After all, her belly bulged just like any other expectant mother. In time, she felt the baby kick like any other expectant mother.

All that self-deceit ended, though, when her doctor referred her to a specialist, a teratologist. She asked what in the Sam Hill a teratologist was. The doctor didn't say. She looked it up in the dictionary and discovered it was a doctor who specialized in birth defects. The word came from the Greek root "terato" (meaning "monster").

The normal-doctor sent her to the monster-doctor. She'd known all along that she was carrying a monster. She had to drive well over an hour to get to this monster-doctor's office, and she didn't like the anxious, dread-filled waiting room. But there were some good things that came from it. For example, the specialist was able to tell her the fetus' sex, (So meticulous was his study of the flow of amniotic fluid around the various nooks and crannies of her baby's body.)

She was having a girl.

They painted the nursery pink. Some women in the office

insisted on holding a second shower, just so they could provide gifts designated for the correct sex. Pink, pink, everywhere pink. It all made the whole thing feel more normal.

As they rounded out the eighth month, she began to worry about the inevitable disclosure. One day, after several months of sullenly and passively accepting whatever care the doctor had to offer, she decided to actually confide in the monster-doc about her worries.

"Mrs. Pruitt, let me assure you that hundreds of mothers in the United States, alone, are raising non evidens kids. There are support groups, there are – "

If she wanted to hear that, she could have stayed with the normal-doc. She interrupted him. "This invisible kid thing. It's just... How can I say this?... It's not an option."

"Well, you know ... there are cases. A *small number of cases*, mind you, where *non evidens* kids grow out of it. In an even smaller number of cases, the children oscillate between stages of being *evidens* and being *non evidens*. I mention that just to inform you that there is a possibility that you'll see your child someday."

"But you're saying that these things only happen rarely."

"Yes, ma'am, that's what I'm saying. Rarely, but I should add, not unheard of. The data we have on the course of this condition suggests that there's a twenty percent chance of it going either into sustained remission or this sort of oscillating remission I mentioned. Both variations of the usual prognosis usually emerge around puberty. Seems like there's some metabolic changes in the body around that time that throw the disorder a curve ball."

"You said only a twenty percent chance?"

"Yes, ma'am."

"And I'd have to wait at least ten years, probably more, to see if that twenty percent pans out?"

"Well, yes Mrs. Pruitt, that's one way of putting it."

Janet sighed. "Then, like I said, this isn't an option."

"You mean, you want a late-term abortion?"

Mental images of the Avon lady (if that was the Avon lady) protesting at the endless clinic-siege flickered through her head. "No, what I guess I mean is ... there has to be something that can be done. Some sort of intervention. Something?"

"Well," the monster-doc said. "Most parents of *non evidens* kids just sprinkle some baby powder on them for the first year or two. Some families jack up the wattage of all the light bulbs in their house so that the kid's shadows are more noticeable. There are all sorts of tricks to keep track of them. When they get older, you can go with various sorts of makeups, too."

"Makeups?"

"Sure," the monster-doc said. "I think I even have some literature here from a man in Indianapolis who specializes in this sort of thing." He handed her a glossy brochure. It had slick color photos of *non evidens* kids of various ethnicities on their graduation day – all of them sporting an obviously-fake, overly-made-up look more appropriate for embalmed corpses from particularly nasty car wrecks. A close look at the company logo revealed that, indeed, the business was "a subsidiary of Hecht's Home for Funerals."

Janet had many objections to taking this approach, but focused on the least unpleasant. "But...I mean ... surely the make-up would wash off."

"Well ... of course ... that is ... obviously. It's more the kind of thing you'd do just for a special occasion."

She began weeping (yes, she tried to hold it in but the pregnancy had eroded her self-control under a tidal wave of hormones). When the monster-doc tried to console her with Kleenex, she took the entire box out of his hands. She whipped out a handful of tissues and presented them back to him. "Here," she said through a stuffy nose, "you'll probably need a couple of these for someone else." Then she walked out of the office with the box and drove home.

She spent the night on the Internet, barraging search engines with any one of a hundred variations on "*non evidens* AND". At two in the morning, she came across the website of Max Harper, a plastic surgeon in California. "The *evidens* is in!" the site proclaimed, "Children should be seen, not just heard!"

The more Janet read, the more she liked. Dr. Harper's artist would draw a composite sketch of what your child *should* look like, based on the most attractive outcome of mixing the parents' features. He'd use computer scans to create a plastic mold matching this sketch, from which an incredibly life-like skin could be manufactured, to be worn as a tight-fitting suit over top of the actual skin. The child could wear it for days, weeks even, before it would need to be washed. It even had a degree of elasticity to allow for the growth process, and if you purchased a lifetime contract they would periodically adjust the skin to reflect the maturing of features. Once the child got old enough, colored contact lenses could be used to complete the anatomical ensemble.

She woke Greg up. Fetched his glasses for him, put them onto his face, and pointed at the screen. "Look," she commanded.

It took awhile for him to clear the cobwebs. "What's wrong? What's wrong?" he said. He kept repeating "What's wrong?", right up until the point he seemed to get what she was driving at. "You woke me up for this? I thought you were going into labor!"

"I'm not due for another two weeks."

"You damned sure could go early. It happens."

"I won't *let* that happen," Janet said. "This baby isn't coming out of my womb until I have a way to fix it."

"I'm going back to sleep. You're obsessed!"

"You're not even paying attention to the pictures. Take a look at those before and after shots!" The before pictures showed *non evidens* kids adorned with inferior treatments, like baby powder or makeup. *Pathetic*, Janet thought. In the afters, the children were practically normal. Hell, better than normal. Downright telegenic.

Greg took off his glasses, rubbed some sleep from his eyes, replaced the glasses, and studied the screen. "Jesus. This has to cost ..."

"We have a house, Greg. We can always take out a second mortgage. You could always take a second job. This is our child's *appearance* we're talking about! I can't believe you're making price an issue."

"We're cubicle-monkeys, honey. We're not poor, but we're not rich either. We get by. This ... this is just ..."

"Look," Janet said. "We're only going to need $5,000 to book a consultation."

"Sheesh. Doesn't insurance cover any of this?"

"An initial fitting at delivery is only $50,000. We could come up with it. We have credit cards. We could sell the house, probably in a matter of weeks, for that."

"Wow," Greg said. "Just ... wow. I can't believe you'd suggest that. Our home is worth three times that much."

"And how much is your baby's happiness worth, Greg? Have you thought about that? Do you want your baby to always have to be seen by a *teratologist* because it's a *terato*. Or do you want her to have a decent appearance?"

Greg frowned. Hung his head down. "Wow," he said. "We're really gonna sell this place, eh? Just ... man ... *Wow.*"

They named the baby Harper, after the plastic surgeon. They'd gone to California for the delivery. Special heat-sensing contraptions were arranged so that the doctor could tell how much of the newborn had made it through the birth canal. (Indeed, delivery itself was the most perilous aspect of a *non evidens* pregnancy). The baby made it through, though, with flying colors.

For Janet, this was one of the oddest moments of her life. The agony of pushing through all that concentrated pressure sure felt excruciatingly real, but the end result seemed to imply it had all been in her head. No mewing, writhing baby. Just the infant's shrieks, tell-tale splatters of newborn-gunk everywhere, and an empty space in the medical staff's arms where she surmised they held her.

At least she had the shrieks. She reminded herself of that. When ladies at the office asked what childbirth was like for her, she would have to focus on the auditory (or else make up a story of what it was like to first *see* her child, extrapolating from having seen such events dramatized on television).

The obstetrician and the nurses cut the cord and put the baby in an incubator. "But the visible skin! My baby needs her visible skin!"

"All in due time, ma'am," one of the nurses said. "Doctor Harper usually doesn't put the skin on until the second or third day."

She scowled. "Then take it out of here. Don't bring it back until it's good and ready!"

"As you wish, ma'am," another nurse said.

She tried to keep as stoned as possible on the painkillers until her baby was rendered normal. In time, she held her. *So this*, she thought, *is what the big deal is all about.* The plastic felt cold on her breast as she tried to get Harper to latch on to feed. She didn't like how there were nothing but shadowy hollows where the baby's eyes should have been. She couldn't wait until she got old enough for cosmetic contacts that would provide the illusion of visible pupils, irises, and scleras. She asked the nurse about it, and she said some moms were able to train their kids to handle them as early as four.

Janet convinced the plastic surgeon to let her try them when Harper was three-and-a-half. The kiddo *needed* them, after all. She couldn't expect her daughter to go off to preschool without them and creep out everyone with those vacant eye-sockets. And her daughter *needed* to go to preschool. Ever since the birth, Greg had to work two jobs to support them, while she stayed home full time with the kid. They weren't able to afford a very nice place yet, but it was a start. Everything was so much more expensive in California than it'd been in the Midwest. Janet reminded herself that it was all worth it, though, to be this close to Dr. Harper in the event the girl fell on the sidewalk or encountered some other catastrophe that tore her skin.

The contacts gave Harper blue eyes, just like her dad. They were the final piece of the puzzle. They completed the look. They made the little girl normal. Janet explained this to Harper over and over, but the toddler somehow still had the insolence to lose the contacts or accidentally tear them, or ruin them trying (for some reason apparent only to the three year old brain) to put them in the eyes of the stray cat they'd taken in. This was a problem.

Janet thought through her options. Preschool was out of the question. What could she do: drop Harper off in the morning wearing contacts, then come to pick her up and find the girl had blinked them out, revealing empty spaces instead of blue eyes? But another income was needed. Pronto. She had to find child care so she could get to work

One afternoon Greg came home for his usual two hour break between his first and second jobs and made an announcement she never thought she'd hear. "I ... um ... left work a little early, honey, to swing by the food stamp office. I have some papers to fill out. Wow, I just ... you know ... didn't think our family would turn out this way."

It had been four solid years of adversity for Greg and Janet. Four years, Janet told herself, without much of a break. Their luck had to change. And it did. It started in a rather unpromising way. Harper had put her contact lenses in the cat's eyes again, necessitating yet another trip to a veterinarian appointment that they couldn't afford. While Janet and Harper sat in the vet's waiting room (the cat tucked away in a carrier, yowling his head off), a lady with dreadlocks and a fashionable leather purse made conversation. She'd brought with her a dachshund wearing a huge plastic collar around his neck. It stared into the cat caddy, trying to make eye contact. The cat curled into the farthest back corner of the carrier, having none of it.

"Your little girl looks like quite the movie star with those sunglasses on," the lady said. "My goodness, she's ... she's just *beautiful*!"

Harper beamed.

Janet smiled, grateful that the lady didn't have a clue as to the real reason she'd made her daughter wear shades inside. She nudged Harper. "Did you hear that, sweetie? That nice lady complimented your appearance! What do you say to her?"

"Thannnnk youuuuu," Harper crooned. She flashed the overly dramatic grin her mother had taught her to exhibit on such occasions.

"Oh my, she does seem to have lost quite a number of teeth, though. Yikes, does she even have *any* choppers in there?"

Janet felt her pulse quicken. The *teeth*. How could she have forgotten them? (She'd been isolated for far too long, that's how. Out of practice in carefully thinking through and pre-planning each aspect of Harper's appearance. It never occurred to her that when she went out in public the issue of teeth might come up.)

She took it for granted that her daughter's teeth had come in. She'd poked around in her mouth herself, every now and then, when Harper was younger. She'd *felt* them. But she hadn't thought of it in well over a year, and now that was coming back to bite her (so to speak). How could she have been so careless!

"You know," the lady with dreadlocks said. "I'm a casting agent. I need a kid to work in some commercials. One's a public service announcement about child dental care. Your daughter looks like she'd be perfect!"

The cat's yowls increased in frequency and intensity. It was always a nervous wreck when going to the vet, anyway. Even more so when it had to endure the visit while afflicted with contact lenses that had veered off into the corners of its eyes.

The casting agent frowned. "Awwww...poor little puddy tat. Whassa matter with him?"

Janet frantically thought through how to best explain things. "Eye problems. Maybe an infection."

"That's strange," the casting agent said. "I never even knew cats could *get* eye infections."

"I think it's a weird genetic thing," Janet offered, trying to defuse the subject. "Anyway ... this commercial thing. It pay?"

"Oh yes, of course. I mean, not much. Your daughter isn't a professional actor. But I'm sure she'll do fine and we will, of course, pay her *something*. Tell you what, here's my card. Give me a call and we'll talk specifics."

"I sure will," Janet said.

Then the dachshund was summoned back for its appointment, followed in short order by Janet's cat getting summoned back for its. The veterinarian wasn't pleased.

"How the hell does your daughter get a hold of contact lenses, anyhow?" He looked at the chart. "This is the third time the cat's been in for this in eighteen months. Your daughter seems ... well, frankly, ma'am ... obsessed with this."

"It's just a phase," Janet said. "Isn't it, Harper?"

"Uh-huh," Harper said. "Just a face!"

The vet took out a variety of instruments and began his examination with a terrible earnestness. "Mrs. Pruitt, you might want to have Harper step out to the play area in the lobby for a moment. The receptionist can keep an eye on her. There's some things ... well, grown-up things ... we have to talk about."

The cat yowled.

Janet walked Harper back to the lobby. She knelt down next to her and whispered in her ear: "Remember, never take your sunglasses off unless Momma says it's okay."

Harper offered an exaggerated nod, indicating she heard and obeyed.

Then Janet walked back to the doctor's office.

"I'm afraid this time is far worse than any of the others. It appears that the contact lenses have lodged in quite a deep recess of the cat's noggin. I think your cat will have to live like that, forever. There's no way for me to really *get them out.*"

Janet bit her lip. Clenched her fists. "Surely there's *some* way."

The veterinarian gave her an anxious grin. "Well ... that is, what I mean ... The only way I can possibly imagine getting them out would be to euthanize the cat, cut it open, and *take* them out."

The cat began yowling more than it ever had before.

"A smart man, Doctor. A very smart man, indeed."

"But ... this is an otherwise-healthy cat."

Janet couldn't afford to purchase new contacts from the plastic surgeon's office. She needed those two little discs ASAP. "But surely, it would be inhuman to let the creature suffer so, don't you agree, Doctor?"

The veterinarian sighed. Arrangements were made. Needles were filled. Lethal injections given. Autopsy instruments employed for a very non-autopsy purpose. The veterinarian only agreed to do all this if Janet paid cash up front, and promised to never, ever darken the doorway of his office again.

Little Harper waddled toward the cat carrier Janet held in her hand, and frowned when she noticed that (aside from a white plastic contact lens case) it was empty. "Where's kitty?" she asked.

"You killed it," Janet said.

The good news was that Harper was an absolute hit in the commercial. The blue contact lenses proved as good as new after getting salvaged from the dead cat's eyes. They just needed an extra day to soak in some solution. The combination of those sparkling blue eyes, telegenic skin and an apparently-toothless mouth wowed the masses (who were used to seeing far-less-telegenic toothless kids on these commercials.) She only earned two hundred dollars for the filming of the dental care PSA, but the job attracted the interest of a talent agent. Janet had wanted there to be another income in the home and now that Harper was acting, there was one.

Greg had objections at first. (Shouldn't Harper be keeping a low profile? What if everyone found out she was a *non evidens* kid? Would she be publicly humiliated?) All these protests evaporated the day he saw his little girl on TV. "That's her ... oh...gee ... She's actually there on the screen. Oh man ... *Wow.*"

Eventually, they went back to the plastic surgeon and explained their problem with the teeth. "Yikes," he said. "I can't believe we didn't think of that." And, in short order, he created a fiberglass "dental edifice" that Harper could wear over top of her own, invisible, teeth. They seemed to fool everyone.

In fact, the edifice expanded Harper's marketability so much beyond the realm of dental care PSAs that she was now working five, six, seven times a week, in all sorts of commercials. It was increasingly difficult to find times to remove her plastic skin, wash it, and give the kiddo's invisible body a bath. Her behavior at bath time didn't make matters any easier, either. She shrieked whenever Janet revealed the carefully-concealed zipper and pulled it down. "I'm really nothing," the little girl said, sobbing. "I'm really, underneath, nothing."

Janet didn't like seeing her daughter cry, of course. It annoyed her. But she was glad that Harper understood the importance of keeping her skin on. During those tear-filled bath times, Janet would comfort Harper by reminding her that, with her plastic skin on, she was something. More than something – an *actress*.

Commercials led to bit parts on sitcoms, which eventually led to the lead on a sitcom. Harper played the role of a plucky orphan who hung out all the time in the lobby of a police station in the hit show *Pigs & Pigtails*. Janet began to worry that millions of viewers would find Harper's performance so convincing that they'd assume she was a real orphan, so she badgered the publicist into getting a puff piece written for *Parents* magazine entitled "The Loving Real-Life Mom behind America's Favorite TV Orphan."

In less than a year, the family moved out of their lower-middle-class digs and into upper-middle-class-digs. After two years, they lived in a mansion. With the paparazzi stalking Harper at every turn, they couldn't afford the risk of going to the plastic surgeon's office for checkups and skin-maturing-adjustments. So, they paid double the usual rate for him to come in and provide house calls. Janet had to make certain she gave all the servants the day off on this day, once a year, lest they become aware of Dr. Max Harper's presence in the home and leak the information to TMZ.

Pigs & Pigtails ran for seven years. After that came the movie deals. Travel to film in Prague, in Vancouver, and – rarely – in New York. Harper blossomed into a stunning young lady. Many a lecherous older man had her eighteenth birthday circled on his calender, in bright red ink. Her publicist tried to convince her to date one of the several teenage boys she was paired with in the movies, as this would give the tabloids something to talk about, but (to Janet's relief) she always nixed the suggestion.

In the midst of all this, Janet hesitated to give Harper the typical talk about the birds and the bees. She wouldn't have felt comfortable with this even under the most ordinary circumstances, but the *non evidens* thing raised the embarrassment factor exponentially. Take this exchange, for example: Janet's attempt to impress on her daughter the uncouth nature of masturbation after noticing that Harper locked herself away in her room for hours on end. "Don't do it," Janet warned, "it's not ladylike." Harper shrugged and agreed to comply. "I don't feel that much down there, anyway. Not with the skin on, at least."

How could Janet not find this conversation mortifying?

If she hadn't had an interest in having grandchildren one day, she might have decided to ask the plastic surgeon to refer Harper to a gynecological surgeon to perform a hysterectomy. But Janet *did* want grandkids, and this meant that she'd have to find a way to convince Harper to lower her expectations in regards to sensation. Or, possibly, to engage in some conversation with the surgeon about how sensitivity might be increased.

Obviously, no mother wants to think of her daughter in *that way*. If she considered it at all, it was in a fleeting manner – associated with the birth of grandchildren. Hopefully, *visible* grandchildren. She reasoned that ordinary sexual functioning had to be *possible*. There was, after all, a special apparatus in the skin that facilitated other, unspeakable functions of the nether regions. The next time the plastic surgeon came for a house call, they'd sit down, like mature adults, and talk about it.

*

He came to the house as planned, but brought trouble along with him. "This is my son, Pax."

"Beg pardon," Janet said. "Did you say his name was, well, Pax?"

"It's Latin," the young buck said, "for peace." The lad had a strong jaw, a handsome brow, and piercing blue eyes.

"It's take your kid to work day, and Pax wanted to see what his old man's job was like. Please, be assured that he'll keep all of this completely confidential."

"I, well, I guess I'll have trust that now, won't I doctor."

The plastic surgeon grinned. "You don't have to worry about Pax. He won't blab to the *Enquirer.* He doesn't want anything to do with the limelight. I keep telling him he ought to go into movies. He's had a director or two interested already."

"I don't want to be in movies," Pax said. "The media gets all up in your business."

"Smart guy," Harper said. "A lot of times, I don't want to be in movies, either."

Janet let out a clumsy laugh. "You'll have to indulge my daughter in her flights of fancy, Doctor. Harper says the craziest things sometimes. I tell her that she can do that here, but outside of this house such statements might be misunderstood. Anyway, I suppose we should be getting down to business. She'll need her yearly adjustment and maturing work done. We also had, well, a sort of private question to ask you. Something that might best be handled without your son around."

"Fair enough. Can we meet in your den? Just the three of us?"

"Just the two of you," Harper said. "I don't want to talk about it. My mom can tell you everything. It's really her question more than mine."

"Fair enough," the plastic surgeon said. "Shall we then, Mrs. Pruitt?"

Janet looked at Pax and Harper smiling at each other. She didn't like it. Smiling led to holding hands. Holding hands led to, well, other things. It felt almost-incestuous, the notion of Harper admiring her plastic surgeon's son. Images flashed through her brain. First dates. Second dates. Someday, a wedding, and the specter of her daughter taking the boy's last name, going around Los Angeles with the name Harper Harper. She felt the need to nip this in the bud.

Janet glared at her daughter. "Harper, are you quite *sure* you don't want to *join us.*"

Harper rolled her eyes. "I. Am. Sure."

Janet fumed. The girl sassed her. For the first time. Right in front of company. Oh, how she'd pay when the doctor and his son left.

Footfalls pounded on the basement steps. Greg ascended them, coming up to the living room for the first time in many hours. "Oh ... hey ... I didn't think ... you know ... think there'd be anyone up here. *Wow* ... it's a party! I mean, we usually don't hang out in the living room on this day – you know, Harper's house call day."

Janet snapped at him. "What are *you* doing up here?" She quickly realized she might make a scene in front of company. She couldn't let herself seem too strident. "What I mean is, I thought you'd be downstairs with your model trains all day."

"Parts," Greg said. "UPS was supposed to bring parts, you know. Have they ... well ... Have they come yet?"

"No dear, I'll let you know when they do."

"Alright then, I'll just go back to polishing the tracks while I'm waiting." He clomped back down the stairs to his man cave.

"Well, Mrs. Pruitt?"

"Yes?"

"You did want to talk, right? I have another appointment back at the office in two hours and you know how traffic is. We need to get things moving."

"Yes," she said. "Of course." They went into the den. Janet explained everything to the plastic surgeon. She emphasized that this was a discussion that didn't have any practical bearing now, but something worth thinking about "down the road ... a few years from now, after she gets married." The surgeon admitted to her that the sort of skin that had been engineered for Harper maximized realism at the cost of sensation. "There's a trade-off there, I'm afraid. We could have a new suit made, of course. One that enhanced her sense of touch, but it would be, by necessity, thinner – less convincing."

"I see," Janet said. She wouldn't allow Harper to wear anything that might endanger her career. "Well, it sounds like for now we'll just keep things as they are."

"As you wish, now is that all you want to say to me in private?"

"Yes, of course."

"Okay, then let's bring Harper in."

Janet went to fetch her. The girl came into the room, grinning like the proverbial cat that ate the canary. "What are you so happy about," Janet said (worried she already knew the answer).

"I have a date tonight."

That night, Janet went down to Greg's man cave. They needed to have a talk. "I'm worried about our little girl,"

Greg's blue-and-white striped conductor's hat wobbled around his head as he followed the course of his Lionel Super Chief. "Well ... yeah, I think any parent would be worried on a first date. But he's, like – What? – the plastic surgeon's son? So ... um, *yeah*. Wow, you don't have to worry about this being some guy who's just after her for her money, y'know?"

"She's going to want to *feel* something, honey. That means she's going to want to take off her suit."

Greg flicked a switch, and the train switched tracks. "But the boy came here with his dad. I mean, well... I guess ... he knows why his dad was here."

"It was a violation of our privacy rights – Doctor Harper should never have been able to bring the boy here. I could sue him for that."

"Well..in that case you'd be, I mean – sheesh, we'd all be – in the news, yanno? *Wow*, you'd really want that?"

"Well ... I could *threaten* to sue and see if his lawyers capitulated, just to teach him a lesson."

"Wow, you'd really do that? I mean – seriously alienate the one doctor equipped to take care of her skin? Just – oh my God – *wow*."

Her husband, for the first time, had won an argument.

Harper started dating Pax when she was seventeen. Under the boy's influence, she became increasingly rebellious. Curfews came and went unheeded. Outfits that had left home perfectly draping Harper's increasingly curvy frame came back in the door with a rumpled, disheveled look suggestive of a roll in the hay.

Worse of all, she began to flatly refuse to do movies.

Janet saw the writing on the wall. She was losing her hold on the girl and the boy was gaining a hold on her. She went down to Greg's man cave one day to commiserate about it. Ordinarily, she couldn't stand the racket of dozens of trains chugging along a football-field-size collection of tracks, but she needed to vent.

Greg didn't hear her approach, and so she had to tap him on the shoulder. He startled so severely he almost lost his conductor's cap, then flicked a switch to turn off the trains so he could hear her.

Janet decided she better not pussyfoot when it came to this topic. She decided she needed to start off the conversation with a hook to snag Greg's interest. "How," she asked, "are you going to pay for all this when your little girl leaves the house at eighteen?"

"Wow," Greg said. "You know, that is ... we have savings, y'know? Put some money away."

"It's all hers at eighteen. She could cut us out completely and give it all to that boy."

"We'll just talk to her, I guess. I mean. Yeah. She's not eighteen yet. So, really, there's nothing she can *do*."

"But it's only months until then."

"Yeah ... um ... we'll talk to her. Yanno? Just ask if we can have some money." He turned the trains back on.

Janet gritted her teeth and tapped Greg's shoulder again. He flicked the switch to stop the train. He trembled. "You really want to keep yammering about this, huh?"

Janet gasped. ("Yammering"?!)

"Look, my goal is for the Super Chief to make five thousand laps today. It's only made four thousand and there's less than three hours left before midnight. So, yanno ... just ... well ... get out and leave me alone." He flicked the switch to start the trains up again. Pulled the conductor's hat over his eyes.

Janet marched out of the basement. Even though the route was familiar, she almost lost her way – so clouded was her vision with tears.

Somehow, Janet's personal cell phone number had gotten leaked to the tabloids. Two weeks before Harper's eighteenth birthday, they called Janet asking for remarks on Harper's imminent early retirement from the motion picture industry. The little bitch must have released a statement to that effect without consulting her!

"No comment," Janet said, over and over again. It was the first time since she'd been in L.A. that she actually *dreaded* the specter of media attention. She felt like the world's worst mother. She had to confess to herself that, for the past several days, she didn't even know where Harper *was*. She tried calling the girl over and over, and always the call went to voice mail.

She had to tolerate news footage of man-on-the-street interviews with fellows old enough to be Harper's father, all of them confessing their attraction for the "healthy-looking" young lady. For two weeks, it was nothing but "Harper This", "Harper That". Harper on the cover of a tabloid. Harper on the cover of a slick entertainment magazine. The entire media seemed to be doing nothing at all except harping on Harper.

Then came the day, itself. The eighteenth anniversary of that day with all the heat-imaging devices and the sounds-but-not-sights and the asking them to take the baby away until it had fake skin on. The paparazzi had the mansion surrounded, anticipating there to be a blow-out birthday party.

But nothing happened. Not even a trace of Harper. Not until that night, when Janet got this email:

Dear Mom:
I'm coming by tomorrow to get some of my things and say goodbye. Today would have been just too crazy, with all the media. But I hear that another coked-up celebrity just bit the dust, so they'll all be covering that now. I'm old news.
    Sincerely,
    H.I. Pruitt

She was "H.I." now, eh? Harper Isabella Pruitt. H.I.P. Janet pondered, for a moment, why they hadn't leveraged the initials into some sort of catchy marketing phrase. Such were the lost opportunities, the regrets of parenting.

There wasn't a paparazzi in sight at ten a.m. the following day, when the doorbell rang. Janet opened it and found Harper and Pax on the other side. They'd brought a U-haul. Janet shook her head. Really, they should have hired *assistants* to do this.

"Well," Harper said. "I guess this is goodbye."

Janet scowled. "Just remember, when the world gets brutal and nasty to you – and mark my words you little hussie, it will – you can always come running home to Mom."

Harper ignored her and went back to her room. Pax brought in boxes. They went to Harper's room and began packing. They closed the door behind them. For ten minutes, Janet heard the muffled sounds of coat hangers clanging, of zippers unzipping, of dull thuds against cardboard.

"The world doesn't like people like you," Janet said through the door. "It will be scary, it will be – "

The door opened. Pax stood on the other side, alongside Harper's skin-suit –which appeared to levitate in mid-air. "This isn't mine," Harper's disembodied voice said. Then, abruptly, something – no, some*one*; an *invisible* someone – shoved the skin-suit toward Janet. "It belongs to you. You purchased it. You wanted it. You never asked me what I thought. That that goes for these, too." Invisible Harper piled two plastic cases on top of the skin that now hung limp and lifeless in Janet's arms – one case contained the latest pair of contacts, the other the dental edifice.

Janet snarled. "Why you ungrateful little bitch!" She let the cosmetic equipment fall to the floor, took the flat of her hand and swatted in the air, trying to slap her daughter right in the face. She missed, and Harper giggled. Pax moved forward, out of the room. "C'mon, H.I., let's make tracks."

"And *you*," Janet said to Pax. "I can't believe that *you'd* allow yourself to be associated with, with this *freak*. What's *wrong* with you that you find an invisible girl attractive?"

"Maybe it's the way her hips feel in my hands when I'm dancing with her," Pax said. "Or maybe it's the soft smoothness of her legs. But honestly, I think it has something to do with the fact that I'm *non evidens*, too. The oscillating type. Why do you think my dad went into a specialty with such a limited clientele? He wanted to help kids like me blend in. But I like to think that if he knew how far some parents would take it, he never would have invented the suits."

"Yesterday we didn't want to come because it was Pax's *non evidens* day," the Harper-monster said. "Today he's *evidens*. It helps that he's visible fifty percent of the time; like, when we want to run errands and that kind of thing. Most people still haven't adjusted to the notion that there are some cars on the freeway that will look like no one's behind the wheel. We try not to alarm people – especially on the highway. That could be dangerous."

"Yeah," Pax said. "We don't want to alarm people, but we don't want to apologize for our lives, either. We just want to be ourselves, and H.I. can't do that here, Mrs. Pruitt. At least, not now. We hope someday you'll change."

And then the two of them started taking boxes out.

Janet began to desperately scroll through her options to rescue victory from the jaws of defeat. "Your father!" she said. "Your father will be *quite* disappointed that you're leaving without saying goodbye to him. You should go down to the basement and see him."

"I'll just catch him on Skype," the Harper-monster said. "That's how we've been keeping in touch the last few months."

Janet fumed. She went downstairs to give Greg a good tongue-lashing. How *dare* he keep secrets from her. He was in the middle of talking to a couple of men in suits. "Oh, um, hey this is uh – my wife."

One of the men in suits, a bald man with a goatee, extended his hand. "Ah, so this is *Mrs.* Railroad Fanatic, eh?"

Janet didn't understand what was happening. "Beg pardon?"

"I made it, honey!" Greg said. "I, um, now have the world record for – you know, most, um revolutions of a toy train around a track in a single day! I, um, *wow* ... I mean, I thought I told you about this earlier."

"You won't mind if we get your husband out your hair for a few months, do you Mrs. Pruitt? We at Guinness World Records would like to take his toy trains on the road – we're making a tour of children's hospitals! Just think how many kids your husband will be making happy!"

"He's ... leaving ...?"

Greg played with his cap, nervously. Rubbed his three day growth of beard-stubble. "Well, um ... you know, with H.I. on her way out of the house and everything, I just thought ... well, you know..."

H.I.? "Fine," she said. "Leave me. I'll be fine here all by myself."

"Oh, wow ... just *wow*, that's good to hear. Okay, then, I just gotta go talk to these guys for a bit longer about the details, yanno?"

"But ... "

The three men started talking again. Janet walked back upstairs.

In a few days, Greg and his trains were out the door – destined to entertain gaggles of waifs and guttersnipes. Janet guessed he was too good to entertain his wife, anymore. Too good to entertain anyone, anymore, unless there was a goddamned camera rolling.

After the toy train tour, Greg didn't come back home. *Must have finally found a way to gather shekels*, Janet mused. She let him go.

For many years, Janet lived alone in the mansion. Maids and assistants left, in a slow trickle. But the bills always got paid. It seems that the invisible-Harper-thing wasn't *completely* heartless. She made some provision for the woman who sacrificed so much for her. She probably looked down her nose at her whenever she wrote the checks to the electric company and so forth, but at least she wrote them.

Years passed without any real contact between the two of them and Janet began to grieve the loss less and less. This new entity, this so-called "H.I." was just a phantom, just a cruel ghost who decided to no longer inhabit the precious skin Janet had scrimped and saved to purchase for her.

The skin was the important thing. One day, when she let her thoughts drift toward the subject, when she let herself feel some flicker of sadness, she reminded herself that she still had *that*. She'd wrapped the plastic skin in a plastic bag and kept it in the hope chest that still lingered in her daughter's old room. "*Yes*," Janet repeated to herself, aloud, "I still have the *skin*!"

This notion energized her in a way she hadn't been energized for years. For the first time in what seemed like an eternity, she left the house to go somewhere other than the grocery store – Home Depot, to be exact. She purchased two large bags of sawdust there, and had a nice man carry them out to her aging Cadillac. When he asked her – in the course of making small talk – what she planned to do with them, she told him she was planning to use them as a remedy, to make her sick daughter well. He gave her a strange look, and walked away without saying another word.

Some months after the trip to the Home Depot, a journalist called and asked her if she had any comment about the tell-all book written by her daughter, H.I. Was she aware that the young lady painted an unflattering portrait of her? Was she aware that H.I. Pruitt had become one of the first celebrities in the world to come out as *non evidens*? Was she aware that she was starting a foundation to help *non evidens* kids? That she was becoming an advocate for the cause?

"There must be some mistake," Janet said. "My daughter's name is *Harper* and she lives here, with me. She's never felt the need to leave home. Each day we have a mother-daughter brunch in the sun room. Each night we have drinks out on the veranda. She's a beautiful girl, my daughter. Hasn't aged a bit since her eighteenth birthday. She's the loveliest girl I've ever seen."

SPACE BLANKET BINGO
by Sandra McDonald

EDITOR'S NOTE
Sandra McDonald's first collection of fiction, Diana Comet and Other Improbable Tales, *was a Booklist Editor's Choice, an American Library Association Over the Rainbow Book and winner of a Lambda Literary Award. Her story "Sexy Robot Mom" recently won an Asimov's Readers' Poll award. Four of her stories have been noted on the James A. Tiptree Award Honor List for exploring gender stereotypes. She is the published author of several novels and more than sixty short stories for adults and teens, including the award-winning* Fisher Key Adventures *and the gay asexual thriller* City of Soldiers. *She holds an M.F.A. in Creative Writing from the University of Southern Maine and teaches college in Florida.*

In "Space Blanket Bingo", she's found a way to bring these 60s icons into the 21st century in a way that will tickle modern sensibilities even while she's evoking a nostalgic blast from the past. And while the main character isn't female, every beach bunny is somebody's daughter. "Kowabunga", Sandra, as Lunkhead would say.

Bells ring, the bright sweet sound of freedom, the fantastic summer upon us, and we burst out of the high school with a rousing rendition of the song "Endless Waves" from the classic 1964 movie *Life's a Beach.* We pile into our convoy of jalopies and woody wagons, the guys bare-chested or wearing Hawaiian shirts, the gals in hot pants and bikini tops, and roll down the road to the golden coast with Danny leading the way. Danny, with his dashing good looks and honey voice, *always* leads the way. Riding shotgun in Danny's yellow jeep is Colonel Frank Merullo, United States Air Force. He's wearing his full NASA spacesuit, including boots, gloves and a closed helmet with reflective shielding. He doesn't sing along with the gang.

Violet Blue adjusts her fur-trimmed bikini and drapes her arms around his neck. "Let go and hang loose, Pops! The fun's just beginning."

*

Her boyfriend Skipper slaps Merullo on the back. "He'll be fine once he catches his first wave."

Danny throws Merullo a dazzling smile, but he's too busy belting out the chorus to say anything.

The Southern California cliffs give way to pristine beach and the limitless blue Pacific. We dump our bags at the beach house and carry our boards over the dunes. The gals claim their territory and break out the baby oil. Most of the guys paddle toward the swells, searching for the perfect wave. Above Colonel Merullo's head, five seagulls whirl and twirl and call out to each other.

"Do you think he'll come around?" Bonnie asks Danny from their blanket at the center of the action. Bonnie is lovely as always, her hair fixed in a perfect flip and her creamy complexion untouched by the sun. Everyone knows she and Danny will soon marry and settle down to a blissful adult life in the prosperous suburbs. She stares at Merullo, her lips turned in a frown.

"Give the man some time. He'll come around." Danny gives her a chaste kiss, grabs his board, and jogs to Merullo. "Come on, Daddy-O! Surf's up!"

Merullo opens his helmet faceplate. He is a middle-aged man with a pasty complexion and reddened cheeks. He says, "This isn't right. I didn't authorize this Vee-Reel."

Danny pats his shoulder. "Whatever that is, you're hanging with us now."

"Is Dr. Naguchi here? Lieutenant Jenny?" Merullo scans the shoreline. "If this is the crew's idea of a joke--"

"Couldn't say," Danny replies. He sprints on down to the water and throws his lean, smooth body into the rolling Pacific. Out at the lineup, Skipper and the others bob in place and wait for the water to rise.

Merullo says, "Computer, exit program," but nothing happens. He tries again. The beach remains firmly in place. The ship's inflight entertainment system is obviously malfunctioning, but the fail safe will engage in sixty minutes. Until then, he'll have to put up with the surf and sand and silly teenage antics. Lieutenant Jenny will be amused at this virtual misadventure.

The weather is always fine at this beach. Beneath the radiant sun, every blanket is shared by a handsome guy and his pretty girl. Lonely singles don't fit the script. The sandscape is painted with surfers, weightlifters, recording artists, loony biker gangs, foreign spies, unscrupulous businessmen and stray comic icons of yore, like Buster Keaton.

"None of this is real," Merullo tells Bonnie at the counter of the snack shack. He removes his helmet entirely, revealing short brown hair that has gone thin at the dome. "A computer is beaming ultrasonic pulses at my brain, creating this illusion. You're all data constructs based on old movies pulled out of a database."

"Really?" Bonnie lifts a tray of hot dogs and French fries. Her bright pink lipstick perfectly matches her sandals and headband. "Are you sure about that?"

Over in the volleyball pit, guest star Dee Ann Lawrence is belting out "Don't Be Fooled by Love," a song that once made the Billboard top twenty. She's singing it to Lunkhead, who is the tallest, dumbest of us all. He has a crush on a girl who claims to be a mermaid. No one else has met this creature from the sea.

Merullo says, "Your character was played by Becky Clark, America's sweetheart. Danny was played by Tommy Suede, a teenage heartthrob. They made a dozen of these movies, but they died a long time ago."

Violet offers Merullo her soda. "How about something cold to drink? The sun's real hot today."

"That drink's not real, either." Merullo checks the chronometer built into the sleeve of his spacesuit. "In a minute or so, these pulses will stop and you'll cease to exist. I'll wake up in the real world, on my ship. In a flight couch."

The five seagulls squawk and cry from atop the roof of the snack shack. Out in the water, Danny and Skipper have caught an eight-footer and are riding it in with their arms outstretched for balance. Their smiles are as wide as the horizon.

"You're still here," Violet says to Merullo.

Bonnie shifts her tray of food. "Danny's lunch is getting cold."

Merullo doesn't move out of her way. "Vee-Reel time is sometimes off from ship's time by a minute or two. It won't be long now."

Violet sips at her soda. Skipper and Danny wade ashore and slap each other on the back. Danny looks for Bonnie, but Skipper has eyes only for Danny. Admiration shines in his expression, as well as something deeper.

Merullo taps the chronometer. "Any second now."

"Good luck with that," Bonnie says. She and Violet return to their blankets and boyfriends. Danny wraps his arms around Bonnie's waist and tugs her close.

"How's the colonel doing?" he asks.

"Still clinging," Bonnie says.

Skipper tries to hug Violet, but she squirms free and reaches for her transistor radio. Skipper says, "He'll catch on soon enough. Right, Danny?"

"Sure thing." Danny pops a non-existent French fry into his mouth. "Give him awhile. The world is a hard habit to break."

Even when the sun sets, the beach party rolls on. The guys shrug into jackets and the gals slip into cocktail dresses. We all gather at Sammy's Pavilion to sip non-alcoholic drinks at tables set around the dance floor. The evening's entertainment will consist of a rock'n'roll band or lip-synching actresses or Little Stevie Wonder. Danny might get up and croon a love ballad. Bonnie might join him in a sweet duet. Afterward some of us will walk the moonlit beach or cuddle in secluded coves. Up in the beach house, there will be pillow fights and risqué sleepwear and the trading of double entendres, but nowhere will there be any sex. It doesn't fit our image.

Skipper has had a romantic misunderstanding with Violet. Lunkhead's mermaid girlfriend has flippered her way back into the sea, leaving him bereft. The two of them meander down to the high tide mark and build a fire. Merullo sits with them.

"I'm sure my crew is working to get me out of here," he says. "They'll have realized something is wrong by now."

Lunkhead leans back and crosses his hairy ankles. "Where's this spaceship of yours going, anyway?"

"To Triton. It's a moon of Neptune. But even with the new propulsion drive, it's several years away." Merullo wedges coconuts into the sand to illustrate the distance between the planets. His bulky spacesuit makes the task difficult. "We're in cold sleep most of the trip, but during the first month and last months of the mission we're awake and can use the ship's entertainment options. Lieutenant Sanchez built a Vee-Reel around Busby Berkeley musicals. Lieutenant Umbo's is based on World War II movies. Dr. Naguchi likes anime. Lieutenant Jenny created this one."

Lunkhead has a goofy grin on his face. "Lieutenant Jenny. Sounds like a dreamboat."

Merullo's expression is troubled. "Mark Jenny. He's my co-pilot."

"Ohhhhhh." Lunkhead's grin disappears. "Never mind."

Skipper plucks at the strings of his guitar. Melancholy notes float toward the stars. "What's your Vee-Reel, Pops?"

"I don't remember," Merullo says. It bothers him, that. He should know. "I don't think I usually play them."

Lunkhead asks, "But you like this one, don't you? Sun and sand. Letting go and hanging loose. What could be better?"

"Sharing it with the one you love." Skipper strums a soft chord. His eyes are dark and unreadable. "So why go blasting off into outer space, anyway?"

Merullo brightens a little. "Eighteen months ago, a comet smacked into Triton. Soon afterward, Voyager 20 did a flyby and detected a strong but irregular radio signal in the Leviathan Patera. Our mission was originally geared to catalog prospects for expanding human colonization beyond Mars, but now we're also going to investigate the possibility of extraterrestrial intelligence."

Lunkhead gapes. "Aliens? Little green men with antennas sticking out of their heads?"

"Hey, everyone," Bonnie says, as she and Danny emerge from the shadows and approach the group. Her lipstick is slightly smeared, and her red chiffon scarf flutters in the breeze.

Danny crouches by the fire to warm his hands. "What's shaking?"

Skipper's gaze slips right past Bonnie to focus on Danny. "We're all some kind of computer program on a spaceship hurtling through space. Colonel Merullo here is the only one who's really alive. And there might be aliens on Mars."

"Neptune," Lunkhead says.

"Triton," Merullo corrects.

"Sounds wild," Danny says, but something in his voice is just a little too casual, and Merullo wonders if he knows more than he's letting on.

But that's ridiculous, he thinks. Vee-Reel characters have no hidden agendas. They ask him if he wants to come sleep in the beach house for the night, but Merullo declines. The program will surely terminate by then. He leans back in the sand, trying not to worry about his spaceship, his crew, their mission. His dreams are full of stars and blackness. That too is ridiculous. Real people stuck in Vee-Reels do not dream.

Surf's up. Five seagulls skim the receding tide, hungry for breakfast.

"Something's wrong." Merullo stands over Violet's blanket, his voice tight with worry. "I have to get out of this. I'm the commander of this mission, my crew need me –"

Violet holds up a bottle of baby oil. "Will you put some of this on my back?"

He tries, but his gloved hands are too clumsy.

She sighs. "Come on, Pops. It's time to ditch these space duds."

Violet brings him up to the beach house, which has already emptied out for the morning. She picks through a pile of wrinkled clothes and pulls out some his size. In the bathroom, Merullo eases out of the spacesuit and scratches at his newly exposed, pasty-white skin. The denim shorts are too baggy. The T-shirt smells like the sweat and musk of other men. He takes a deep breath.

From the door frame, Violet says, "You don't like girls much, do you?"

Merullo flushes. "I don't know what you mean."

She gives him a humorless smile. "Sure you do. Skipper's that way, too. He keeps promising to change. But I don't think it's something you can change, like your haircut or the way you dress. Do you?"

He busies himself by hanging the spacesuit up on a rope that stretches over the bathtub. "I wouldn't know. Things like that aren't allowed in the Space Corps."

Violet rolls her eyes. "You're not in the Space Corps right now. You're in a Vee-Reel. Or so you say."

She brings him back to her blanket. Merullo tries not to stare at the guys in the volleyball pit as they leap in the air or dive for the ball. Violet watches the strong, lithe bodies with her eyes shaded by sunglasses. He thinks that he could tell her about himself, that Vee-Reels are often the repositories of hopes and secrets, but this isn't his program. It belongs to Mark Jenny.

Lunkhead bops on by. "Kowabunga, Colonel! Come ride the curl!"

"You should go," Violet says. "Clears your mind."

Merullo wades into the water, but it is cold and deep and he prefers dry land.

Later, a straight-laced reporter drops in to conduct an in-depth report about The Mind of Today's Teenager. A rich heiress falls in love with Danny and tries to whisk him away to Greece on her yacht. A drag race goes awry, a bikini contest turns ugly, and Lunkhead trades places with a British rock star who could be his long-lost twin. Life on the beach is wacky that way. The Vee-Reel refuses to disengage.

"Even if the crew can't turn off the system, all they have to do is pull the power on the unit," Merullo tells Danny. He scratches at his sunburned chest. He took off the T-shirt somewhere but can't remember where. "Mark knows the ship's specs backward and forward. But what if he's not awake? What if all of us are stuck in the entertainment system, or something is wrong with the ship itself – "

"You know what you need, Pops?" Danny drops his board into the surf. "Let go and hang loose. Learn to surf. I'm just the fellow to teach you."

Merullo's fists clench. "Maybe this Vee-Reel isn't what it appears to be. Maybe none of you are constructs. That radio signal from Triton – "

Danny snaps his fingers and juts out his hip and launches into "Dig Those Waves," another teen anthem – fast, breezy, easy to shake your hips to – with Bonnie singing backup and the rest of us pitching in on the chorus, and an unseen band providing the accompaniment. Everyone on the beach is bopping and twirling and shimmying, and for two perfect minutes all the world is young and in love, and the endless summer reaches the pinnacle of perfect happiness.

While we're singing, Merullo walks away.

Bonnie and Danny quarrel. She wants an engagement ring. He thinks that they have their whole lives ahead of them, so what's the rush? Merullo overhears part of it. They are so young, he wants to say. So naïve. He wonders if he's ever been married, if he's ever been in love. Life outside the Vee-Reel is slip, slip, slipping away. Later he finds Bonnie sitting alone on the beach, building a lopsided sandcastle.

"I was never very good at this," she admits. "The tower always falls over, or the moat caves in."

Merullo sits and starts helping her. The sand is warm and gritty, and gets under his fingernails. "I heard you fighting with Danny."

"He thinks we have forever. I think forever's over before you know it."

Out in the water, five dolphins breach the surface and quickly curve under again. Danny and the others are out bobbing in the lineup, but they are indistinct, fuzzy. The sunlight is very bright. Merullo thinks of Mark Jenny, and then dumps more sand into the pail.

"When you wake up and leave the program, could you take me with you?" Bonnie's expression is suddenly shy. "I think seeing a real-live spaceship would be groovy. There's an astronaut club at school, but they don't let girls join."

"This is where you belong, Bonnie."

"This isn't a place." Bonnie lifts her head and looks out toward the ocean. "It's just a stopover on the way to something bigger. Don't those movies of yours have endings?"

Indeed they do. First there will be a climax of sorts. It might be a zany motorcycle chase, with Danny and chums capturing the bad guys who never posed much of a threat anyway. Or maybe a skydiving sequence, or dance marathon, or some other test of young adulthood.

Then there will be a luau full of singing and dancing, one last hurrah of summer, before the credits roll.

"So maybe your ending is coming." Bonnie rests her soft hand on his. "Or maybe this whole thing will just start over. Do you know what's going to happen?"

Merullo squeezes her hand. "I don't know much of anything, anymore."

Rival surfers from another beach challenge Danny to a surf contest. Merullo watches the action from the high rocks near the water. Some of the contestants look like his crew – a Japanese man doing a handstand on a rushing board, a dark-skinned woman on the shoulders of a man Merullo's age. Some others look like his family, or friends long gone. Their names are lost to him. The outside world is so far away now that he might never get it back. He needs something to hold on to.

"My suit," he says to Violet, who has come to stand beside him. "It's the only proof I have."

"Proof of what?" Violet asks.

He's already sprinted past her, heading for the beach house. When he gets there, the bathroom clothesline holds only wet underwear and damp socks. The NASA spacesuit is gone.

"Where is it?" Merullo demands.

"I don't know," Violet says.

Lunkhead comes out of the kitchen, munching on a bag of potato chips. "Lose something?"

Merullo overturns mattresses and empties duffel bags. He digs through closets and cabinets. Over at Sammy's Pavilion, where Tiki torches flicker under the sunset sky, he sees Bonnie and Danny dancing cheek to cheek in the middle of the crowd. Becky Clark and Tommy Suede eventually grew up, grew old and died, but these two will be young forever.

Merullo grabs Danny's arm. "Where is it?"

"Where's what, Pops?" Danny asks.

"My goddamn spacesuit! What have you done with it?"

Nobody uses profanity on the beach. The music dies off and the dancing stops.

Merullo turns in a circle, challenging us all with outstretched hands. "Who are you? You brought me here, you trapped me, you won't let me leave – "

His voice cracks and fades. We shake our heads.

Danny steps toward him. "You can't leave because you won't let yourself. Because you haven't finished what you came here to do."

Bonnie's voice is just as compassionate and sympathetic as Danny's. "Look at the water, Colonel."

Five seagulls lay at the border of water and land, the wind ruffling the stiff feathers of their corpses.

"No." Merullo's legs fold under him and he lands on his knees. His eyes are wet. "Don't you understand? I'm in charge. I have a crew and ship to keep safe. We're on our way to Triton ..."

The seagulls fade into the sand. Where guys and gals once stood, there are only faint indentations in the sand. Sammy's Pavilion is gone, and empty beach blankets billow toward a sky that has gone silver-white. But the rolling blue ocean remains constant, and our hand is warm on Merullo's shoulder.

"Let go and hang loose," we tell him. "Surf's up."

"There was an alien radio message," Merullo insists.

"No. There was a malfunction on your Voyager craft. It detected and reported a distorted version of its own transmissions. That was all."

In the lineup, the water is flat and calm. We help him sit up and say, "When the wave comes, lay down and start paddling toward the beach as hard as you can while leaning forward. If you lean back, that'll just slow you down. But also keep your chest raised."

Merullo's fists tighten. "What happened to my ship?"

"An accident. It could no longer support you." We ruffle his thinning hair. "It wasn't your fault."

The water rises. We help Merullo to paddle toward the shore, pull himself upright, and stand low with his gaze held high. There's no blue screen backdrop or Vee-Reel special effect for this ride. Physics and balance rule the world. We're riding the perfect wave across the cosmos of time and memory, through the heart of a crippled spaceship and the five corpses secreted aboard, and toward the speck of beach that has always been nothing more than a temporary accumulation of sand and sorrow. The sun burns away all regret. The salty water lifts us up and makes us sing.

Merullo sees Mark Jenny standing on the shore.

"I've been waiting for you," Mark says, as Merullo emerges from the surf. Mark's suntanned face crinkles with affection, but there is concern there as well. "Where have you been?"

"Letting go. Hanging loose." Merullo has a wild grin on his face. He cups Mark's face with his strong, wet hands. "I'm sorry I never told you."

Mark smiles. "You don't think I knew?"

The story, as with every beach movie, ends with a kiss.

Thieves Don't Scream
by Janett L. Grady

Editor's Note

Sadly, Janett died shortly after we accepted "Thieves Don't Scream" for publication. Her husband has been kind enough to continue to work with us to bring "Thieves" to print. Janett lived and wrote with her husband in Palmer, Alaska. Her stories have appeared in magazines, anthologies, and on websites all over the States; and in a few publications based in Canada, the United Kingdom and Australia.

"As to how she came up with 'Thieves Don't Scream'," her husband says, "I have no idea, except to say I'm not surprised. Janett's venture into writing speculative fiction was brought on because she got bored with writing all that other stuff – religious, regional, history and so forth. If something weird or off-the-wall on the news caught her attention, she'd turn it into a speculative fiction piece – science fiction, fantasy or whatever ... with quite a bit of success, I might add. Working on spec stories is what kept her going, tweaking her imagination to the point of coming up with some really weird stuff."

Janett, we love and miss you. Nobody else does it quite the same.

She was not your average, run-of-the mill ghoul lurking in the shadows on dark and stormy nights, nor was she the blood-thirsty vampire you read about in horror magazines. No. Amy was something else. A bit weird, yes, but a careful and well-educated woman who thought of herself as being a decent person, a hardworking law clerk who just happened to have an obsession, an uncontrollable hunger for the occasional crunch of human bone, marrow soft and gummy with a touch of crisp.

How Amy acquired such a taste was a mystery even to her, but it might have had something to do with being born of a wicked, cannibalistic old hag who had finally been caught and lynched. Amy was born having a full set of permanent teeth, no growing and discarding of the usual baby-teeth, and two of her teeth just happened to be set one inch apart and a bit longer than her other teeth. However it happened didn't matter. Amy had never thought much about it, but had simply enjoyed the quirk of her off-the-wall appetite. She did, however, live in fear of being caught and hanged.

"Get right with God," she said. "I think you're dying."

She then left the bleeding drunk behind a dumpster. Amy half-walked, half-ran out of the alley and into the street, homeward bound, eyes scanning for cops.

Approaching her building, she smiled prettily at the old bum on the stoop, walked inside and hurried the four flights to her apartment. Only after she was inside, the battery of locks in place, did she lean against the wall and take a deep breath.

But there was still work to be done. She hurried into her bedroom, stripped, examined her skirt and blouse for traces of blood. Stains, still damp, were on her blouse. She stuffed her skirt and blouse into a laundry bag for the cleaners. She walked into her bathroom, brushed her teeth, paying particular attention to the gum line. Blood and something gray swirled into the drain. Amy then pulled on a robe, moseyed into her living room, poured herself a glass of brandy, plopped onto the couch and started sipping her drink. Now she allowed herself to remember.

She saw herself strolling through the alley toward her prey. Her skirt was short, slit to the hip. Was her blouse unbuttoned? It might have been. The smile. The nod. The feeling of power when she spun around and struck, slamming her fist to the back of his head, kicking at his groin as he fell, tearing open his shirt, stabbing her fist into his gut to rip out a bottom rib.

The sense of power was basic. It was, after all, easy to subdue a drunk. What amazed her, what completely amazed her, was the texture of gum-like flesh on her tongue, the scratch and break of crisp against her teeth, all somewhat rancid but thrilling. Now, recalling what she had done, she felt that sense of heightened intimacy. Captured in passion, Amy closed her eyes, drifted into a long and peaceful sleep, and dreamed the sweetest of dreams.

Morning light awakened her. She glanced at the clock on the mantel. 7:10 A.M..

"Damn, I'm going to be late."

Dashing into her bedroom, Amy tore off the robe.

Rummaging through her closet, she stepped into a pair of black slacks, buttoned a white blouse all the way up and pulled on a jacket, which matched her slacks. She checked herself in the mirror. The slacks were a bit wrinkled, so she quickly kicked them off, stepped into a pair of panties and pulled on an ankle-length skirt, which matched her jacket. She rechecked herself. She looked neat and well-groomed.

Amy raced out of the apartment carrying her bag of dirty clothes.

After dropping her laundry at the cleaners, Amy stood anxiously at the bus stop waiting for the bus that would take her to her job at the courthouse. There was no sign of the bus. If the bus was late, she'd be late, and the old judge would put on his sour face and say, "Late again huh?" It was the same old monologue, day in and day out. Abruptly she crossed the street before she could change her mind. She hurried to a Quick In-Quick Out store, fished for the cellphone in her purse and found a secluded spot near the pharmacy.

"Carter? Amy. Listen, tell the judge I'm not coming in. I'm going to the clinic. No, Carl, it's a female problem. You wouldn't understand. Yes, I'll do that. Thank you. Goodbye."

Carter had sounded pissed. For one brief moment, she had second thoughts. But it was too late now to reconsider.

She walked out of the store, stayed on the same side of the street. For the rest of her day off, Amy strolled, watching people and window shopping, her mind mostly on the drunk of the previous night. A-a-ah, the thrill. By three o'clock, Amy felt terribly anxious, hungered for the crunch of bone, the texture of marrow on her tongue.

She walked into a department store and wandered around. She turned right at Gloves and Purses, then paused, scanning the aisles for a potential victim. A bum with a hangover? A guy who looked lonely? That's when Amy saw the young girl, about twenty, shoulder-length hair, kitten-cute in a short white dress and shorter brown coat. The girl was at the jewelry counter, eyes darting warily about, and Amy knew what the girl was going to do even before seeing the small white hand close over the necklace, slide quickly into the coat pocket.

Amy followed her through the doors and into the street. "Hold it right there," Amy said. "You forgot to pay for that necklace." The girl stopped in front of a window filled with naked mannequins. She turned to face Amy, eyes downcast, pretty little jaw trembling. "I saw you take it," Amy told her.

"Oh, please," said the girl through quivering lips. "Please let me go."

"Can't do it," said Amy. "You're a thief."

"Here," said the girl, reaching into her pocket, "take it."

Amy raised a protesting hand. "Can't do it," she said. "If you get away with it once, you'll do it again."

The girl fumbled through a small brown purse and brought forth a fifty-dollar bill. "I'll pay for it," she whined. "Please ... please take it and let me go."

"Well ... " There was hesitation in Amy's voice, but the hand that snatched the fifty showed not the slightest pause. " ... all right, but there's more to it." she said, tucking the bill into the pocket of her skirt. "We're going back to the store," she said. "I want to see the clerk ring it up."

"But ... "

"No buts," Amy cut in. "Let's go." She latched onto the girl's arm and dragged her along, walking swiftly until coming to the alleyway of the previous night. "Through here," Amy insisted, and pulled the girl into the shadows.

A setting sun to the west kept the shadows from becoming too dark in most of the alley, but on a short stretch, tall buildings screened off the light. When they reached the darker stretch of alleyway, it was like walking into the ladies room of a rundown bar. Dim light. Eyes slow to adjust. Steps cautious. As they made their way through the shadows, stepping around barrels of garbage, something scurried in the trash behind them.

"What was that?" the girl asked.

"Rats," Amy answered. "They live here."

"I don't like rats," the girl whined. "They're scary."

Amy almost felt sorry for her, but not quite. Her arm felt warm and vibrant in Amy's hand, and Amy gave it a final, sudden squeeze. Then she struck, punching gut, an uppercut to the chin. The girl fell back and Amy pounced, yanking hair, grabbing a wrist and chomping down on a pair of fingers. Squirming and flailing her other arm, the girl was moaning and groaning but not screeching and screaming. Amy thanked God for that, and, after one long chewing on bone, Amy climbed off.

"You're one tough chick." Amy grinned. "Forget about going back to the store," she added. "I want you to squeeze off the bleeding, then make your way to the street, find help and head for the nearest emergency room."

Amy felt proud of herself. She hadn't hurt the girl too-too bad, or at least there was little chance of the girl bleeding to death. Amy thought of herself as a good person.

Leaving the girl whimpering behind a trash bin, Amy felt somewhat satisfied but still a bit hungry. She walked out of the alley and into the street. She hailed a cab, and the yellow sedan slid to a halt at the curb. Amy ordered the driver to drive her around. She had some serious thinking to do. She reached into her pocket and pulled out the fifty. She stared at it, amazed that her victim had actually paid her. Amy toyed with a new idea. Unlike the bums and drunks, her usual prey, shoplifters couldn't afford to be screaming for the cops. There'd be less danger of getting caught. She brought the fifty up to her lips and kissed it. Her day off had progressed amazingly well, and there were reasons to believe the rest of her day held promise. She ordered the driver to take her back to the store.

BIRTH
by Victoria Hooper

EDITOR'S NOTE

Victoria Hooper is a writer and editor living in Nottingham. She's a huge fan of all things fantasy, science-fiction, paranormal, magical, weird and mythical, and is a staff writer for Fantasy Faction. *She also happens to have been my editor on two novels. She loves video games and cheesy movies, and can easily be bribed with chocolate brownies. Find her on Twitter @VickyThinks, or on her blog: vickyhooper.blogspot.co.uk.*

"The beginnings of this story started fermenting after playing one of the inspiration games on Chuck Wendig's blog," says Victoria. "The idea is to roll dice three times to select certain elements from a list, and then combine them into one story. My rolls bagged me these beauties: childbirth, weird, and insects. But it wasn't until I was talking with a friend that the whole thing came together. We were discussing which things might be particularly difficult to make scary in a story, and she reckoned kittens could never be creepy. Challenge accepted!"

And a challenge fulfilled. You'll never look at kittens the same way again.

Suki leaves her bowl and totters over to her bed by the radiator. She's dragged the faded old rug from the sofa, arranging it into comfy peaks and hollows in her basket, twirling in circles until it's patted down just right. She mews at me, a little pathetically, but she looks contented enough. I join her on the floor behind the sofa, caressing her head as she squeezes her eyes tight in pleasure, crooning to her softly as she purrs back.

I wake in the dark, the sun down but the moon bright through the blinds. It's almost full, a heavy moon ripe and bloated with promise. Like Suki. It won't be long before each of them peaks. Just a few days now. Suki is asleep and purr-snoring in her little nest.

I pull myself up, walk over to the window and peer out. It's only 6.30 pm and the street below is unusually quiet. There's an odd yowling sound, like a cat but harsher and meaner, the kind of noise that raises the hackles. This is not the first time I've heard it, and I wonder vaguely if the neighbourhood has a fox problem. No-one on the street seems to notice, hunched and bent forwards against the cold, hurrying home.

Shadows move across the roof tiles opposite, like a creature skittering, or tree branches scraping the night. Living on the third floor affords a great view of the rooftops, and of the odd ornamentation found on some of older buildings in the city. Like the gargoyle face two houses down, angled out as if peering along the street at my flat. Not a gargoyle like on a church, but a tiny, pale-stone creature, half cherub and half something whiskered, with sharp teeth. One side of its face has crumbled, giving it a lopsided look.

I twist the rod and the slats inch shut, slicing the moonlight into bars before snapping it out. I flick on the lamp, and choose a book for the evening; creepy stories for cold nights. I settle down. Suki chirrups gently in her sleep.

Outside my breath forms smoke-creatures; in the underground it's perpetually stuffy, as always. The trains on this stretch of the Piccadilly Line have been canceled, which means taking the longer route, losing enough time that I'll have to powerwalk the last steps to work. I hate arriving in the office disheveled.

I hear cats in the underground. Softly at first, in the distance, then closer. At first I think that Suki has somehow followed me, then I realize that it isn't her sound. This is throatier, and besides, it comes from more than one direction. Could there be cats living in the Tube, I wonder. And, am I going mad? I miss Suki; I hate leaving her at this time. She's a first time mother, still surprised by changes in her body, and I'm *Suki's* mother. I should be with her. But work hardly grants time off for cat pregnancies.

There are shadows bobbing at the end of the tunnel, where the rail stretches into darkness, and I hear chittering. I half expect to see the milky glow of eyes reflecting the station lights, but it's just the train that arrives, ordinary, shuddering to a stop. I shake it off. *Reading too much horror before bed.*

I should be working, but instead I'm reading up on cat births on the internet. What to expect. What can go wrong. The websites are written in a reassuring, friendly tone, but my anxiety is a contrary monster. Reassurance only seems to feed it.

"Kel?"

I wonder if I have everything. Suki could pop at any time and I need to be prepared, and *oh god what if she's already in labor*, all on her own in the empty flat?

"Kelly?"

A shadow falls across my screen and I close the browser guiltily.

It's Jo; who else? She stares at me for a few seconds, her eyes knowing and pitying and smug all at once. My nails bite into the underside of the desk.

"Cat sites again, eh?"

I don't answer.

She perches on the edge of the desk.

"You shouldn't stress so much, you know," she says. "You'll have kittens." She grins as if she's made the greatest joke in the world.

I stare back at her, and a flicker of annoyance passes through her eyes.

"You need to get a grip Kelly." She smiles, but it's almost a sneer.

As she walks off, I turn back to the computer, gazing straight through the blank screen. She's right about one thing; I need to find a way to de-stress. I can't help Suki properly when I'm this jittery.

I bring up the browser again and type "kittens" into Google images. Nothing like a kitten-in-a-mug photo to ease the blood pressure. The site is painfully slow to load, one of the drawbacks of image surfing on company time.

The page begins to reveal, peeling downwards slowly, and something is wrong. A ragged ear, disjointed little faces, insect-like joints. As the pictures inch into visibility, the kitten-creatures only become more horrific. One stands with legs splayed, the fur on its back bulging and splitting open to reveal a grey carapace below the surface, like a giant bug hatching from a walking corpse.

The kitten in the image turns to look at me, and in unison so do the others. Skin undulates and ripples as what's left of the kittens transforms.

I jab at the mouse, minimizing the window, and squeeze my eyes shut until purple tendrils stain my vision. *No!* I hear Jo's voice: *You need to get a grip Kelly. Get a grip.* Suki nurses her baby as it stretches, testing fibrous wings. Suki lies in her basket crying, as barbed claws rake at her belly from inside. *No!*

I open my eyes and the Internet window in one quick motion. The kitten pictures are just kittens. Fluffy, saucer-eyed, mammalian. I breathe out.

Shakily, I open up a new window and type 'signs of stress' into the search bar.

The minutes drag like lifetimes, minutes in cat years, and the clock above the coat-pegs drums steadily to the beat of an unborn heart.

It's dark outside; Helen's impromptu team-meeting kept us almost two hours. The temperature has plummeted since yesterday, which was already cold enough, and the air reeks of impending snow.

I hurry through the busy streets, squeezing past Christmas shoppers dawdling by the windows. Normally a cacophony of noise and color, London has faded into the background like the world observed through water. Reality is rippling, and there seems to be nothing I can do to prevent it.

At the underground station, commuters dissolve into the walls. The ceiling drips faces like stalactites, and they chitter at me as I wait. I am relieved when the train arrives. It restores rigidity, if only for the briefest moment.

It's only as I reach the turnstile that I realize something is following me. Padding, cat-like, in the shadows, it keeps its distance until the subway steps, then flows upright and continues beside me as a person-shaped billow of darkness.

I glance sideways, but the creature doesn't turn. I walk the rest of the way pretending that I have not seen it. It doesn't seem to mind. The silence is almost companionable.

At my door I risk another glance, but the shadow is only shadow and nothing more. I turn the key and hurry inside, dead-bolting the door behind me. Outside, a fat moth lands on the window with a thud. It scrabbles at the glass, and is soon joined by another. Together their wings form eight lidless eyes, peering in with arachnid intent.

I close all the blinds.

In the living room, Suki mews her greeting, but she is too comfy to get up to greet me. I walk over to her instead, and massage the soft fur behind her ears.

"Such a good cat," I tell her in my babies-and-animals-voice. "Sweet cat. You're gonna be such a great mother." She purrs at me and rubs her head against my hand. "We're gonna put all your kittens in little mugs and take pictures of them, yes we are!" (Purr)

I leave Suki snug in her basket and walk through to the tiny kitchen, flicking the kettle on and grabbing a new box of Suki's treats from the cat-goodies cupboard. I pour her a bowl, grimacing at the little brown and pink nuggets, shaped like organs – hearts, kidneys, livers, stomachs... since when have fish shapes gone out of fashion?

I pad back through into the living room and yelp in surprise. My laptop, which had been turned off, is open on the coffee table, light pooling out from it onto the floor. I inch over to it, afraid to look. The screen shows my desktop, but the background image has been changed to a mother and her kittens, all huddled together in a giant ball of fur.

As I watch, the image alters, horribly. Bones in the kittens' backs snap upwards and long, angled limbs emerge. Fur gives way to chitin and shell. The mother wakes and looks at her monstrous offspring adoringly, licking the tops of their half-morphed heads.

No. Not again. With a shaking hand I reach out and close the laptop. *It's not real.*

I open the lid. The laptop's power is off.

My shoulders slump. I turn to Suki, but something's not right there either. She's snoozing, as sweet as ever, but her fur is moving oddly, rippling under the skin like there are thousands of insects scurrying beneath it. I stare at her in horror.

I jump as the blinds clack, and I realize that the window is open. It's colder in here now, naturally, but also darker, as if the light is seeping out of the opening. I hurry over and slam it shut, staring fearfully out into the night. The neighbor's gargoyle glares back at me.

When I turn back to Suki she looks normal again, dozing peacefully, and the growing sense of menace has gone. I tell myself that I'm going crazy, but I only half believe me.

Suki opens one eye and gives me a quizzical look. I return it with a lopsided smile.

"Your owner's cuckoo, huh Suki? Mummy's a fruit and nut case." She purrs.

I thought I would have nightmares, but when I do dream it's warm and cozy. I am Suki's kitten, fuzzy and small, curled into Suki's side. Suki smells musty and sweet, and I have a strong sense of safety. Suki licks my head, her tongue like gentle sandpaper. It's both protective and oddly sensual. I turn to look at her, and her beautiful amber eyes fill my world.

I wake, shivering. It's so cold in the flat, and I long for the warmth of my dream. I look over to the window. It's open, but the air is soft and still.

There is a figure at the edge of the bed.

It's the same creature that followed me home, I'm sure. I lie, rigid, unable to move or to take my eyes away from it. It's facing away, only a small part of its face visible in profile, but the moonlight catches the tilted jaw, painting one curved mandible silver. It turns, slowly.

As it drifts towards the door, the world blurs once more into sleep.

I call in sick in the morning. Suki is restless and agitated. She mews repeatedly, and paws at her blanket. I don't think it will be long now.

I can't eat breakfast. Instead, I sit backwards on the sofa, my cheek resting against the back as I watch Suki. I don't want to cause her further stress by sitting too close, but I can't bear to be far away either. The yowl outside has returned, perhaps in sympathy pangs for

Suki. I ignore it.

I'm glad to see Suki get up to eat. Her belly drags almost to the floor now. She looks exhausted already. I want to snuggle beside her and soothe her, but I know she is best left to herself, for now.

I stretch, arching my back and yawning deeply, and in her basket Suki yawns too. Yawning is a cross-species infection; I hope insanity isn't as well. At least the flat is finally warm. I blink, half close my eyes, and feel myself beginning to doze.

Suki yelps in pain, and I start, wide awake again. She frets a little more, then settles. It's not time yet, but soon. Very soon now.

I get up to stretch my legs. The flat is warm enough that the windows have fogged up, like we are being enchanted away from the world, sealed into our own little bubble. I feel slightly dizzy, and have to lean on the chair by the window.

Something presses against the glass. It's thin, like a twig, but I know what it is. Another joins it, and another. Fingers scrape at the window-fog, and though the condensation is all on my side of the glass, I am not at all surprised to see a clear circle appearing. A face pushes up against it and stares through at me, a face of shadow and moonlight. Its whiskers twitch.

I stare back at it, willing my gaze not to slide to the handle, but the creature seems to have no interest in coming in this time. It morphs and oozes, skittering across the glass and then solidifying again, gazing past me at the sofa. It remains there, occasionally shifting form, clinging to the window like a cricket. Eventually I turn my back and return to Suki, the hairs along my neck bristled despite the flat's warmth.

As the hours crawl past, Suki totters up twice to use her litter box, and each time the face at the glass follows her through to the hallway window, then back. I begin to feel sick with anxiety, remembering the pictures on the internet. Suki is only hours, maybe minutes from birth, and I still can't truly acknowledge the terror that's freezing me from the inside out: I have never let Suki out of the flat. She's a pampered house-cat, and there's no flap on the door. What is she carrying?

I close my eyes, then look to the window. The creature is still there, poised against the glass, a horrifying synergy of insectile and feline, watching Suki. It has separated itself now, and in the fading light there is a shadow at every window, with scurrying and skittering in-between.

Suki makes an odd sound, and I whip round. It's begun.

Suki's labor is short, but it seems to last all night. She is very quiet; the whole flat is eerily quiet in fact, and the babies, whatever they are, do not cry or squeal as they are born. I can't look too close. I hover at the edge of the sofa, but leave Suki to cope as she will. She will let me know if she needs me.

When it's done, Suki licks the tiny things clean, then curls herself around them. There's a newborn smell on the air – musty and sweet. I remember my dream, and I can't keep myself from Suki anymore.

I approach the basket, and, steeling myself, look inside. Suki has five kittens, beautiful little things, with teeny-tiny paws and noses, and thin, stubby tails. One of them squeaks slightly, and Suki gently licks its head.

They are perfect. Five ordinary kittens, helpless and cute.

I stumble to my bed and flop, crying with relief into my pillow until I fall asleep.

I dream again of Suki, curling her paw around me protectively and keeping me safe from the world.

I wake at a noise from the living room. A small thud, and another. I slip out of bed and hurry through, hoping there is nothing wrong with the kittens.

The kittens are all out of the basket, standing together in a line. As I come into the room they gaze up at me in unison, their eyes bright and intelligent. These are no newborns. I stumble backwards and grab the edge of the sofa for support. As I watch, the kittens enlarge, their paws stretching and thick fur sprouting along their backs. They would be adorable if they weren't so creepy.

They huddle together and begin to tumble over each other,

as if playing some kind of sinister kitten-monster game. I watch as their bodies begin to merge, fur billowing and skin oozing, joining limbs and faces together. The kitten-blob turns to me, and still I'm rooted to the spot as it bends upwards, morphing into something vaguely person-shaped. One moment its skin is like oil, deep and purple-black, fluid underneath loose, greasy skin, and the next it's as if the creature is formed of a million skittering beetles, their quivering antennae all watching me at once. Then a sharp crack as bones begin to harden and snap into place. It bubbles, and features form on its face. I shake my head as it changes, solidifies into me.

For a second that feels like the whole world, I stare into my own eyes. Then I'm falling, a sense of crushing weight washing over me as I shrink down to the floor. My thoughts, for a moment, are doubled, tripled, confused, before I slide apart. I gaze, uncomprehending at first, and then with dawning horror, at my own sets of paws.

The kittens who are now me look down at the me who is now kittens. It stoops, Kelly stoops, and tickles gently behind one of our ears as we cuddle into our mother. Kelly seems as tall as the sky, and just as strong. We know we trust her.

"Such pretty kittens," Kelly croons, her voice loud but sweet. We purr.

DREADFUL DAUGHTERS
by Tantra Bensko

EDITOR'S NOTE

Tantra Bensko teaches fiction writing through UCLA Ex. Writing Program, WritersCollege, and her own online academy. She obtained her MA from FSU and her MFA from Iowa, while teaching at both universities. She has two books out (with one more slated), four chapbooks (including from Rachel Kendall's ISMs Press), and 200 stories in journals and anthologies, such as Red Fez, Mad Hatters Review, Birkinsnake, *and* Surreal South. *She publishes chapbooks through LucidPlay Publishing, maintains a resource site,* Experimental Writing, *published* Exclusive Magazine, *and runs the FlameFlower Experimental Fiction contest. She lives in Berkeley and maintains a web presence at lucidmembrane.weebly.com.*

Tantra's piece was written specifically for this anthology. Here's what she says about her process: "I let myself go hedonistically full strength into playing with the subconscious tone of my own failings as a daughter, my regret that I wasn't there more than I was at the end of Mama's life. My wish to apologize to her haunts me daily. But rather than hold back and be polite and try to write the kind of thing her hypothetic ghost would approve of, I tend to write just the opposite: bizarro, sensual, transgressive literature I know would make her belch. I want somehow this seemingly impossible thing: I want her to stay herself yet also move into some place of acceptance for me and all the things about me that disturbed her. Like the mother in the beginning of the complex of narratives within the story, she wouldn't even pet my head because she thought it would make me a lesbian. She wouldn't let me play with a girl at elementary school any more because I said I loved her.

"She was an integral, loving woman with strict, old-fashioned tastes, and that's fine; she was a fabulous mother. It wasn't her fault, but the family dynamics did contribute to my developing anorexia nervosa when adolescent. I made myself as trembling small and perfect and quiet as I could back then, but in this story, I'm letting it all out, being big and loud and wrong. And I hid the supplements she gave me to take all those

years growing up to make up for not eating, because it was physically impossible for me to swallow them. Mama never forgave me for that. That's where I began the narrative, going into the guilt I felt about those things and I let it carry me into my subconscious where zany, bizarre dream-like stories were having a wild party dancing with fun to forget the real pain of wanting to make Mama happy.

"For me, going into my subconscious through an authentic feeling is the best way to find the strangeness I enjoy most which speaks most relevantly to other people's subconscious. And perhaps if you get something out of the story, maybe some universal bit of Mama floating through you embraces me too. After the intro bit, none of my short story elements are true. But just writing it let me face that I am a dreadful daughter indeed, who loves her mother so very, very intensely she could cry the whole world out her eyes."

There are layers upon layers of meaning in Tantra's story – layers of sadness and anger and regret and boldness and fear and bravery. I've read it several times, shook it out, looked at it from different directions, pondered the mother and daughter – so locked together, so alike, so different. So much like we are, trying to make sense of relationships buried in the silt of the past, braced against the future wreckage.

1.

Every shining supplement Mama gave me, I pretended to take, putting them in my hands, my hands to my mouth, making all the gulping and extensions and satisfactions of my muscular structure galore. I kept them in my curled white boney hand, gracefully, eating with one hand, never gesturing with the curled one, hidden in the red veined long toothed farting maw of the inability to swallow pills, nesting between my adolescent thighs. Drooling as the pills heated in my sweat.

One story about Mama's life, glued inexorably to the next. Stories I'd heard a thousand times, yet I asked warm questions, absorbing the brown sandy past of her and eccentric ancestors through my dilated pupils.

I learned I could enter the world of strange people and humor them further than anyone else could. They appreciate it. You keep your eyes open and brain-waves synced in true wonder. You ride the Wonder-Horse, the Hell-Hen, the Gander-of-Forever, into the night skies, the stars the stars, with them. They want you to.

If they turn to the right when they're talking, head down, you follow them. They'll turn all the way in a circle, and you follow them all the way around. You're Joneses.

I carried the supplements to my room and opened my minion hand onto the closet, the horror-fingers opening to plop out whites and yellows, greens, too big for my crooked throat no one had yet looked into and seen. Unlike anyone had ever seen in there. Because I have a crooked head, an unhinged jaw, and the top of my skull is fallen: a dentist pulled too many teeth when I was forming. I am I, as long as I pouf my hair before anyone sees me, and cover up the lack of a top of my head with my comb, backwards furtively against the grain of wheat colored hair, teasing.

Some girl at school stood behind me at lunch and combed, getting out knots of matted matte, no matter how often brushed.

I didn't eat dinner for weeks at a time. My dinner, I'd tell Mama, I'm taking to the creek for a picnic. I'd open it out criminally onto the ground for the raccoons to eat, food she has made me with her money-love and tells everyone about – well, everyone being – no one. She has no friends but me. She makes the most beautiful food, like art. It's her life, cooking for me. But if I eat it, you won't be able to see my bones and braces, my tremble slender, my dance bird, my poem skin.

I don't let the girl at school, who almost never talks to me anyway, brush at the top of my head. But what if she did brush it, while my attention got caught up in the food someone was eating. I ate nothing, ever, for lunch. What if I became mesmerized by someone's salad and she unpoufed my tease, and the monstrosity of my freak-skull avenged itself upon the table full of "friends," and not-friends.

I can't tell Mama the girl brushes my hair. She'd tell me to never speak to her again. Even *she* wouldn't pat my hair, because that's gay.

2.

Letter to the Editor:

My mother is after me today because I used the word "single" in her presence. She says I'm a mollusk, a comquit muskeedine, a quince squished on the road, a road apple. She leaves such notes all over the house. I'm going to use them as a suicide note, spread over me like leaves in the Fall when you go jumping in the burn-pile. Should I set them on fire? Or would that destroy the evidence? Would my ghost be mingled with it as I rise up with the smoked notes, my ribs intersected with "scum of the scullery", "drudge of doom", "horror of Nicwick Alley" and "turd"?

Last week she came after me because I borrowed her heating pad. The notes might as well bite my earlobes off and chew them up for spit. So, in case I burn them, you'll know you can print this. If I don't burn them, let them speak for themselves, over my scorched and withered body, wearing the word "single" burned into me with a blow torch, a picture of my mother glued to it with my melted flesh.

Here's the picture. Her name is Cynthia Webbern.

Yours always,

Letty

3.

Oh when we saw the Docent's Daughter, we vibrated our tendrils at her, elongated our tongues, scented the air. The Docent. Our friend, who has rendezvous with women in our park after hours, always picks places where only grass grows to lay her down in the moonlight. He's careful where he hops the fence, so he doesn't trample any plants, just the dirt around the shrubs. He's so darling to us, singing in falsetto what he calls his "Megalomaniac Song."

Father's Day today, we hear, and he brought his little girl, named Mollypolly, in a dress with little raised white dots, on yellow. The dandelions quivered in response until she prescribed us medicine and dumped some gooey liquid on us. The toads blinked and gulped close by until she put a tiny collar on one of us, and dragged it behind her chubby legs. The native plant section sizzled in despair when she pulled out her toy tuba and caused us to decay at a fast rate of brown, around her frilly monstrosity of delight, that poufy dress, those rounded sleeves, that nothing in the ears but horrorsound, loud inside the stomata too, loud inside the centers of the flowers, delicate, porous.

She yelled at the vines and pulled us down, laughing, and rolling into a ball, tied up by us. We became like a ball of fetal twine, attached to the ground, rolling around the ground with the tiny hairs of the vines grasping at nothing, air where their world should be, her giggles blasting their leaves.

She painted two turtles' backs and threw us over the bridge into the pond, to clap as we swam inside the spreading holocaust of color. She swallowed a slug.

The Docent knew everything about the park, so what could we do? His clear observances and keen eyesight kept magick at a minimum. No raucous blustery, no levitational device, no flinging off the bended branch.

His woman, we wanted to whisper to the girl. Her perfume is our fragrance. Smell it on her, and never want to smell us again. Realize she is your mother's devil, and flee this place of hedonistic iniquity. But we loved the Docent, and didn't know his wife. If we'd met her instead, perhaps we'd have no loyalty to his secrets. If he didn't water us on weekends. If he didn't cry on us after hours, after the woman leaves.

What could we do? We ran. All the grasses, and trees and squirrels. All of us ran in her dream, as she napped on the bench waiting while he drank his rye in the bathroom. Some of us ran at her, some ran away, as we didn't have time to plan it out. The rushing of the waves of glasses one way and another served to dizzy her so much that on awaking, she ran into a tree and broke her noggin, and was no longer such a problem little child.

4.

After that livid day when my chest hurt so much I turned inside out, and my veins took over, and my blood ran away, and my brain got stuck, and I couldn't get out of bed, no one talks to me any more. It's been weeks, and my daughter keeps lying on top of me in bed. She smokes. I never knew that. And drinks. Makes me wish I were dead.

That boyfriend of hers with the long hair has been lying in bed next to me. They roll over and have – belch – sex right on top of me. It's the most dreadful behavior I've ever imagined in my 80 years. They must be trying to hurt my feelings more than I imagined possible by pretending I'm not here.

They pretend to be me, belching, and laugh, falling over each other, like I'm not there. She says she just wanted me to have heart surgery so I'd stick around and take care of her father, so she wouldn't have to. She says she sends me energy every day to send me on my way. It's like she thinks I'm supposed to float up to the ceiling or something, the way she turns her eyes up and I can see the whites under them – belch.

She says she doesn't believe in flowers on the grave, only sex. She says she wishes she hadn't inherited my fat gene, and she could have been happy. She says she hypnotizes herself often to believe she had a different mother. One who held her little body up to the sun, saying Be kind to this little one, oh world. She says as long as her subconscious believes she had a different mother, she has self-confidence, and can give better sensual massages to her clients, on my bed, on top of me. I can't understand how I'm so flat, but I sure like it better than being fat.

5.

I went in crying, and told our daughter you were giving us almost no money these days, so when it came time to determine the amount of alimony you're supposed to pay me, so I could live in the state to which I'd become accustomed. Know what she said? "But shouldn't you be able to go without food for a long time, and live on all that fat?"

I said, "Oh! You don't know what you're talking about."

"And she said, "Obviously, I know more about it than you do," and she turned her perfect double-lemon bottom in the air.

6.

I told her not to go down to the interstate spur in all this snow, on top of all those days of rain. The ground is like quicksand, where they're constructing the road. So, why should I be expected to go down and rescue her? Didn't she tell you I said you girls couldn't go down there today? I guess it's not your fault, so just have some hot chocolate, and tell me what it's like for her. How far down in the ground her legs had sunk by the time you freed yourself from your boots, and ran in your socks in the snow through the forest, up the hill, to our chocolate house? Here, have some whipped cream.

How long have her legs been stuck in the ground, which is freezing around her boots? You say she tried to wave down a plane? How cute, except I *told* her not to go down there. How sad except now I'm supposed to put one piece of cardboard down after another, like mobile snow shoes, for miles down the woods and ravine and construction site, and pull her out of the ground and onto me on the snow, going down into the mud, my bottom stuck down inside the mud the last minute before the squush turns to solid gripping eternity of cold.

7.

The frog jumped into her lap as she read the personals, on the park bench, looking for another ghost to try to get to know. So it would tell her where it stashed the wealth. Maybe a caregiver position, or a marriage proposal. You could always tell which ones were written by ghosts who hadn't realized they were dead. They were the easiest to con cause they really didn't have it goin' on any more. They were a little slow.

She found one written, surprisingly, by her own mother. She'd suspected her mother didn't know she had croaked. "Oh, sorry about the language, froggie," she said, figuring frogs are telepathic. But by that time, it had already peed on her privates, and bounced down.

She lifted her bottom up to let the pee run down her little triangle, in the perfect spot to make a statement to anyone wandering by in the park of such perfectly trimmed hedges. She'd had sex in those hedges by the playground where her mother had taken her when she was little. In fact, her mother had been sitting in the swing, by herself, taking in the fine March wind on her upturned face, swinging thoughtfully, humming.

She knew it was her fault her mother had died of anorexia. Well, she almost had, too. They almost had become two sides of one skull, fused, the parietal bones breathing slowly with the pumping of the cerebral spinal fluid, pulse pulse. They had both almost disappeared, when her father had withheld money from them before the divorce. They had both felt no right to exist, had tried to win his love by smallness, tenderness, inexpensiveness.

She, however, was not going to let that stop her from writing back to the personals ad and finding out what she could. Maybe just find out what her mother would tell a perfect stranger about her, when asked. Maybe to find out about money she'd hidden away. Maybe to pretend to want to marry her, and get her going, show her what a hold passion can have, show her how it can twist a life up like it did hers, how even her mother has a weakness for the right suitor. She knew just how to compose the letters that would make her mother melt, drip, perungulate. She knew how to woo her so hard, she'd understand. She'd love her. She'd understand.

8.

Hiding her suicide note from her mother in her fat hand, she gracelessly fell into the mud when her mother reached out her snow-littered gloved hand. She roundly fell on top of a frog, pounding it into the slushy freezing mud, where it began writhing to escape its fate. Her mother used all her weight and pulled her out of the mud and made her sit down on the park bench while she patted the snow off of her.

She knew her ghost, from after she killed herself, was watching from the future. She saw her ghost hover over her mother, crying. She saw the ghost, from behind her, reach around, moving toward tapping her mother's arm, and warn her about it with a premonition. "Piss off," she said to the ghost. Who slunk away flat footed, stepping on the frog, without realizing it, who had just freed itself from the mudden grip.

HEADS WILL ROLL
by Rachel Kendall

EDITOR'S NOTE
Rachel Kendall is the editor of Sein und Werden. *Her second short story collection,* The Bride Stripped Bare, *was published by Dog Horn Publishing in 2009. Her first,* Her Black Little Heart, *was self-published in 2004.*

"This story was originally written for the 'Pharmacopoiea' issue of Sein und Werden," *said Rachel. "I was thinking of the phrase 'heads will roll' when a whole gamut of bodily/visceral phrases and clichés started to form themselves into a story in my head. I love the idea of a person's sides actually splitting, or someone wearing guts for garters. Sometimes clichés, though they should usually be avoided, make for the best surreal tales."*

I rather lost my head over this particular story, myself. If you find it, please return to the Dog Horn offices.

I knew I was in love the day I lost my head. It took me completely by surprise, both the head-ejection and the question that came before. I'd only known him for two weeks, so when he asked me to move in with him it would be completely in keeping with my usual responsible character to laugh it off as a bad joke. Instead, on this particular day, my mind tumbling like a dinghy on the high seas, I opened my mouth and vomited the word "okay". Immediately, POP, WHOOSH, my head left my neck and shot six feet into the air, coming down to land in a thorny shrub. It left my dress quite blood-soaked, and my body disorientated. I didn't know if I was coming or going for a moment. However, my love retrieved my head, a little bruised and scratched but otherwise in fine fettle. He gave it a slow, sensuous kiss on my responsive mouth and then placed it carefully back upon my neck.

At which point I immediately retracted my leisurely consent with a shake of my wobbling head. It was a ridiculous notion, I told him, as I felt my head slot comfortably back into place. He sulked.

He complained. But I knew I'd done the right thing in order to retain my sanity. We couldn't live together yet. We didn't know each other. We hadn't had time to experience and then put up with each other's weird little nuances, the things that tortured us, the neuroses and fireworks. So I knew I'd made the right decision in the end and over the days and weeks that followed, the steadfast hold of my head on its column was confirmation of a right decision.

But his love began to waver. He grew physically distant and emotionally recalcitrant, as though he really couldn't cope with a little rejection. And soon, as though in response, I began to feel a loosening around my neck. If the car in which I was a passenger turned the corner a little too fast, or if my bump 'n' grind became a little *too* bumpy, my head would threaten to topple. I needed a permanent solution, before I lost my head again and did something silly to remind him he did indeed love me terribly.

I decided to go to the "Heads Will Roll" barber-sturgeon on Cutting Street.

His place of office was hard to miss. The slowly-turning barber's pole beside the door and the window display of perfectly polished surgical instruments confirmed his medical/aesthetic creativity and I was in no doubt he'd be able to help me.

He barely glanced at my precariously-balanced head before grunting, "You need stitches. Why didn't you come to me immediately? Ridiculous. Sit down please." He motioned to one of the barber chairs. Beside me a young man was being de-loused.

"I didn't realize it was that serious," I said, honestly. There was also the fear, of course. Not of surgery but of this particular sturgeon. He was rude, foreboding and smelly. He treated his nurses with contempt and, I'd heard, wouldn't hesitate to draw blood when working over the five o'clock shadow of an enemy with his cut-throat razor.

There was also, of course, Aunt Mabel, who lost her mind in 1973. Back then, medicine was not as advanced as it is today and it left her holier than Emmental. The trepanabotomy technique had its flaws. After much skull-duggery and whole-body scans it turned out her mind had completely relocated to her womb, which explained the beginnings of her prolapse. That pink flesh showing itself was the result of extra pressure inflicted by her heavy mind. There always *had* been a lot on it – affirmations, contradictions, salutations. Its decision to rove was quite inevitable really, a complete hysterectomy the only possible solution and now, carrying around a hole in her belly as well as a hole in her head, Aunt Mabel was really nothing more than an empty snail shell, her sticky innards scooped out and discarded.

"It's starting to rot," said the barber-sturgeon, as his nurses helped him on with his gown and stretched it around his humungous body. It stuck, in patches, to his wet skin.

"Headaches, you say?" he asked as he tapped my head on one side and then the other to assess the speed and angle of my head's wobbling trajectory.

"I'm not surprised. Sit forward please." As I did so I got another whiff of that awful gone-off fish-smell.

An angel fish wearing a yellow surgical mask that flattered the yellow of her beautiful tail tied up my hair, while another fixed a brace to my head to keep it firmly in position. A local anesthetic was given while the sturgeon threaded a needle with fishing wire. I held my breath as he began to sew and watched in the mirror, trying to alleviate my anxiety by creating familiar images in the mess of his blood-stained gown. I was looking for animals, flowers, shoes. Instead all I could see were agonized screams and instruments of torture.

But when it was done it was done, and I was happy with the results. It was a neat job. The criss-cross pattern was attractive, despite my reddened neck beginning to swell, and I was pleased with the effect.

"Now," said the big fish, "how about a trim while you're here?"

I ended up with a complete new head of hair - colored, cut and curled – to mark the occasion of my new level-headedness, and left the barber's with all my anxieties gone. I felt good.

So when my boyfriend came round that evening to tell me we were through, I didn't take it too badly. Though I could feel my stitches straining, my head desperately trying to detach itself, I didn't lose my cool. I took his following compliment with grace and then asked him to leave, before sitting down to watch a crappy romcom called *Pretty Woman Ever After* with a box of tissues and a bottle of wine.

*

I learned to love being single. I no longer cried in front of the TV. Instead I got myself a social life. I loaned it from the library and it came with a CD of soothing music and affirmations of self-love. I began to immerse myself in ever-growing circles of friends, or acquaintances at least. I went to parties, slept with strangers in public places, wore outrageous clothes and shaved my head. Things were going swimmingly.

Until I saw him hand-in-hand with another woman. A tall, striking, blonde woman (though upon closer inspection she did have bad skin). They were standing outside a shop-window, looking at the display, then each other, then each other's reflections. Then they kissed, smiled. They oozed smug and I oozed anger. I strode over there, stood behind them, between them, so they could see my reflection and I could register the look on his face. Which, I should say, was everything I could wish for. The shock and sudden dawning of recognition, and then the slow slump, like the life had been squeezed out of him. He turned around, his face all wrapped up in a fake smile. "Hey," he said. "How've you been?" and before I could open my mouth to retort, my head blasted off my neck with such force, my body was thrown backwards and my poor shaved head was lost in the ether.

When I woke up I was blind. I was lying on something hard; I was cold; I could hear whispers and groans and footsteps approaching.

"You're awake. Oh good. Just in time to try out your new head for size."

I was pulled to my feet by cold hands, and I shuddered as a lump of something hard and unfamiliar was placed onto my neck, and then turned and screwed and tightened until it could tighten no more. I was pushed in front of a mirror.

I had lost weight. I was bones and skin and hairy legs poked out beneath a knee-length white nightgown.

"Oh, don't worry about the way you look. You've been in an insulin-induced coma for three months," the nurse said cheerfully.

"You're bound to have lost some meat. But what do you think of your head? It's not brilliant but it's only a temporary solution. When the doctor decides you can go home, we'll get you a brand new shiny fully functioning realistic female head, size small. In the meantime, you can see, and hear and speak. But your head won't move so you'll have to shift your whole body rather than turn your head to the side. You'll get used to it dear."

My "head" was a football, wrapped in brown paper. The features were drawn on in black marker – wide open eyes, exaggerated eyelashes, a small nose and a smile, exposing slightly crooked teeth. The hair was a few strands of yellow wool stuck to the "scalp".

It was hideous. I backed up, sat down back on the bed. Then curled myself into a ball and tried to cry but couldn't.

As always, though, I adjusted. Life on the ward wasn't too bad. I had talk therapy, art therapy, hydrotherapy and occupational therapy to learn ways of controlling stress, and lessons in "how to live like a normal person". The ward motto was, in fact, "A Stitch in Time Saves Mine", sewn by a wavering hand into what looked like blackened flesh, and exhibited above the entrance to the toilets. The ward was made up of men and women with mental illness, and those who suffered from clichés. Many of the patients were, like myself, waiting for a prosthetic or reconstructive surgery. There was one man, for instance, who kept splitting his sides whenever he became manic and was waiting for a new, wipe-clean plastic torso; then there was Mary, who'd gutted her husband's mistress and refused to remove the section of gut she'd worn for many months as a garter. That is until the restricted circulation meant her leg had to be amputated. She was waiting for a new, tattooed limb, complete with stiletto-heeled foot. There was an ex-soldier who'd jumped the gun and shot himself through the foot. He was receiving therapy for post-traumatic shock, whilst also learning to walk on shattered bones. And another who'd bitten the bullet. He'd had his entire face reconstructed. Then there was Henry, who kicked the bucket and put his back out. His frequent suicide attempts meant he was a regular on the ward.

My head served its purpose. It allowed me to eat messily, hum tunefully, listen curiously to the hisses and gripes of the other patients, and smell retchingly the shit and piss whiffs that wafted through the ward. I bided my time. The paper bag over my football head became patchy with grease from ointments and sweat and the woolen hair was soon plucked out by the other patients with their fiddly fingers and nervous energy.

I "got better".

And then came the day of my release. My new head, I'd been told, would be a feat in precision engineering, the first in a new phase of prosthetic surgery. I would be packed off to a new home, my very own little flat, with my new head, and a little money in my pocket. Ready for a new life. They kept me waiting till two in the afternoon, post-siesta. Not that I slept. I was too excited. I had slipped into my old coat and shoes at six that morning and sat on the bed all day, waiting.

At last they came. Two men and a box between them. They removed the head which had been my temporary skull, brain and four working senses for the last 18 months. I became blind once more and the bile rose in my throat with the fear that I might remain like this forever. Blind, deaf, mute. What if it had all been a lie? But then I felt warm, gentle hands prodding, placing, screwing, hammering around me and upon me. It was like a sexual act in reverse. I was becoming whole again, being refilled.

And now I could hear the constant hissing of steam, smell the heat of hydraulics and see, in the mirror, my new head.

Upon my neck sat the most amazing piece of machinery I could have imagined. The ball-bearing eyes blinked and rolled; the lids could become seductively heavy or enthusiastically wide-eyed, just like any real oculus. My lips could stretch open into a smile or squeeze together into a pout. My nostrils could flare as well as any mare's and I could even wriggle my ears, raise one eyebrow and curl my tongue – tricks I'd not been able to do before. The head was set onto a thick metal pillar where my neck used to be, with criss-crossings of staples and nails to ensure my head wasn't going anywhere.

The head was made of a single piece of titanium, with pulleys and cranks, gears and levers to produce every possible facial expression. I learned that when I was comatose the surgeon had placed electrodes deep in to my gut (the small brain). These were now connected by a number of wires to my new head, and were able, through instinct and reaction, to control the expressions on my face. These were tested immediately by my having to watch a series of films – films that repulsed me, saddened me, made me laugh, yell with surprise, feel a deep-seated guilt, and films that made me afraid. The tests were recorded. My results showed an 80 percent success rate in terms of perception and production of the 'correct' facial response to visual stimuli, although it seemed as though the doctors were merely testing my levels of compassion. Once again, everything comes down to being "normal".

I was discharged from the hospital under one condition. This prosthetic (and the term was used very loosely, considering the many functions of the head) was brand new. I was, in fact, the first patient to use it. Also, it was incredibly expensive and much data had to be collected before funding could be acquired to make another one. The condition, therefore, was that every now and then, something would occur that would have once made me lose my head. Perhaps I would witness something horrific, they said, or be told some tragic news that was not necessarily true. My movements would be recorded, and I would have to keep a note of anything and everything to do with reaction ... In short, I might be monitored for the rest of my life.

But this head, this was so much better than I could have hoped for. This was everything to me. I looked good, I felt good, I was going to get my life back... I signed the consent form, grabbed my bag containing a bottle of sertraline, a blister pack of mycophenolate, a macaroni necklace, an ID-Card and a small wad of cash. And then I stepped out the door.

It took almost five minutes for a nurse to come dashing out. I hadn't actually left the entrance to the building. I was standing watching the automatic doors open and shut as I swung slowly from one leg to the other. Watching, waiting. I wasn't sure what to do. I didn't remember what my plan of action was, if I ever had one. I'd been so excited about the new head I hadn't thought about what would happen next.

"Oh, you're still here, good," panted the nurse who'd run the length of the hospital to find me. "You need to come back inside please."

"Is there a problem?" I asked, my new mouth becoming dry.

"Please just come inside."

I followed the young woman back into that horrible, smelly, noisy ward where a small huddle of patients watched me through barely opened eyes.

"I'm sorry to break this to you," a doctor had appeared behind me. "But we're not quite ready to send you on your way. We've discovered a problem with your prosthetic and we need to make some readjustments. I'm afraid it may take some months."

I backed away from him slowly. I tried to speak, to yell, to scream, "No, no, no you can't do this to me," but the terror had left me momentarily mute.

My head strained. It hurt like a thousand hammer blows to my small metal eyes. I began to back up, back up, and back up until I touched something soft. I turned around quickly and found I had backed into the surgeon. He took my hand in his. "Well done," he said. "You've passed the first test." I didn't speak. I stared, I gawped at him. "That was the first test of your reaction," he said. "You did very well. You didn't lose your head. Well done. You're free to leave."

I saw red. Then I saw black. I shouted, "you fucker. You motherfucking bastard!" However, what came out of my mouth was actually, "you little tinker, you naughty man, you, you horrible person."

I gasped.

"Oh yes, one other thing I forgot to mention. We've removed your ability to curse. Your potty-mouth earned you little respect on the ward so we decided to decode the swear function. There's so much more we can do as well, if necessary." He leaned close to me as he said this, threateningly.

"Now," he said, "off you pop. And remember, keep your chin up, otherwise we may have to revert to other methods". And with that, he steered me back out on to the street.

POMEGRANATE SEEDS
by Roberta Chloe Verdant

EDITOR'S NOTE

Roberta Chloe Verdant is London-born and currently resides in Devon in the UK. She facilitates creative writing workshops. In the past this has included a series on working with archetypes. In the future this will include sessions in "Writing from the Body". She loves myth, fairy tale and storytelling. She also enjoys free-form dance, kickboxing, spending time in nature and eating vegan ice cream. Her writing is widely published in the independent press – under this name and others – and can be found in venues such as Mung Being *and* Sein Und Werden.

She explains her inspiration for "Pomegranate Seeds" as follows: "I have always been fascinated by the myth of Persephone. So many human issues and conflicts seem to be represented within it. Rites of passage, the mother/daughter bond, the dawning of sexuality, the treatment of women within society (Zeus gives away his daughter, Persephone) and the lure of the Shadow. I am strongly influenced by Louise Gluck's poem 'Persephone the Wanderer' and the philosophical questions she asks of the Persephone myth within that.

"Writing the story, I had one particular question in mind: does Persephone choose Hades or is she raped? I opted for the former, whilst acknowledging that any notion of choice for Persephone within the myth is limited. However, I depict a protagonist who is not entirely a victim, who is empowered enough to have desires of her own. I wrote that twist in a spirit of reclamation which fits my own Feminist sensibilities.

"The Persephone ('Sephi') of my story is eighteen years old (so older than her more common depictions) and smothered by the love of her mother, Demeter, the original 'earth mother'. Here is a Persephone hungry for experience. Although she fulfills her father's bargain, she is captivated by the shadowy, sexual underworld where Hades (in my text, 'H') dwells. To say she goes willingly is troublesome in a narrative where her father has sealed her fate. So perhaps I will simply say Sephi enters the underworld (or the 'Below') with interest.

"Sephi proceeds to meet a Hades who is flawed, a victim in his

own right. She experiments with this other life (or death) as so many teenagers – and humans – experiment with that which though not good for us is undeniably compelling. Eventually she will learn – as we all must – that however alluring the darkness is, it cannot sustain life. Whether this is her salvation or any kind of salvation at all is for you to decide."

Roberta's images are lush and captivating, luring the reader in, not unlike Sephi was lured into the Below. It's a unique take on an old, old myth, making the young goddess's struggle and her choices as fresh as an eighteen-year old girl walking in the spring.

My father was a rapist. My mother was unbearable. I left home to copulate with the king of the night in unlikely positions.

I was the perfect daughter. Lithe, golden-skinned, a skip in my step, murmuring tunes beneath my breath. Beloved of my parents (but my father so often away!). Poets sang my name. Minor gods and goddesses tickled me under the chin, proclaimed my loveliness. Sephi the maiden. Sephi of the wildflowers. Sephi, her mother's treasure, her father's darling. I was eighteen years old, the perfect maiden. Apollo wrote me verse, promised he would always be true to me. Hermes hovered near in his golden sandals, whispering enchantments. My mother covered my eyes with flowers, plugged my ears with flowers and sent them both away. Smelling like an orchard, I waited for my life to begin.

I used to walk alone at dusk praying for something to happen. I used to lie in bed at night-time, a mirror between my legs to reveal myself, ripe red as pomegranate seeds. I waited. –

One evening in the meadow, I was skipping with the ocean-faeries, small earthquakes inside me. The virgin Goddesses by my side, my keepers. My father, my father who said I was the apple of his eye, my father who was always far away, my father he sold me. My father sold me to Death. I skipped. I knew. I ceased to be innocent.

The earth split open, a subtle thing. A crack like a vulva in it. I looked to the sky, the sun still visible. I looked to the cracked earth, to the Below. All I could see inside the earth was inky black; a mystery. Was it a choice I made? I slipped off my undergarments, I took in a breath and silently I leapt down into the Below. Something happened.

That first night, that first evening that bled into night (there is little distinction down here. The sun does not shine. The whole world is inky. We who dwell here have bade farewell to daytime). That first evening, he offered me his hand, no assumptions. I took it. I was already wet. He raised his other hand to my head, stroked my hair just once. He offered me purple-black liqueur and told me he expected nothing.

I slid the alcohol away, met his gaze and simply said: "I want to." That first time, I gushed thick water and dug my nails deep into his skin. Just one of us bled that night. Somewhere in the lands above, the bards were gathering to sing my story, my mother beginning her exhaustive wander for her stolen daughter. I was far away, learning to scream when I came, drawing the letter H with my wet tongue over the back of a man's neck.

It was weeks until I noticed the scars. I'd been feeling them all along. Where his veins are, there the scars are. In this flickering candle-light, shapes distort, reality remakes itself every night. I find a map on his wrists, feet, forearms. Gently he takes my hand when I trace the patterns, leads it South, or leads me elsewhere; leads me anywhere but there. Those patterns aren't whole deaths in themselves. He who is already Death, all else is just echoes. With monstrous needles he sticks himself full of trance. Night-times become deeper night-times and he practices forgetting. There I meet him.

In caves, in pitch-black drinking holes, in his screaming bed we toss and turn together. There is no time here, no beginning and no end to this. He tells me this is not for me. It is already too late. I have written his name all over my skin, I string my hair with pomegranate seeds, I have forgotten the living and he is my addiction. In our bed I marry Death like a seizure. The first hit makes me dance like a maenad, makes me shiver and shake, makes me finally climb atop him, dancing. "Mine." I whisper as I rock my hips. Mine, mine, mine.

*

In the other world, my mother sends out search parties. Her over-full breasts shrink from watermelons to apples and finally to wrinkled berries. Her hips cave in. Harvests fail. Dead leaves strew her hair as she traverses the planet, moaning "Sephi! Sephi!" My father is fucking Danae, Leda and a slew of forgotten nymphs. My father is angry and shape-shifting. My mother weeps, offers sacrificial rams who seep pomegranate blood. The bards sing my story, but now that story is of Lost Sephi.

The bards' stories say he raped me, did Hades. My mother goes deaf in order not to hear them and she walks the barren earth roaring my name. Echoes of the bards' stories reach these dark Below spaces, carried down by the dead. H tears his indigo hair, says he did this to me. I bite lightly at his skin, then harder, harder. *I wanted this,* I answer. There is little for me here but intoxication. There is still less up there for me in the world above. I send no answer back. My bountiful mother, she wanders and her hair turns grey. I live only in the right now, in this place of forgetfulness. No-one can find me here. I did not come here to be found.

Below the worlds visitors lust for blood in dreams of wholeness. We move like shadows and I drift about; a myth. H has been drowning since long before the first storyteller dreamt of me. Death is always a drowning. Discarded needles, last night's ashes and dregs of alcohol, blood stains on our blankets. I toss and turn, thinned and un-maidenly and H sings me songs that will haunt me for the rest of my days. This is what death sounds like: a slow seduction. Above this world my mother roars and rages and even down here I can sense it in my belly. Something is coming. H has me sip these underworld waters and I feel it coming. Sunshine: I feel it nearing with no emotion at all. My mother the harvest is calling for something. Sometimes I too roar a little. Sephi, with a viper's tongue, pointed teeth and a fetish for screaming. I am a sold-off daughter. I am every girl who has wanted to drink up the darkness.

*

In the worlds above, the earth is still dying. Without my mother's blessing the crops fail and the animals die of strange diseases. My mother's eyes are dead, she wears beggar's rags as she presents herself to Helios, God of the sun, screams my name, screams my name until the world shakes on its axis, ready to split open again. Helios breathes his bright light all over her. The sun spells out that my father sold me, that I am beneath the worlds and all is lit.

The people scream like a chorus, the starving children, the half-dead adults. The sun is brighter than the world can remember. The earth is weeping, my mother is roaring and the Gods and Goddesses are calling my name: *Sephi, Sephi!* In the Below I am waking. In the world above my father raises a single eyebrow, shoots lightning at the Below, a message to H that I am to be returned.

H shakes and shivers and I tell him this is my choice and he asks me: wasn't this always my choice? I feel like a sacrifice, lover to Death, daughter to a man who moves the world with his eyebrow. I sigh and choose the sunshine, though is this a choice I am making? I put down a needle and I too shiver. *Sephi, Sephi,* whispers the earth, calling me back. I place a hand on H, lift his arm, lick seven tiny blood-drops from his wrist. Without words we meld. I am Sephi. I am life and death and I move towards the sunshine like a crumpled butterfly.

In the world above, the harvest returns. My mother, ripe as the Spring-time, wraps me in her arms and the earth rejoices all Spring and all Summer. I am Spring, I scatter my seeds and flowers blossom. I am she who knows Death and six months a year I return to H, carouse in Death and the world falls into a coma, sleeps as I toss in slumber. I am Sephi, mystery, keeper of secrets. I am Sephi. Do I make choices? Is this a choice I am making?

THE LAST OF THE SACRED MONSTERS
by Amelia Mangan

EDITOR'S NOTE

Amelia Mangan is a writer originally from London, currently living in Sydney, Australia. Her writing is featured in many anthologies, including Attic Toys *(ed. by Jeremy C. Shipp);* Blood Type *(ed. by Robert S. Wilson);* Drag Noir *(ed. by K.A. Laity);* Worms, After the Fall, X7 *and* No Monsters Allowed *(ed. by Alex Davis);* The Bestiarum Vocabulum *and* Phobophobias *(ed. by Dean M. Drinkel);* Carnival of the Damned *(eds. by Henry Snider & David C. Hayes); and* Mother Goose is Dead *(eds. by Michele Acker & Kirk Dougal). Her short story, "Blue Highway," won* Yen Magazine's *first annual short story competition and is featured in its 65th issue. She can be found on Twitter (@AmeliaMangan) and Facebook (facebook.com/amelia. mangan).*

"This story more or less came about as a kind of meditation on glamor and excess, decadence and artifice, and the importance we place on ritual even when the meanings behind those rituals have eroded and been forgotten," says Amelia. "Think of it as 'The Masque of the Red Death' via Hollywood Babylon."

Debauchery carried to its most twisted extreme is how I think of it. A tale of supernatural sin and corruption in the land of the fallen angels, the main character is all the more horrifying for her complete and utter self-absorption as the world tumbles down around her. I think I'd rather be the lobster.

It was almost November now; that much, at least, her body was not yet too numb to feel. Needles of ice worked beneath her skin, tripped up and down the ridges of her bones. Electricity. The sharp taste of rain in the air, in the mouth.

Someone, back in the days when she had been surrounded by someones, had told her that it never rained in California. It never had. Until a day came when it did nothing but rain, and the rain had a color, a sick yellow color, and its taste was bitter as dust.

Long time ago. Time passing, passed, and gone. What was now was not real. Just a pose. How long could it be held? How long before the legs began to cramp, before the arms seized up, before the face twitched and spasmed, before the eyesight failed and all the world went dark?

Not a life. Not a real life. Only an image of a life.

Celluloid. Growing dull and dim. Too many shadows muddying the image. Fading, fading, fading to black.

In the morning, she dressed herself in her gold leather bikini, her Versace thigh-high stiletto-heeled leopard-print boots and her fly-eyed Gucci sunglasses, and walked her gold-plated lobster around the pool.

It took a long time. The animal was so weighed down with splendor that it could barely move. It had no name, and she watched it struggle over the marble with idle disinterest. Its stiff body cast glittering shadows over the wet white stone. Soon it wouldn't be able to walk at all, and when that happened, she would have it cooked and eaten. Her chefs would dip it in liquid nitrogen; she could almost see herself cracking open its dazzling shell with a delicate ivory hammer. It would all be exquisite, just too, too exquisite.

The lobster shifted, set one claw on the next flagstone with a sad, defeated click. It stopped. She clucked her tongue at it. Time crawled. Her bleached hair snapped in the wind. The lobster took one more step.

Slow, so slow. But she didn't mind slow. It gave her time to think, at least in theory.

Skeletons were gathered around the poolside. Wire strung through their bleached white bones. Frozen in poses they might never have struck in life. One with arms raised to the sky. One lounging in a chair, reading French *Vogue*. One with a fleshless leg dipped in the pool. Smiles, lots of smiles all round. Fixed grins. Their teeth were perfect.

She did not look at the skeletons. She would not. She stood on the edge of the pool instead, and looked out. The sky was churned and boiling, dark gray. She looked down. She could just about make out the ruined "H", turned on its side. All the other letters – the O, the two Ls, the Y and so forth – were gone. She wondered if they'd fallen. If they'd landed on anyone. Had people been crushed? She'd have heard something about that, wouldn't she? And anyway, it didn't seem likely. Who would have been there to be crushed? There was nobody left to hurt.

The chemical bath. That came next. Every day, no matter what. It kept her pure.

The tub perched atop a flight of golden steps, a ziggurat of steps, an impossible height; it looked like an Aztec altar, and of course it did, because she'd had it made to look that way. Lotuses floated on gelatinous green water. Their roots were thick and dark and strong, and dead; had died the moment they touched the poisonous chemical stew.

She dressed herself in her Chanel cat-eye sunglasses, her Swarovski diamond necklace – the one that looked just like Marilyn's in *Gentlemen Prefer Blondes* – her gold Louboutin heels and nothing else, and she climbed the steps, and she eased herself into the water, her face perfectly made up to mimic solemnity. Down below, crouched and huddled on the peacock-patterned bathroom tiles, were the Daughters.

The Daughters. Once, they had been her servants, her handmaidens, and in a way they still were. When their limbs had succumbed to malformation and their minds turned to dirty gray slush, she'd ordered them wrapped in muslin, swathed in glitter, rolled in leather and vinyl and snakeskin and rubber. One wore a porcelain Carnivale mask over its face; another an impenetrable beaded curtain; another a zippered leather hood. Her remaining designers had been eager to create the couture; they had no desire to look upon their own fates and despair.

The Daughters. They moved in hunched-over silhouette, twisted spines and locked shoulder blades. Hard angles. Wet sounds. Choking gurgles, garbled shrieks, hidden mouths. Even sitting, they were never still. They went nowhere, did nothing, but still they had to move.

She kept them warm and fed, and alive, after their fashion.

Sandor, her butler, had once observed them and made a discreet suggestion, veiled in metaphor, and she had declined. She couldn't end them. There would be no one if she ended them. They were *hers*.

What she did owe them was a performance. An entertainment. One last story before lights-out.

"When Lupe Velez, the beautiful Hollywood movie star, made up her mind to die ... " she began, easing deeper into the chemicals: "My Daughters, she did it with *style*. Her hair was perfect. Her makeup was perfect. She wore a shimmering silver gown and high heels to match. Surely, she was the most beautiful thing anyone in California had ever seen. Maybe the most beautiful thing in all the world."

The Daughters writhed. One spat. Another made a thick, tubercular sound, coughing, or laughing.

"She had a banquet prepared. A banquet to put the feasts of Rome to shame. A banquet Nitocris herself would have envied. A last meal, my Daughters. The finest wines, the richest meat, the freshest fruit." She dipped down, raised one toned, tanned leg, arching the calf muscles and admiring the water as it sheered away from her skin. "Can't you just taste it?"

A Daughter gibbered, howled, and clutched at its skull.

"So. In the one hand, a forkful of rich dark cake, dripping with chocolate sauce and fine white frosting. In the other, a bottle of pills. The old-fashioned kind. They called them 'dolls', once. Isn't that a cute name? And so Lupe took the cake, and the wine, and the dolls, and she lay down on her bed of satin and velvet, elegant arms crossed over her beautiful breasts, ready to die glamorous.

"Unfortunately," and she leaned forward over the lip of her bath, reaching out one dripping arm, drawing her Daughters forward: "Unfortunately, my dears, Lupe hadn't counted on the cake and the wine and the dolls not getting along. Deep down inside. Lupe felt sad. Lupe felt sick. Something wasn't right. This suicide wasn't going at all well!

"Yes," she continued, as she climbed out of the bath and held out her arms. Down below, Sandor was mounting the steps, thick fluffy towel over one arm, silken kimono over the other. "You guessed it, my Daughters. Lupe's gorge was rising. She had something coming up, and I don't mean a new picture. Lupe staggered off the bed and into her beautiful black-tiled bathroom, and that, my dears, is where she was found the very next day."

Sandor toweled her dry, his touch light and careful and soft. He knew he was polishing a masterpiece. Something rare.

"Oh, yes indeed," she said, as Sandor slipped her into her robe. "Lupe was a star. Lupe was a beautiful, shining star. Everyone wanted her. Everyone needed her. She had only the best, the absolute best of everything in all this world and all the worlds there are.

"And do you know what, my Daughters? She died with her head in the toilet bowl, just the same."

The Daughters applauded. One, who held a champagne flute in mangled fingers, bit into the glass. A crack, a splinter. Blood oozed down its vinyl suit.

She took her bows and departed the stage.

There was no time here, but she decided it was Wednesday, and that meant it was the day she acted out her own death. Her designs for this event were elaborate, and often beautiful.

She dressed herself in a belted Marc Jacobs bikini – white, just like the one Ursula Andress wore in *Dr. No* – and scarlet Vivienne Westwood rocking-horse wedges, then wrapped her whole body in a straight-jacket, Kevlar and chains. She stood on one side of the pool, belted up and helpless. Black and white images flickered beneath the water. A screen had been set up at the pool's bottom, long ago, and now, if she didn't mind the distortion and the lack of sound, she could, had she wished to, be watching *Last Year at Marienbad*.

Sandor stood on the other side of the pool, and shot her in the chest with a diamante-encrusted antique revolver, and watched as she plunged into the deep end. Her heart slammed against her bruised ribs, deep in the tomb of iron and Kevlar and water. She saw and heard nothing, breathed only chlorine. Her limbs spidered around her, working and fumbling and twisting against Delphine Seyrig's exquisite black-and-white face, masked by white feathers. She felt her bones click like locks.

When she disentangled and re-emerged, she tried to feel

reborn. But all she could feel was cold water, closing in on her from every side.

In the afternoons, she walked around the gardens. She had seen the mansion from every angle; knew every spiral, every curlicue, every blank-eyed angel and every carved stone pillar. Every staircase and every fountain. Every sunken pond and every rockery. Every plant and every flower and every thorny tangle. The stones and the shadows. The moss and the dry rot. The damp and the peeling paint. The orchids and the weeds. The yellow pall of rain on cracked gray walls.

Every so often, bodies were found in the gardens. Even now. Under bushes. On the lawns. The front steps. Soaked wet through by the sprinklers. Sandor had them removed. She rarely had to see them up close. She watched from her balcony, sipping her morning coffee. Pinky out.

She never saw the process. Only the result. A brand new skeleton, posing beside her pool. With her for always.

There were no rhythms, no patterns any more. Chains once forged had rotted; links rusted and fallen away. There was nothing connecting one day to the next; no way to chart the soul's evolution, or devolution.

This was the price one paid to live in a dream. The privilege of privilege. You never had to think about what it cost you.

She could feel herself vanishing. Day by day by day.

She stood on her balcony. Leaning over the side. The servants were removing another body.

Sandor came up behind her. "Would you like something?" he inquired. "Anything?"

"I doubt it," she said.

They said nothing, for a time.

"Sandor," she began. Her perfect brow puckered. "I feel ... "

Her lips quirked, unused to the phrase.

"Don't worry, ma'am," Sandor said. "It'll pass."

And a thousand thousand slimy things lived on, and so did I.

On the rare nights her sleep was not drugged, she dreamed. And this was the dream, and this was the law of the plague:

She dreamed the memories she had lost. She dreamed that forgetting was the first symptom, that forgetting you had forgotten one of the last.

She dreamed the changing of bodies, of hair and muscle and fat and blood, once so lovingly tended, so carefully sculpted, cultivated like secret gardens, growing wild, refusing to do as they were told. She dreamed of perfect faces warping and twisting. She dreamed of words turning to shrieks, turning to wet.

She dreamed that she had had parties once, in a dazzling town filled with light, parties filled with perfect faces and perfect bodies, toned and groomed and shaved and suited and silked and satined. She dreamed she'd been somebody. Somebody's daughter. Somebody's love. She dreamed she had laughed, and made people laugh. She dreamed that the laughing people had been some of the first. She dreamed they fell away. She dreamed she had not fallen away. She dreamed that there was a night beyond the night, a night riven with streams of yellow rain and thunderheads of yellow cloud. She dreamed that all the world was yellow, except for her.

When she woke, she remembered nothing. Increasingly, inevitably, she remembered nothing.

This was the law of the plague.

"Anita Berber," she told the Daughters from the depths of her bath, "was the toast of Weimar Berlin. She danced on tabletops in black jewels and nothing else, and pissed on anyone who didn't pay attention to her. She seduced ... She seduced ... "

The thought sank. Drowned in the chemical bath. She looked down into it, at her own flesh, biting her lip.

"She seduced a lot of people," she said. Her voice wandered. "And she died. There were syringes all around her. Statues of the Virgin. That's ... that's about it. That's all there is, really."

She dressed herself in clothes. Just clothes. They had labels on them that told her who'd designed them, who'd sold them to her, what they had once been worth, but though she knew they signified something, she couldn't summon the meaning. They had none. Only words, only symbols. Hieroglyphs. Cuneiform. Scratchings on a mausoleum wall.

She dipped her fingertips in gold. Molten gold. She'd had them melt down her jewelry, all of it. It was just warm enough to burn her fingerprints away. She smiled. Sandor stood at her side, looking worried, looking sad, but she didn't know why. He shouldn't be sad. Her hands were beautiful now. But so heavy. So heavy.

Once, in the valley of night, there had been a city that pulsed and glistened and dazzled with light. Now there was nothing. A canyon of silent darkness. And out of that darkness a strange wind arose; a cold, sick, yellow mist that stole across the grass, the flagstones, the still waters of the swimming pool. It licked at the window panes behind which she slept, and dreamed, or did not dream. It clawed with quiet hunger at the glass. But when it slipped between the bones of the skeletons, they swayed and clattered and chattered.

"Not yet," they told it. "Not yet. Soon. Soon."

Bones clicking and chattering. The Morse code of the ruined body. The secret sign language of the dead.

FOX BONES. MANY USES
By Alex Dally MacFarlane

EDITOR'S NOTE

Alex Dally MacFarlane lives in London, where she is pursuing an academic life. When not researching, she writes stories, found in Clarkesworld, The Other Half of the Sky, Heiresses of Russ 2013: The Year's Best Lesbian Speculative Fiction, Beneath Ceaseless Skies, Shimmer *and* Zombies: Shambling Through the Ages. *Her poetry can be found in* Stone Telling, The Moment of Change *and* Here, We Cross. *She is the editor of* Aliens: Recent Encounters *(2013) and* The Mammoth Book of SF Stories by Women *(forthcoming in late 2014). Visit her online at alexdallymacfarlane.com.*

Of "Fox Bones. Many Uses", Alex says: "It grew from a novel opening written purely for fun while I was working on a farm in Australia. The novel opening focused on a young male character, Fenh, whose mother had disappeared when he was very young. A while later, I started wondering what the mother's story was. As I started writing about Za, I realized that she wasn't going to disappear."

I love this story. The prose is as lyrical as Ashlyn's cover art, the conflict and the action overlaying each other in a manner that is both compelling and thought provoking. The words cast a spell, pulling us into a world of moonlight and danger and death and a simple magic bound with a mother's love.

A fox's foreleg bones: humerus, ulna, and radius.
Main use: attack. Also used for treating colds and headaches.

The two imperial men were walking in an alarmingly accurate direction.

"Let's go," Za said. With only a glance in the direction of her basket, safely hidden among rocks where no one could see it, she opened the fox-ear pouch she wore at her waist and pinched ground foreleg bones from one compartment. *For fur-bright fire*, she thought as she licked it from her fingers. She made saliva to swallow it down. *For strength.*

Her brothers did the same, and together – full of power, bursting with it like a rice-wine container over-full and leaking – they descended into the gully and chased the imperial men, with fire at their fingers.

The men had swords. Za and her brothers laughed and circled them, marking how their eyes went wide.

"You're going to die," Za said in the Nu language – the imperial language – and traced arcs of fire through the air with her fingers.

"So are you," one of the men replied, "but only after giving the emperor all your silver, little animal." He lunged at her, his sword swinging sudden as a midwinter wind.

He fell, covered in Za's fire, and only screamed for a moment before it burnt away his throat.

The other man died under her brothers' fire – but he reached for something in his bags and hurled it into the air before they finished killing him.

The siblings stood over the bodies, their power fading, and stared up as a white ball flew straight into the sky, far above the trees, and began to blaze like a small sun.

In the men's bags, they found a map that marked a village high in the hills.

"It's too close." Tou moved his finger marginally along the hilltop to where their village truly lay.

"Look." Za unfolded the map further, and with each piece of paper she exposed, she felt more and more sick. Villages dotted the high hills. "They're all too close."

From the mountains in the far north, where vast spirits kept the snow from ever melting, the green hills stretched out like numerous fingers towards the lowlands where the Nu lived. Only two hill-fingers away from theirs, a perfectly placed dot marked the village where Koua, Za's closest childhood friend, had gone to be married. Imperial men had been there, almost two years earlier – forcing the people of the village to reveal the location of their silver mine, forcing them to work it until their bones filled the empty tunnels.

"Take the bodies to the river," Za said. "Just in case that thing up there burns out before more of them can arrive. Then scout more, in case they weren't the only group. I'm going to see if I can find out any good information."

"How?" Tou asked, just curious –

– but Pao knew. "If you trust a word that comes out of that man's mouth, you deserve to join these men in the river!"

"He hates them almost as much as we do!" Za snapped back, wanting their mother's strength to smack him into silence.

"So he said! To win you over, to – "

"Enough," Tou said. "They will come anyway. If Za can convince that man to tell us anything useful, she should try."

"You're an idiot," Pao spat, but he didn't stop Za as she ran back to her basket, where her infant son was bundled with the bamboo shoots she had been harvesting.

She began the long walk downhill to the trade town, hating Pao, hating the Nu, trying to ignore her son's complaints at her long, jostling pace.

Fox-skull.
Many purposes, including the acquisition of the fox's ability to see at night and its strong senses of smell and hearing.

Za had hunted the fox when she was still weak and sore from childbirth, but no one else would do it for a half-Nu baby.

"Perhaps it's for the best," her mother had advised as the boy, small from his premature delivery, cried feebly beside Za. "He will only last a few days. And because of his size, he has not hurt you."

As soon as night fell on the boy's second day and everyone slept, Za wrapped herself in clothes and gathered what she needed: her bow and arrows, her fox-ear pouch, her mortar and pestle. She touched her baby once on the forehead, gently, so as not to wake him, and set out into the snow that coated the ground in a fine layer like cotton.

Her pouch still contained fox-skull.

It cast the forest in a pale grey glow. Za sniffed the wind. Foxes sometimes hid in winter, but they didn't hibernate. They needed to hunt too.

Za tried to put aside her mother's words. "It only works half the time, and who knows what his Nu blood will do? It probably won't work at all. He's small and sickly – let nature run its course."

"I want to try," she had said.

"Listen to wisdom for once in your life, child!" Temper had flared in her mother's voice – the same anger that had made her strike Za to the floor when she revealed the pregnancy, although later she had apologized with grief in her eyes. "Your life will be normal again. Don't you want that?"

In the snow, an hour's hard hike from her village, Za crouched. Something rustled. She nocked an arrow and waited, still as a rock, until she saw what her nose had found: a male fox, searching for food. Za drew the bowstring back and released, and her arrow struck it in the rump, only wounding. It ran off – slowly, dripping blood, and even sore tired Za managed to follow it until she had a clear second shot.

She finished it with her knife and flayed it on the spot, rolled up the hide to carry home, and began stripping away the flesh. The hide would help to make her son's first jacket, she decided, and the flesh would go into a stew for herself, to restore her energy and enrich her milk. But before all that, she needed the bones.

Out of respect for the fox, she ground its bones there, setting her mortar and pestle in the snow and forcing her cold fingers to co-operate. First she ground the tail-bones, murmuring the words her grandmother had taught her early in the pregnancy: *For a strong heart. For strong lungs. For strong arms and legs. For strength. For strength.* She poured the pale powder into a small pouch. Then she ground the other bones, separating them as use dictated, and picked up the hide and meat and set off home with steps full of fear: that the tail bones would not strengthen her son; or that they would, and her mother would hate her for it.

A fox's hind-leg bones: femur, tibia and fibula.
The speed that a sprinting fox longs for.

Further south, the hills were entirely cultivated, and the trade town sat among them like a curious outcrop of bare fat trees. Za followed a narrow path from an outlying village. On either side, terraces of rice and corn stretched up and down the hill: over a hundred large steps from the top of the hill to the valley, and again on the other side.

If she glanced north, the imperial men's orb still shone in the sky.

With several weeks until the next trade day, the town's streets were almost bare. Men and women worked in the surrounding fields while children helped or watched animals or played near their houses. A few people recognized her, with her half-Nu son; she hurried between the houses with their anger at her back.

She remembered liking this town.

At its far side, a house sat slightly apart from the others, identical in construction – walls of wood and a roof of dried banana leaves – but far smaller. Almost at its door she stopped, biting her fingers. She needed information. She didn't want to talk about anything else – she wouldn't let him. Fixing her village firmly in her mind – her grandparents, her parents, her littlest sister who liked to chase the chickens – she took one step forward, and another, and soon she stood outside the doorway, looking at the man bent over his paper with ink staining his fingers dark like indigo, as if she had never left.

Hello. I hate you. No I don't. Why was I stupid in the fertile part of my cycle?

"Why are there imperial men in the northern hills?"

The brush in Truc's hand clattered to the paper, ruining his words. "Za," he said, then thought better of whatever he'd wanted to ask first. Silence grew awkwardly between them. Her son stood up in the basket, trying to pull himself up to see over her shoulder, and Truc's agonized expression worsened. "He's mine?" he asked softly.

Za glared at him. *What other Nu man was I fucking?* The father couldn't be a Hma man – the differences between Hma and half-

Nu babies were small, but they'd been pointed out enough that Za doubted anyone could miss them.

"Tell me about the imperial men," she demanded.

"What imperial men? Um, do you want to come inside? I have some soup and tea and ..." His words withered. "Come inside, at least, Za, and sit down." Several stools sat by the wall, un-used. If Za's shoulders had hurt less, if her feet hadn't needed to carry her to the town so quickly, she might have refused him. Instead, she stepped inside and gently put the basket on the floor beside her and sat on one of the stools, longing for the silent emptiness of the forest.

Truc stayed at his table, stiff-shouldered, not quite watching her or her son.

"You must know about them," Za said. "You're still one of them – someone would have come to you. What did you tell them?"

Sighing, he said, "They came to me with a map and asked me to confirm its details."

"A map." From among bundles of uncooked rice and freshly cut bamboo shoots and some corn she had traded in the last village for extra shoots, she removed the map: wet on the edges, from rainfall and her son's brief mouthy fascination, but unmistakable.

"Yes." Truc looked directly at her. "That orb in the sky is theirs. I assume that when you took this map, one of them managed to set it off."

"You told them where to go." *Deny it,* she thought. Then, *Tell the truth.*

"No. I promise you, no. I told them nothing, even though they threatened me. I threatened back. They left. And now that orb is in the sky, confirming their suspicions." He sounded genuinely unhappy.

"What are they doing?"

"Looking for silver, of course, but that is not all. What I managed to get their leader to say indicated tensions in the imperial court – they need an enemy to fight for a while, and your secretive, silver-rich people suit their needs perfectly."

"Why? There's so many people in their empire."

"And they are busy fighting most of the others, too." Truc smiled wryly. "This is why I left, remember."

"I remember you saying that my people would be safe."

His meager humor faded. "I thought you would be. That map ... I don't know where they got that information."

"How do we stop them?"

"I don't know."

Two years ago, after the destruction of Koua's new village, he hadn't been able to answer. He had promised to think of ideas, to use his exiled life in ways that benefited the people of the hills – but Za's mother had been right. None of his fine ideals made a difference.

"Are there more of them?" she asked, because nothing mattered except getting information.

"Yes. A small detachment – about one hundred, I believe. They are probably in the hills north of here already."

One hundred imperial soldiers walking faster than she could, guided by the orb.

She stood up and took her son from the basket. "Good bye."

"Za," he said as she turned, and he filled her name with an intensity of emotion that surprised her.

"I need to tell my people," she said without looking back. "I need to travel fast."

Many more questions hung in the air between them. She answered just one.

"His name's Cheu." She didn't tell Truc that sometimes, on days when she looked at her son's face and saw every small way he differed from little Hma boys, she called him Fenh – a Nu name, one of Truc's many.

Outside the town, she tied her son to her chest and swallowed ground hind-legs.

A fox's tail vertebrae.
Used to sustain life.

Za breathed a story onto the ground tail bones:

"Long ago, all our people were created in the mountains, by a great spirit who had already created many animals. When the time came for the spirit to make people, a different animal oversaw each of our births: foxes watched the first Hma man and woman be stitched from the air, ants watched the first Daren, snakes watched the first Pinoh, and so on.

"Many years later, the spirit grew weary of our company and sent us away, and we moved south into the hills where we settled comfortably and developed our own ways of life. Even we Hma are different. Some of us, whose clothes are bright as every flower combined, live in the same hills as many other people, and are probably the most numerous. Some of us, whose clothes are almost fully black and whose cheeks are tattooed with lines as thin as hairs, live in small numbers in hills far to the west. We, the only hill-people to live where snow sometimes falls, are scattered across many hills, always in the north, always hidden."

She pressed more powder to the baby's tongue.

I will make you fully Hma, she thought. *I will fill you with our stories – then you'll have to be Hma, and this will work, and you'll live, and everyone will stop hating you.*

Blinking away tears, she began another story.

A fox's scapula.
Pleasant when smoked with tobacco.
Said to promote health in the elderly.

Za stopped at the last Hma village before hers, a place where two rivers crashed together and bamboo grew thick-stemmed on the shore. The white peaks of distant mountains hung in the northern sky like clouds. She put away her fox-speed at the village's edge and appeared in front of an old woman who sat on a fence surrounding a small corn field.

"That's a good trick!" the woman said, grinning toothlessly. "Although I don't think your son likes it."

He still wailed against her chest.

"He's fine," Za said. The sudden stop had jarred her. She blinked, expecting the village to blur like the road behind her. She kept herself still.

"Will you be staying long?"

"No."

"What do you want to discuss then, little mountain one?"

The noises of the village and the eternal river wrapped around each other in a distant knot. Here, with only her son's quietening cries and the faint sucking of the old woman on her pipe, she didn't feel like she stood in the village. She preferred being here. In the village they often derided her for sleeping with a Nu man, the girls with their Hma husbands and their first Hma children with perfect little Hma faces.

"Would you at least like a drink?"

"No." Za felt stable enough to talk. "My village is in danger. I have to hurry to them."

"The imperial men," the old woman said unhappily.

"What do you know about them?"

"They have been in this area, hunting silver." Anger simmered in her eyes, but sadness kept it from boiling. "We told them we don't know the location of any mines. We trade the silver for our corn, for our little chickens that hatch as easily as the sun rises. So they stole as much of our silver as they could, and moved on."

Za looked at the woman's jacket, so brightly stitched that she hadn't noticed how little silver adorned it – only two small discs, which would sit side-by-side if she fastened the jacket at her throat. And she wore just two narrow hoops of silver in her ears. Compared to her, Za felt like a silver mine. One thick band of stitched colour – red and white and yellow and black, and the russet of magic-rich fox fur – circled her indigo-dark jacket at her chest, and a row of silver discs ran above and below it. A similar design circled the end of both sleeves. Nothing decorated her dark trousers or boots, but thick bracelets clustered at her wrists and a large hoop hung from each ear. Even her son, whose jacket bore thick bands of fox fur for protection, owned more silver than the old woman.

Za's village knew a good silver mine, as bounteous as the summer sun. A sick suspicion clenched in her.

"You told them," she hissed.

"No." The old woman spoke firmly. "We don't know where you live, so how could we give them any details? They're far away, we said.

They come to us but we don't go to them. And then, a month later, one of our men went hunting and never returned."

Of all the people of the village, a hunter would best be able to guess the village's location.

"We still don't know where he is," the old woman said. "Perhaps he lives, in one of the stolen mines. Perhaps his ghost wanders the mountains, lost."

Za shivered. "They're coming for us."

"That light in the sky is theirs, isn't it?"

"Too near."

Za realized she was holding onto her son, like a child with a new fur. *You will be safe*, she thought. *At least, from the Nu.* What would they do to a half-Nu child? Throw him into the forest with the other infants, too small to work in a mine, left to cry at pines and rocks for food? Keep him? Sneer at him, just like everyone else?

"He's a handsome child," the old woman said, smiling. "A year?"

"Almost." Za swallowed. "Thank you." She couldn't remember when someone had last complimented her child. She stroked his hair absently. "I have to go."

"Safe journeys, little mountain ones. I hope you impale many imperial soldiers on your claws."

Za grinned. "Oh, we will."

Some people stared as she jogged through the village, but the wind stole their words – she slid back into her fox-speed and ran with the forest blurring at her sides. She heard her son scream.

"Hush," she said, gasping, jarring again from fast to slow. "Please. We need to hurry."

The wails tore at her ears.

Za opened the pouch at her waist and frowned as, for the first time since the days after his birth, she fed him fox-bone. *At two years*, her grandmother had said. *Wait two years. It is powerful and dangerous; wait, unless the baby's life is in danger.* Well, it most likely was. The Nu would laugh as they tore the silver from his jacket and threw him aside. Stupid to think otherwise.

His eyes went wide and he inhaled as if trying to breathe all of the journey ahead.

"All you have to do is stay still," she told him, "and try to enjoy it." She felt very strange, talking to him like this. "Can you do that?"

He wriggled and stared into the forest, so Za re-bound him to her chest, facing out, and hoped he didn't get too many bugs in his eyes and mouth. Slitting her own eyes, she ran, and her son pealed with joy.

Fox hide.
Use varies depending on how it is stitched.

Za sat nearly alone in her family's house, winding a long braided strip of fox hide around her son's head: one loop for every week he had lived so far and for every decade she hoped he would live. Ten weeks accumulated around his head, with its tufty dark hair. Soft as a fox cub's, Za thought. Ten decades – though none lived that long. He watched her, with dark eyes in a face that seemed to get plumper every day, slowly gaining the fat he should have got in her womb.

"For sixty healthy years," Za said, on the sixth loop.

No one joined them for this ritual, except for her littlest sister who sat just inside the doorway, crouched and wary. Misbehaving Bao, who ignored their mother's order.

Za didn't shoo her away.

"For seventy healthy years," Za said, on the seventh loop.

Her son watched her with such contentment, such a simple kind of happiness: fed and warm and full of fox-strength, wrapped in it tight as the linens, woolen blankets and the fur stitched with every protective strengthening thread Za knew. As she began the eighth loop, he made little noises of pleasure.

Her hands and her mouth worked, put magic into him, but she turned her head away.

At Bao's ten-week ritual, her extended family and almost everyone else from the village had crowded into their house or peered in from outside, through the door and windows. They had prepared a feast. They had sung and beat on the fox-hide drums brought out only for this day: small drums, with threads as white as snow and as grey as rocks criss-crossing the deep, rich russet of the fox. Ten weeks!

They had hung ten amulets in the house, to keep the ten child-spirits sweet, and they had stamped ten times to send death away. Stay, ten-week baby! They had named her.

"For ninety healthy years," Za said, unable to keep the tremor from her voice. She imagined her family gathered around her son, and tears rolled over her face like an icicle melting.

"For a hundred healthy years."

She sewed the braid fast with sun-yellow thread, brought the thread round and round and round the join so that it bulged like a strange stone. She kept her hands steady, though her tears splashed on her son's face.

Her son, who needed a name.

Possibilities tangled in her head: Hma names, good names, beautiful names, Nu names. Little half-Nu boy who no one but her – and Bao, who remained by the door, probably just curious about a part of her life she couldn't remember – would acknowledge. Her mother wasn't even speaking to her any more. A Nu name would suit him. Why couldn't he look Hma? Why couldn't the stories she'd poured into him with milk and powdered fox bone, a uniquely Hma magic – why couldn't her milk, her fully Hma milk – why couldn't all of it make him Hma and not Nu?

Za picked up her son, held him out – to the family that wasn't there. Her hands shook. "Your name," she managed, before sobs replaced the name she'd picked at random. She thought, wildly, *I'll drop him and he'll die and my family will talk to me again.*

"What's his name?" a small voice said.

Old enough to want to be helpful, little Bao put her hands under Za's son, steadying Za's hands. Such a serious expression for a three-year-old's face.

"Your name," Za said softly, "is Cheu."

"Cheu!" Bao said excitedly. It was a common name; Za suddenly remembered that a boy Bao's age had that name. His parents wouldn't like her for this. Za decided she didn't care.

"Be strong, Cheu. Be brave, Cheu. Be loving, Cheu. Be healthy, Cheu."

Bao echoed her words as closely as possible and kissed Cheu's head afterward.

He wouldn't tolerate being held up for much longer; his face scrunched and he cried for milk. Za returned to the edge of the room, where her blankets and cushions made a far more comfortable place to nurse, and rearranged her jacket around him. It didn't take long for Bao to grow bored of watching. The girl wandered away and Za was alone once again, with the fox hide around her son's head scratching uncomfortably at her chest and only the drip-drip of her tears for company.

Fox teeth.
For tearing enemies to pieces.

"We must move the village," said Yi, the old woman who took charge in times of difficulty. She sat on a little wooden stool in the open space between houses, where early winter sun fell on the gathered villagers like an offering. Everyone stayed silent as she talked. "It was last done when my grandparents were children, also to escape the Nu. We must gather our possessions tonight and leave at first light tomorrow, and when the Nu soldiers arrive they will find only empty houses to burn to the ground. If they find our mines, they will have to work the silver themselves."

Or have other Hma work them, Za thought. *Or us, caught while we're fleeing.*

She bit her fingers, reluctant to speak out – to have the entire village stare at her, with her son fidgeting in her arms. But she couldn't let them agree to this.

"Mother-Yi, may I talk?"

When everyone stared at her, she did her best to ignore them, focusing on old Yi with her smile empty of teeth.

"Of course, child. You have brought us such valuable information. Speak up!"

Murmurs spread. Not everyone agreed with Yi's generosity. Za clutched her son tighter and spoke.

"They are only days behind us and I probably didn't take their only map. They know where our village is. With a hundred of them, they'll find it. And they'll find our trail – not even we can hide the movement of a whole village. A stray heel-print here, a dropped thread there, and they'll follow us into the mountains, and we'll never be able to live in safety.

"But if we kill them all, or send them running, by the time they try to find us again, our tracks will have faded. Winter is coming, in only a month or two. Perhaps the snow will fall again." And they would go into it, towards those higher reaches where people were no longer supposed to dwell, where mountains birthed icy winds and spirits slept. How far did they need to move to be safe forever? How far would the mountains let them?

"So keen to kill the people who are just like your baby's father!" one of the men exclaimed.

Laughter fell around her like slung stones.

Since her son's birth she had stayed away from the other people of the village, had split her time between household work and going far from the village on patrol. They laughed and she wanted to run back into the forest with her son, wanted to throw him aside and beg their forgiveness. Hated herself for both thoughts. Hated them.

Yi glared at the villagers and reached for her staff, no doubt to stamp it on the ground and demand their respect.

Someone mentioned trust and whether spreading her legs for a Nu man made her Nu too.

"Shut up!" Za screamed, and realized it had been Pao and that their mother had smacked him so hard he lay on the ground, moaning. "He's not – " He was. Little half-Nu boy, ugly little boy, from loose-legged Za. She felt it all, rattling around in her skin like knuckle-bones in a cup. "He's Hma!" she shouted, as Yi drew the conversation back to its main subject. Some people went quiet. "He's Hma! He's Hma and he's mine and I'm Hma, I fed him fox-bone, I told him all our stories while he drank my milk, and if you don't shut up you can drink my piss!"

Everyone stared at her in silence.

She shook, held Cheu to her chest, said, "Why don't you ever shut up?" And for once, they did.

Her mother put a hand on her shoulder. "I think Za is right. If we all flee together, they will follow us. Some of us must defend the rest – but not by killing them. We cannot. Count every healthy adult in the village who possesses enough skill and power with the fox-bones to fight, and you will not find fifty, or forty, or even thirty. We could surprise them, and then they would recover, and kill us, as our finite power fades.

"However, there is something else we can do: destroy their supplies, and perhaps kill a few of them, to put the fright in them. Without their supplies they cannot follow us. It will be dangerous and difficult, and perhaps each soldier sleeps beside their food – " her voice faltered there, at the difficulty of their task " – but I think this is our best chance. And I will be honored if Za is with us."

Whatever Pao might have said next was silenced by Tou, who kicked him in the ribs.

As the village agreed with Za's mother's plan, Za wiped away tears with the fox-fur on her sleeve and returned to the ground, tucked away among other people.

Later, her mother murmured angrily, "You are Hma, even if your son isn't, fully."

Za stroked his hair.

The village split in two, its very walls taken apart – small parts bound to backs, transported ahead to be the first walls, shelter for the young, the elderly, the infirm. Its nearby stores were opened and emptied, sacks of rice put onto two wagons, sacks of dried corn added to the wagons where possible, added to baskets and hefted by all but the weakest of the group who departed. The two buffalo, used to plow the lower-altitude rice terraces at certain times of year, were brought from their pens and tied to the wagons, touched fondly by passing people. *Be steady. Be strong.* The further food stores, kept separate from the village for safety, were not touched. In safer times, people would return and find what remained. Children accepted bags of pots, herbs, any spare clothes. Adults hefted baskets full of not just food but fabric, medicines, silver. The graves of the dead were honored one last time.

The group who departed began their journey throughout the morning: wagons and children and the elderly and infirm and adults who possessed little ability with the magic and some adults who did, protecting their mobile village.

Za watched Tou walk away with her son in a fabric-filled basket on his back. "Time to go," her mother said.

"Yes."

With pouches full of fox-bone, they left the village behind.

The forest opened to them like a fox-ear pouch and they pierced their tongues with teeth. They swallowed foreleg bones and hind-leg bones and skull.

They spread out. The forest crunched under Za's feet and she knew it crunched under twenty-one other pairs of feet, knew that her mother ran nearby, that Pao and Xi ran together, her with a tiny child curled in her womb like a fleck of dust. This fight would determine the new lives of many, and Xi did not consider her new life more important than those, though she hoped it would survive.

Za bared her teeth, thinking of the village's future – and of her son, more distant with every step. She felt Tou, who had swallowed fox-skull to sense the forest around the fleeing villagers, holding him.

She knew when Xi killed a Nu scout, tearing his chest open before he even realized she stood in front of him. She knew when another scout fell, and another.

She knew when the first of their group found the army, camped on a flat place where, generations ago, their village had grown rice.

"There are small tents, for the soldiers," her mother said, and everyone heard despite the distances between them, "and bigger tents. Perhaps they contain supplies. We must burn them – and burn the small tents too, if possible, in case they also contain supplies, and because the soldiers will not survive the high-hill nights without them if they still pursue us."

At her wordless yell, they burst from the forest as one.

The first soldiers ran, terrified, and two of the larger tents shone in the night. But the soldiers regrouped, with weapons no one had anticipated. They gathered together to defend their remaining two large tents, holding swords like teeth, and threw gourds full of something that exploded and tore apart even fox-fast limbs. Za felt two deaths – brief agonies that left her gasping. Nearby, Xi screamed. Pao lay lifeless in his blood. The soldiers readied to throw more of their gourds, and Za dashed forwards, grabbed Xi, pulled her away to safety.

If only the fox-bones let them throw their fire like gourds, over the soldiers' heads, onto the tents.

"We need to lure them away!" Za's mother said.

Their group crouched among tents and the old ridges between rice paddies, holding themselves still, putting more fox-bone on their tongues. Xi's tears dripped onto her fingers and she chased the smeared bone with her tongue. Za hurt, too – she hadn't wanted Pao to die, hadn't wanted to see a former friend torn open. "We'll get them," Za whispered – to Xi, to all of their group. Movement. "Look. Those men by their tent." Not all of the soldiers were in big, safe groups after all. Za and Xi ran forward, pounced on three men, killing one of them – and dragged the other two away, towards the forest, and others ran out of cover to circle them, tracing fire-shapes in the air as if they planned to torture the screaming men all together.

Several soldiers broke away from the two groups. Shouts told them not to, but they ran forwards and they were captured too, or killed. Even more followed.

Za felt her mother and six others emerge from hiding, and in the fear and frenzy they reached the tents, and the fires began to warm the night. The soldiers scattered, afraid again, and the Hma ran through the camp, laughing, igniting the smaller tents. "Run south!" Za yelled at the soldiers who fled her fire. "Run south!" *And give us enough time to escape!*

Someone screamed.

Za knew that scream. It was as if Tou stood beside her, as if he had come down from the fleeing village, but –

No. *No.*

They slowed, they looked up into the hills, as if they could see clearly the ambush falling on their moving village.

They ran.

A fox's heels.
Mixed with certain herbs, an abortifacient.

Throughout the pregnancy, Za knew where to find the necessary herbs: carefully dried, hanging from the ceiling. They wafted in the breezes that drifted through the house, as if beckoning her. Once, she tore off enough leaves and held them over a pot of boiling water, and imagined how easily the barely developed baby would leave her body. No half-Nu child.

When only she knew about the pregnancy, she had found happiness in the thought of a child, though it hadn't come according to her plans. But neither had Koua's death; neither had meeting Truc. She had accepted it. Then – shouting, fists, silence.

She didn't know what to do. She dropped the herbs to the floor.

She didn't decide and then it was too late, and her son came out of her, bringing with him a knifing hurt at the way his eyes folded more like a Nu than a Hma, the months of silence from her mother, the looks and the comments from her village all the way down to the trading town, from people who had always smiled at her.

A fox's pelvis.
Used in several healing remedies.

Yi led the defense: burning bright with her fire, tearing away pieces of wall-wood and hurling them in flames at the soldiers. Others – old, young – clustered around her and in smaller groups, protecting anyone unable to fight.

Bodies lay along the ground like rocks.

Za's mother directed the returning group: encircle the attackers, kill as quickly as possible. "Do not look down. Later we will mourn the dead."

They all looked.

Two little girls lay on the ground. Not Bao. Za blinked away tears at the sight of such young deaths – and there were babies, too.

But though she ran faster than storm-winds and left soldiers clutching their burnt throats behind her, she couldn't find Tou or Cheu.

Her father and grandparents stood with Yi, and Bao hid at their feet. Za circled around them, fending off soldiers, who scattered, finally outnumbered.

As her fox-bone ran out, as her senses and speed and fire-hot fingers returned to normal, the cold night fell on Za and she collapsed. "Cheu," she gasped. Around her, the village rearranged itself for the next few hours: healing those who could be saved, honoring those who could not.

Za's father brought a bowl of hot stew made with ground pelvis and helped her drink.

"Tou felt Pao die," he said, "and then they attacked us. He ran after some soldiers, away into the forest, and he hasn't come back."

"Cheu."

Her father stroked her hair. "He was with Tou."

Though every part of her body protested, stiff and sore, Za got to her feet.

"You need to rest, Za."

"No."

The forest kept its secret for so long that she stopped crying. She forced one foot in front of the other, knowing that eventually she would find their bodies, and bury them, and move on into the mountains with the rest of her village. Branches scratched her face. The cold ached in her fingers. Battle-wounds worsened; she limped, but she could still walk. The moon gave her poor light to see with. High above, the orb had finally dimmed, and the other soldiers hadn't carried a replacement – or it had been destroyed. Za managed to smile. Maybe the village had enough time now.

Something cried.

She looked to one side, at a dark shadow: a cave.

In it, still-breathing Tou curled unconscious around the basket. Cheu cried hungrily.

"Oh." Za sank to the ground, to pull him from the bundled cloths and silver and hold him close.

*

As the village moved into the whitening mountains, Za felt as though someone looked at her and Cheu with mistrust as often as snowflakes fell around them. She carried a basket as heavy as anyone else's, she cried together with Xi at the memory of Pao's death, she hunted and cooked and sat with everyone else, turning hides into mountain clothes – yet the looks didn't stop.

Most of the time she walked with her mother, who out-glared them all, and stayed utterly silent.

Cheu babbled sometimes, apparently fascinated by the cold, exhausting, hungry process of fleeing. Wrapped in hide and spare fabric, nestled in a child's basket padded with pine needles for extra warmth, fed as much meat as she could spare, he didn't feel any of it. Za made sure of it.

No soldiers had attacked; with a week between the village and the ambush, many began hoping for safety. Many began to talk more decisively of where to build their new village. They needed to survive the winter, but then their lives could begin anew.

In a few months, Cheu's noises would be words. *Mama. Papa?* Za wrapped her arms around his basket, torn between shushing him – how they looked at her whenever he babbled, how they looked at him – and letting him practice his infant-babble.

He deserved better. And not just, Za thought, from the village. From her. That old woman had called him handsome. A handful of people looked at him differently. Limping Tou ruffled his short hair. Xi gave him pine cones to play with, snapping off some of the scales to make them look like people. Za's mother started smiling at him in the evenings, when he pottered around their fire pointing at sparks. Za's grandmother winked at him as she carried her remaining chickens.

One night, Za couldn't sleep for crying, so angry at herself.

The next morning, as she heaped snow over the ashes of their fire and hoisted her baskets onto her back and front, she began to sing to him. People glared at her. She flushed and fell silent. But as the village began to walk, they looked away; quietly, so that only Cheu could hear, she gathered up her courage and sang,

> I ground the fox-bones
> for you,

I hand-stitched the jacket
   for you,
I walked into the mountains
   for you ...

THE CITY BUILDERS
by Michele Lee

EDITOR'S NOTE

Once upon a time Michele defended a Borders bookstore from an infestation of flesh-eating, book-look-a-like monsters. On a stormy April day she once single-handedly wrestled a bear into a bathtub and even got him to sit still for a nail trim. Mostly, though, she writes stories of heartbroken werewolves ("Wolf Heart"), zombie with souls ("Rot") and rock star hyena-girls (you'll see). Follow along at michelelee.net

"Like a lot of my weirder stories, 'The City Builders' came from a dream I had; I was an apartment building trying to help a victim of domestic abuse," says Michele. "It was so odd I had to see if I could make it work for readers."

It's a haunting story, a complete world in just a couple thousand words, a dream that quickly turns into a nightmare. The questions it poses about the price of survival are riveting. How much would you pay for survival? For yourself, for your society, for your species?

When we moved to Pando we were a desperate, fragmented race. The treaty with the Naibians had just fallen through and we found ourselves cut off from our own home world, out-maneuvered by politicians better at the game than us.

They said Pando, a lifeless hunk of mineral and metal, could be our paradise. We thought they were crazy.

They said we still had our health, and our minds, our spirit, even if we'd lost our jobs and our homes. The divide between those who stayed under Naibian control, those who fled for hopefully greener pastures, and those who accepted the handouts given to us – consolations for our planet, our culture and our lives – threatened to bring about another solar war. We nursed dreams of working our way back up to a global middle class, at least, and reclaiming something of our past.

When we got here they looked at the ruined black landscape

and begged us not to fall into hopelessness. Clonal colonies, they said, would save us in this dark place.

They lied.

I watch the fragmented metal skin of J'aul glittering in the never-ending lights of the city. There might come a day when we would glitter in the stars that glowed in the night sky, but the people of the city chose to supplant the glory of the stars with their own need of perpetual light. To never have to face the shadows. To never have to know they were alone. They danced in the streets, drinking and feasting, reveling that they were concerned with no one's well being but their own.

J'aul fell last week. Already there is less than half of him left. The metal poachers stole some, making off with his guts before the city closed off the site and posted extensive surveillance. The city began clearing the site the next work day, whisking his bits off for other uses. Waste not.

His heart is the part I missed the most. I should have had his heart, since if it hadn't already been in use it would have been mine; and mine, his. But the people tore it out, removing the tender bits of flesh inside. Then they entombed the flesh in a box, buried in the empty earth and raised a monument to J'aul's centuries of labor, at the edge of the city where I could not see. Where people rarely traveled.

I wonder if the people in the walls could feel my sadness over J'aul's loss. Did the lights dim slightly, as the world had when he fell? Or did all go on as they perceived normal? Life perpetual and everlasting. Life unquestioned and unconsidered.

Rats scuttle through the remains now, chasing the last bits of food and flesh left behind. They find little, as J'aul warned those of him long before his strength failed and he collapsed to his knees in the empty streets. They took with them what they valued, but from the early squeals of the vermin digging through J'aul's skin they'd left behind enough. Unwanted pets, immovable aquariums, the dented cans and expired boxes of their food stores, not even metal could resist the rats' gnawing these days, though it was the last thing to go when more delicate meals could be found.

*

Pando, it turned out, was as rich in gases, minerals and metals as the earth has once been in lifeforms. We struck mile-wide veins of rhenium, under mountains of tungsten that looked painted with oil slicks in the softest light of dusk. Great chunks of columbite, tapiolite and tantalite made the original settlers rich and no doubt made the Naibians regret exiling them to an outworld planet dismissed as a death trap.

But in the spirit of our ancestors we were determined to pull ourselves up by our bootstraps and make the most of what we did have, which was a few life-sustaining ships, vicious determination and a wicked way with science. After all, the Naibians had already ripped our culture apart, gentrifying us and our planet in their own image. What they didn't have was a creative process and a willingness to cannibalize their own for the greater good.

Today the people choose J'aul's replacement. But it's a mistake of a word. Replacement. The very idea that he could be removed, gutted and emptied, only to be grown again, is laughable. Cruel.

There was a grand ceremony, any excuse for a celebration, as we watched and shook in anger, or sadness, around them. Parades and ponies, the roasting scents of meat and vegetables, musicians in the streets and hanging from the balconies and calling from cars and trains, threading through the feet of the city. All day they laughed and cried out until the sun slipped past the horizon and the mechanical lights of the street burned, glowing off the walls and the curves of bodies and machines alike.

A heralding blast rose up from the streets and the crowd. People, so many vermin themselves, squealed and cheered together, a cacophony of noise. Over the corpse of J'aul sparks burst, red green gold silver. Fireworks scorched the air where he fell, where he lay alone for three days, unaided, until his last breath left him. Had he felt me reaching for him, though he forbade it?

The song grew louder as the people approached, the soft discussion among us drowned out. Paraded through the streets, they left the drunks and the old and the young and tired behind in their revelry. They shed members and gained them. They pounded the streets, unforgiving, with their feet, with their dancing, arms open to the night air and the stars they would never see.

Above the city lights I watched as they approached the body of J'aul and the gates fell away with a flourish of The Architect's arms. Above the city lights I saw the stars, trying to reach in vain to J'aul's ruins.

During the wars with the Naibians we spliced ourselves with beasts of prey, creatures of the air, bacteria and bear mites. Among us we had families who could photosynthesize, children who had the crushing bites of hyenas and the claws of bears. Women with the willowy, spineless shapes of cephelopods who used to be able to breathe water before the Naibians fouled up the waters to stop ocean attacks.

So it seemed only natural that in an environment that, at best, discouraged life, they'd splice us with other things. Aspen did the trick. With a few reconfigurations, membranes and cytoplasm became living steel and rebar.

We rebuilt ourselves. Down to the metal in our cells.

The moon in her mercy tried to light up the shell of J'aul's heart, a hollow sphere that rose, dirt spilling away like liquid, and came to rest before The Architect.

He cried out, in tiny words that were swallowed by the crowd's cheers. I couldn't remember what he'd said anymore. It had been too long since his lies were dedicated to me.

Then another, smaller form, only the thin white dress and the wreath of pink flowers in its hair betraying that it was a girl, a young one at that, though I had lost the ability to tell the significance of such things. But they like to use young ones, so that we last longer. They fed the girl, whether she was scared or accepting in her fate, to J'aul's heart.

They all heard the girl's piercing scream as the connections within jabbed their way into her fragile flesh and began pumping.

The crowd sent up a cheer of pleasure that sounded an awful lot like a scream. It ended suddenly, when J'aul's heart closed around her, cutting her off from the rest of her species. I remembered that I had screamed for a very long time, before my voice failed forever, neutered by the growth of circuitry in my veins. As it had risen the heart sank, planted and left to germinate in J'aul's carcass until she grew into a new life, in service to the city.

In a few days the sprouts would push up through the soil, the girl's immune system building and repairing biometal in great cells, forming the tissue of the foundation and walls. In a few months, she would be inspected and deemed habitable, then, like J'aul and I, she would stand as long as her heart beat and the twisted system her biology had become would echo with the cries and laughter of the people within her.

They told us it would be immortal steel flesh that wouldn't die. They said we'd be honored and loved, genetic code cycled into fetal codes for the barren among us. It wasn't even really a sacrifice, they said, because no one died.

But they lied.

I pulled my awareness away from the streets and the celebration and the blind mess of them all. I wondered again if the humans inside my walls could feel my pain, my weakness, my rage. J'aul had warned those who he had lived in service to, the families who had found shelter under his roofs. He had told them when he felt himself fading and unable to hold up and regrow the biometal compound that had become his skin.

But I remain silent in my weakness, in my heartache. I know it's coming soon and I wonder; when I fail, would the screams of the humans who made me their home finally give a voice to my rage before I fall to silence beneath the lights and stars?

WEREWOLF OF SAPPHO
by Deb Hoag

EDITOR'S NOTE
This is the first story I ever wrote specifically for a Dog Horn publication. I've had many stories in Polluto *magazine since then, and two novels as well. This is still one of my favorites, pointing out that one can never be too careful about first impressions.*

Florescent light gave a subtle purple gleam to the straight black hair of the woman in the booth. Kate, her waitress, held the menu clutched to her bosom like a shield as she approached the table. She reluctantly gave up her cardboard armor, opening the menu and placing it in front of the black-haired woman.

"Hi. Would you like me to bring you something to drink while you decide what you want?"

The woman gave Kate a brief glance, full of amusement.

"What, no 'Hello, I'm Bambi and I'll be your server today?'"

While her voice was ironic, there was warmth in her eyes, and Kate gave her a shy smile. "Guess not, but I'm Kate, anyway."

"I'm Fay. Nice to meet you, Kate. What's good in this joint?" Fay held her palm up before Kate could reply. "Don't answer that, and you won't have to lie to me. Give me a burger, rare. Really rare. I want it to look like it could jump off my plate and start mooing any second. Whatever looks good next to it on the plate. And a Coke."

Fay flipped the menu shut and handed it back to Kate.

Having exhausted her repertoire of polite chit-chat, Kate snatched the menu and fled to the kitchen.

While the aging cook was searing half-a-pound of hamburger and tossing fries, Kate surreptitiously studied Fay from the safety of the service window.

There was nothing strange about her clothes; plain, straight-legged black jeans, buffed black leather work boots, a plain black shirt, crisply tailored and tucked into the jeans. Small gold hoops at her ears, a serpentine chain around a slender neck, nestled gently between her breasts. Kate couldn't quite make out the pedant dangling from it, except for a small purple amethyst that glowed against Fay's creamy skin.

Her nails were plain and short, her hair was smooth and long, flowing like water over her shoulders. Her eyes . . . were looking at Kate with amusement. Kate felt herself blush from the crown of her head down to the tips of her toes. That was what happened when you were red-headed Irish. She could blush at the drop of a hat, until her face was nearly as red as her hair.

Jane rang the "order up" bell, even though Kate was standing right next to her. The cook studied her own handiwork dubiously. "You're sure she said *very* rare, right?"

Kate eyed the burger. Little pools of blood were oozing up the surface from the center of the sandwich. Both Jane and Kate had been raised to believe the credo that you cook meat until it is brown all the way through, or else God knows what could happen. Salmonella, hair on your palms, knock-knees, you name it. A number of ooky diseases could be blamed on eating meat that had not been cooked all the way through.

Reaching out to grab the plate, Kate gave the burger one more worried glance, and managed a small shrug. "That really is what she said, Jane."

Kate swung through the saloon-style doors that opened into the dining area, and went to face her customer.

Fay ate like she hadn't had a meal in a week. When Kate came by to see how she was doing, she was just in time to see the last french fry disappearing into Fay's mouth. There wasn't a single crumb left of the burger. She blinked in amazement at Fay. Most people were still getting their ketchup applied when she did her first "everything okay here? Can I get you anything?" routine.

Fay sighed in contentment as she pushed her plate away. "Kate, that was an amazing burger. I take back everything I was thinking about this place when I walked in the door. Small town diner, but your burgers rock!"

Kate gave Fay another one of the shy smiles that illuminated all the beauty in her face. "Don't eat here during the day, then, or you'll have to change your mind again." She collected the twenty Fay gave her for the bill, and went to ring it up and make change. When she turned back around, Fay was gone. Kate stuck the money in a plain envelope and wrote Fay/Kate on it, then lifted the register tray and placed the envelope underneath it. Maybe she would come back.

Two nights later, she did. Another quiet evening, two middle-aged guys drinking coffee together in a corner and talking about wives, families, taxes. Easygoing Jane on the grill, Matchbox Twenty on the juke. Kate thought that she might possibly make it through the night without falling to pieces if she was just allowed to keep pretending nothing was wrong.

She stopped believing that when she approached Fay's table, and saw that the smile blooming on Fay's sharp pale face had stopped as soon as she got a look at Kate. "You look a little under the weather tonight, Kate."

Embarrassment made her sullen. "How I'm feeling is none of your business. Would you like something to drink while you're looking at the menu?" Kate slapped the menu down with unnecessary force.

"I don't know. If I ask for a Coke, you promise not to spit in it before you get it out here?"

Surprised, Kate glanced up and got her eyes tangled with Fay's, who looked amused, insulted and sympathetic all at the same time. Kate's lips curved up. "If I was going to do that, I'd wait until I was standing right in front of you, I think."

"And what did you do to the creep that clocked you in the face?"

Kate's hand flitted to the skin that was split over her cheekbone, the bruise that was creeping down from her left eye to join it, the puffed and swollen flesh under her left brow. Danny had caught her damn hard. For a second, she remembered the impact of the blow, the thud as her head bounced off the wall she had been pinned against. The next second, that flash of memory was gone, and Kate was standing under a crummy florescent light, while a woman she hardly knew reached up and clasped her hand with more tenderness than

Kate knew what to do with.

After Kate had brought Fay a burger that looked like it should still be wandering around munching hay, she tried to give Fay back the change from a couple of nights before. Fay looked at her incredulously. "It was a tip, Kate. A Tip. T-I-P. Jesus. You hung on to the change for two days to give it back to me? My priest isn't that honest. Take it and buy a baseball bat and use it on that asshole that hit you!"

Kate's lips curved up again, even though it hurt to smile. "Thanks, Fay." They both knew she wasn't talking about the money.

Fay was back in a few days later, and Kate was beginning to think of the rare burger she ordered as "the usual." Fay's eyes swept her face, and small traces of worry disappeared when she saw there were no new bruises.

"Hey, Kate, whatcha know tonight?"

"I know you."

Fay looked at her, eyes dancing. "You think you do, maybe. What do you know about me?"

"I know you're Matt Spark's big sister. You left after you graduated from high school, and no one heard from you for a long time. Some people said you went to college, and some people said you got knocked up. One of my friends told me she had been at a party with you and you got drunk and hit on her. So I figured the 'knocked up' story probably wasn't true."

Kate stopped and waited to see how Fay would respond. She hadn't meant for everything to come gushing out like some kind of challenge. Fay had seen Kate walking around with the evidence of her problems on her face for every stranger to see – and Fay hadn't said a damn thing about herself. Then she remembered Fay's gentle fingers twining comfortingly with hers, and wished she could take back what she had just said, but she couldn't, so she stood and waited.

To her surprise and relief, Fay laughed out loud, and ran a long-fingered hand through that mass of black hair. "If your friend was Jill Abbot, you are absolutely right. I did not get knocked up, did not go to college. I did not get married, did not pass "Go" and did not collect two hundred dollars." She looked at Kate, and one cheek dimpled. "From the looks of you the other night, I'd say missing out on the whole family thing was no big loss."

Kate let out a snort of laughter. "You can say that again. So what have you been doing for the last ten years?"

Fay smiled again, this time slow, and tilted her head as she looked up at Kate. "That's too long a story to tell while you're standing there looking at me. I went to Europe for a while, kicked around, had a few adventures. If you want to hear more, you'll have to find some time to sit down and let me tell it the long way. What do you think?"

Kate knew exactly what she thought. A small shiver of excitement and recklessness flicked through her. "I have some free time tomorrow afternoon."

Fay was still smiling that slow deep smile. "How nice. So do I."

Danny was out of town until Sunday night. The blow to Kate's face hadn't been any more intentional than any of Danny's other violence, and she was glad to have a weekend to pull herself together before having to face Danny again.

Kate and Fay sat in one of the snowbird cafes, where there were more snowbirds than locals, and drank wine and giggled softly to each other. Fay had an amazing memory for the people she had left behind, and had no trouble keeping up as Kate told her about the small-town antics that had taken place in her absence.

Finally, the conversation wound down, and Fay reached a casual hand up to smooth back one of Kate's red curls. Kate's breath caught in her throat, and for a moment her eyes stung, as if tears were going to come gushing out any second. She blinked them back, and looked steadily at Fay. "Would you like to go, now?"

Fay smiled back. "Yes, I would."

Fay's mom had been moved to hospice shortly before Fay arrived in town. Her younger brother Matt was supposed to join her in a few days, so they could get the old house closed down and spend some time with their mother. So they went back to Fay's childhood home, carrying a bottle of wine with them.

They made love in rooms full of dust and doilies, sun motes

dancing in the air as Kate lay on her back and felt Fay's tongue sliding on warm flesh. When Fay came, a cloud of hot, perfumed air came off her skin, a scent that Kate breathed in greedy and deep. It made her feel more drunk and luscious than the wine ever had, and she curled close to inhale the lingering fragrance of her lover's skin.

Afterward, they lay on a faded carpet of mauve cabbage roses, and twined their fingers as they talked softly in the twilight. From above, a cabinet full of porcelain figures watched them benevolently, while the headlights of passing cars shone brief illumination on a full breast, the curve of a slender thigh, red curls tangled with long straight strands of purple-black hair.

Two days, too short. Danny was coming back Sunday evening. On Saturday night, they lay in the guest bed that used to be Fay's and now was again, and touched gently. There was never enough of that gentle, fragrant touch for Kate, who felt she could shatter from the pleasure at any time, and then float away in pieces, happy at last.

"You haven't asked me about Danny," said Kate at last.

Fay shrugged. "You haven't asked me about what I did in Europe. What you want to know, what you want to tell, is up to you."

Kate looked at the floor, then back at Fay. "There are some things I need to tell you before Danny gets back."

"There are probably a few things I should tell you, too, Kate."

A tiny frown creased Kate's brow. "Things like what?"

"Kate, I've had some really strange experiences since I left town. Really strange. And because of that, I can tell you absolutely, unequivocally, you do not have to stay with Danny, or take any shit from Danny, ever again. I can protect you. I can show you how to protect yourself, so that Danny can never, never bother you again."

Fay looked at Kate, waiting for a response.

Kate was astounded. "You would do that for me? Stand up to Danny for me? Aren't you afraid that you could get hurt, too? Maybe even killed?"

Fay shook her head. Her hair flowed like a live thing. "Of course I would, Kate. Danny can't hurt me. Not in any way that matters. If you're ready to end it, I'll help you do it, in any way that is in my power. And that's not just idol talk, Kate. I mean every word I say."

"I can't believe you'd do that for me. You've only known me for a few days, and you're ready to put yourself between me and a monster. You have no idea what Danny is capable of, Fay. You couldn't possibly know."

Fay shifted impatiently. "You aren't listening to me. That doesn't matter. What matters is: Do you love me enough to leave this mess and start a new life? Here and now, and with me. Tell me yes, and I'll make it right. I'll make everything right for you, Kate."

Kate looked out the window, as if the answers might be written on the face of the moon, and sighed. "Tomorrow, okay? I'll need to go home and take care of some stuff, and Danny deserves to hear what is happening directly from me. Not to just come home and find me gone."

Fay's glance followed Kate's out the window. "Tomorrow. I'll come over around eight."

They went back to the sturdy old bed, and made love in the moonlight.

At eight o'clock, Fay pulled up in front of Kate's house. Parked in the driveway was a lovingly restored International in cream and a lush, dark green. Leaving the doors unlocked and the keys in the ignition in case they needed to take off in a hurry, Fay got out of the car and walked up to the door. She knocked briskly, but there was no sound from inside. The house was dark and silent, and she knocked again, more urgently.

When the silence continued, Fay turned the handle in her hand and quietly opened the door. Stepping through, she glanced cautiously around. Nothing looked out of place, no signs of a beating or worse, as far as she could tell. Everything she could see was spotlessly clean, and the aroma that hung in the air told Fay that Kate had actually cooked for the son-of-a-bitch.

Something stirred down at the far end of the hallway, but Fay couldn't tell what it was.

"Kate? Is that you?"

"Just one more minute, Fay," whispered a harsh voice. Fay

wasn't sure whether it was Kate or not. There was a skittering noise, something hard scraping across the wood floor.

Fay waited, and watched – the indistinct movement in the hallway, the moonlight that flooded the room, the second hand of a clock with an illuminated face. Her hands were bunched in her pockets. She felt like the ticking sounds of the clock were moments of her life that were passing away, being pulled out of her against her will.

Kate's face, pale beautiful oval, became clear in the moonlight as she crossed the room. Fay allowed herself to relax, the smallest bit, as Kate's smile bloomed. Suddenly, a small shape barreled towards her from the hallway, darting around Kate. Fay started at the sudden burst of motion, but wasn't able to move quickly enough to get out of the way. She had a split second to register the shape as vaguely dog-like, and then it was on her, teeth deep in her throat.

The gun she had clutched in her pocket spilled down uselessly to the floor. The werewolf ripped open Fay's slender neck – the creamy column that Kate had trailed kisses down only that morning.

As Fay died, Kate came closer, watching regretfully as the light faded out of her eyes. "Danny never really meant to hurt me, Fay. She's just a teenager, and God, you must remember what that's like. Hormones go crazy, the moon comes out and *Bam!* But she's always sorry the next day, and she's getting much better at controlling her changes."

She leaned forward and patted her daughter fondly between her large, inky black ears. Her own pelt was starting to sprout, a fine, foxy red.

"See, Danielle, I told you I would bring something nice home from the restaurant. But, I swear, if you spill one drop of your dinner on my nice, clean floor, you'll be eating leftovers for a month."

Danny made an agreeable rumbling noise low in her throat, and kept chewing.

BIG SISTER
by Janis Butler Holm

EDITOR'S NOTE
Janis Butler Holm lives in Athens, Ohio, where she has served as Associate Editor for Wide Angle, *the film journal. Her prose, poems, and performance pieces have appeared in small-press, national, and international magazines. Her plays have been produced in the US, Canada, and England.*

She found inspiration for this flash piece in a common cliché. "Sometimes it's fun to take a moribund metaphor and give it new life," says Janis. "E.g., 'My brother, that little monster.'"

I'm reading this book about life on other planets, and suddenly I hear a tapping at my window. "Who's there?" I yell, jumping to my feet.

"It's me!" my little brother shouts. He's climbed the tree again, despite Mom's saying not to. I open the window and let him into my room.

"What's the matter with your neck?" I ask. There are funny blue scabs on the skin above his collar.

"I dunno. It just itches." He scratches, and a gummy powder sticks to his nails.

"Your legs look really weird," I say. He's got scabs there, too, but they're a dark gray.

"So what?" It's clear the little monster is in a bad mood. "I'm hungry," he complains, scratching his head. I can see some purple scabs between clumps of hair.

"Well, Mom'll have lunch ready in a few minutes. You'd better wash up." My own stomach growls. I close the book on my desk. "In fact, you could use a bath. You're beginning to stink."

"Oh, shut up, stupid. You're the one who stinks." He bends down to scratch his feet, which are covered with black scales. His fingers are now blue and joined by stretchy webs.

"Ha, ha, ha," I sing. "You stink, and you're weird." I hold

my nose and go "Eeeeuuuuwwww." I'm being really mean, but my brother drives me crazy.

"Kids, it's time for lunch!" Mom yells up the stairs. The little beast looks upset, and I begin to feel bad. His nose has morphed into a snout.

"Look, I'll say you're in the bathroom. As for climbing up the tree, that can be our secret." I'm a pretty good big sister when I decide I want to be. "Be right down, Mom!"

My brother's making dopey noises. Of course he won't say "thank you," but I can tell he's grateful. Still, I worry about him. What's going to happen when his sister's not around?

As I move toward the hallway, I'm shaking my head. "You'd better start behaving," I say, just like Mom, "or one day you'll find yourself in really big trouble."

EASY'S LAST STAND
by Nancy A. Collins

EDITOR'S NOTE

Nancy A. Collins has authored over 20 novels and novellas, numerous short stories, and worked on several comic books, including a two-year run on Swamp Thing. *She is a recipient of the HWA's Stoker Award and the British Fantasy Society Award, and has been nominated for the Eisner, John Campbell Memorial, World Fantasy and International Horror Guild Awards.*

Best known for her ground-breaking vampire character, Sonja Blue, which heralded the rise of the popular urban fantasy genre, her works include the best-selling Sunglasses After Dark, *the Southern Gothic collection* Knuckles and Tales, *and the* Vamps *series for young adults. Her most recent novel is* Left Hand Magic, *the second installment in the critically-acclaimed Golgotham urban fantasy series. She currently resides in Wilmington, North Carolina with her fiancé, Tommy, their Boston terrier, Chopper, and an indeterminate number of cats, only two of which she admits to having anything to do with.*

"Easy's Last Stand" was originally published in Cemetery Dance Magazine, *Vol. 3, #2 (1991). In* Women Writing the Weird I, *Nancy wowed us with "Catfish Gal Blues", a sleepy southern folk tale about a woman done wrong. You could practically taste the mint juleps as you read. She switches up here with a fast-paced story about murder and mayhem in the big city and a larger than life heroine who knows how to take it ... easy.*

Somewhere In Middle-America, 1981:

"I want to fuck my mother; isn't that naughty of me?"

"I really can't say, Floyd, until you give me your credit card number and its expiration date."

"Tell me it's naughty! Tell me it's bad; the worst thing in the world! Tell me it's the worst thing you've ever heard!"

"Floyd ..."

"I won't give you the number if you don't tell me it's bad."

Sandra rolled her eyes. If it was up to her, she'd hang up on the little perv. She'd never seen Floyd before in her life. Never would. She pictured him as a middle-aged CPA in Sans-A-Belt slacks, leather oxfords and the wrong color tie. But she also imagined he had a platinum AmEx card, and that's all that really mattered.

Her employers, the Gazzola Brothers, liked to eavesdrop on the line every now and again, to make sure everyone observed proper procedure. It wouldn't do to have the girls insulting the customers – or giving away too much for free. She could tell from Floyd's shallow, nasal breathing that he was whacking off – a definite no-no on the toll-free line – but she didn't dare drop the call before getting his card number.   "Yeah, it's the most horrible thing I've ever heard," she lied. This seemed to be what Floyd wanted to hear, as the sound of one hand clapping rapidly increased and he moaned something under his breath. "Now, about your card number ..."

click

She swore into the mouthpiece of her headset. She should have known better. Why give the cow your AmEx number when you can milk yourself for free? Usually she was better at spotting the jerk-offs, as they were called: the callers intent on getting their rocks off before you could snag their credit card numbers.

She'd been working for Easy's Hot Talk for three months, long enough to give her relative seniority in the call room and gain a boost in pay. Not bad for work that consisted of sitting on your ass and talking on the phone. Granted, you had to talk to some really sick puppies but, as Gloria was fond of saying, "you knew the job was dangerous when you took it."

Easy's Hot Talk was a phone sex joint. Well, not really, as the women harnessed to the state-of-the-art telemarketing headgear and multi-line telephone banks weren't the ones who helped lonely, faceless men achieve long-distance sexual fulfillment, although the classified ads salted in the back of skin mags like *Hot Milk*, *Big Bad Mama*, and *Catfight Quarterly*, certainly gave that impression:

"Hi! I'm Easy! I've got a HOT, NASTY TONGUE and I want to make U cum! I know what Men Like and I've Got what

Men Want! I'll make you EXPLODE with PLEASURE! Call now for WILD UNTAMED HOT TALK! Call anytime! I'm ALWAYS there for YOU! 1-900-555-8255.

The come-on, crass as it was, hooked them but good. Hundreds of hot and horny readers called the 900 number, the vast majority of them after dark. But instead of the oozing, cooing sex-doll shown cradling a telephone receiver at an inappropriate angle for conversation, the callers got an operator with a prepared speech designed to be mildly titillating without being actually obscene. Each "Hot Talker" was under orders to sell the caller a list of "secret phone numbers" for a nominal fee (charged to their credit cards, of course) along with "candid photos" of the infamous Easy frolicking with her friends.

In reality, the phone numbers 'sold' to the callers were simply pre-recorded tapes of Gloria reading letters from Penthouse. To top it off, the callers were billed three dollars a minute, including for time spent on hold, to listen to the canned messages. It was a blatant rip-off and the Gazzola Brothers made money hand over fist. The operation had been around since the mid-Seventies, but what with the increase of herpes, penicillin-resistant gonorrhea, and AIDS, business was booming like never before. Barnum was right; there *is* one born every minute. But she wondered how, since it seemed half of America was into one-handed telephone conversations.

She decided it was time for a brief respite from the perverts of America's heartland and removed her head-set. Gloria frowned at her from the foot of the conference table. Sandra mouthed the words "gotta pee" and made her way to the hall.

The Gazzola Brothers' operation wasn't illegal, but it didn't exactly have a Better Business Bureau sign hanging in the front window. Easy's Hot Talk was located in a nondescript one-story single-family dwelling that had been converted into what amounted to a twenty-four hour answering service. The house lay just beyond the city limits, in an unincorporated section that was a no-man's land of third-hand auto dealerships, after-hour pool halls, and tail-gate flea markets.

Sandra glanced back into the call-room and at the cigarette smoke that hung over the conference table like mosquito netting.

Most of the women chain-smoked while on duty, herself included. Non-smokers tended to quit after a couple of days. If any of the poor sweaty-handed bastards who surrendered their Visa, MasterCard and AmEx numbers (the Gazzolas didn't accept Discover) could see who was answering the phone for Easy (she of the silicone injections and artfully spread labia), they'd probably never get it up again.

She'd interacted with enough desperate college students and terminally aroused hicks to know most of them thought they were going to interact with the woman pictured in the ad, or one of her so-called "close personal friends", when they called the 900 line. In reality Easy was just some bimbo who posed nude for a sleazy photographer sometime during the Seventies and had signed a model's release. Not even the Gazzola Brothers knew who "Easy" actually was.

The Hot Talkers fielding her Easy's eager suitors were a world removed from the buxom sex-kitten in the ad. At twenty-seven, Sandra was one of the youngest women working the phones. Doris was a grandmother of three, and routinely knitted sweaters for her husband while reciting her spiel into the throat mike. Muriel was in her mid-forties and chatted incessantly between calls about her various ex-husbands, of which she had an impressive collection. Nora was in her early fifties, with cat-eye glasses and a bouffant, and constantly snapped a wad of Dentine. Then there was the Head Honcho: The Big G. If anyone could be said to dominate the call-room, it was Gloria, who weighed close to five hundred pounds and sat on two folding chairs. She also sounded like Marilyn Monroe in heat. She'd been with the Gazzola Brothers since the start and was the de facto Night Manager.

When Sandra had answered the ambiguously phrased ad for "telephone sales woman", the first thing Gloria told her was: "We got three rules here: we don't take calls from minors; we don't take calls from women; and we don't take calls from guys with numbers on the Hot Card list." It seemed like a simple enough business philosophy.

Gloria ran the show from eight in the evening to three in the morning, which was the heaviest call volume period, and didn't tolerate goofing off on her shift. Despite her insistence on treating Easy's Hot Talk like a legitimate business, Sandra and the others still liked her. Gloria, unlike the Day Manager, wasn't scared of the

Gazzolas and wasn't above making jokes at their expense. She would also send one of the girls out for doughnuts or order pizza if the mood struck her, something frowned on during the day, when the Gazzola Brothers often stopped by in person to check on business.

Just then the bathroom door opened and ZuZu stepped out, tugging on her leather miniskirt. Of all the Hot Talkers, she was the only one who looked like a pin-up girl, if you ignored her magenta Mohawk, the yin-yang symbol tattooed between her breasts, and the collection of rings piercing her ears, nose, belly-button and lips. ZuZu fronted her own all-woman punk band, ZuZu's Pedals. She claimed the only reason she worked for 'pigs like the Gazzolas' was to raise the cash for a Stratocaster. She'd been there almost a year.

"I better get back to the yoke before Big Mama starts losing her cool!" ZuZu said with a wink.

A few minutes later, as Sandra washed her hands at the sink, a shadow flickered across the bathroom's frosted window pane. She hurried back into the call-room and tapped Gloria on the shoulder. The Night Manager looked up and frowned, causing chain reactions in her chins.

"We got company, Big G."

"Shit! You sure about that?" Gloria growled.

"I saw something moving outside the bathroom window."

Gloria grunted and pressed her deceptively small hands against the tabletop, levering her vast bulk onto elephantine legs. Not only did Gloria weight over five hundred pounds, she also stood six-foot-six. The metal folding chairs seemed to groan in relief as she stood up. Sandra stepped back, momentarily overwhelmed by the body heat radiating from the other woman. Gloria seemed to sweat all the time, even in the dead of winter.

"Better wake up Carl, then. I'll call the Brothers."

Technically, Carl was one of the Gazzolas, but in the same way Gummo was one of the Marx Bothers. He was the youngest and least motivated member of the family, and his sole function was to chase off unwanted visitors. It was an undemanding job, it kept him out of trouble, and, theoretically, involved him in the family business. The Hot Talkers, for the most part, did not resent Carl's presence amongst them as, unlike his elder siblings, he actually proved useful on occasion. While the Gazzolas didn't advertise their comings and goings, the location of Easy's Hot Talk was something of an open secret in the local community Jealous boyfriends and outraged husbands were fairly common problems for Hot Talkers, as well as the occasional lust-struck caller hungry to meet Easy in the flesh. Usually the sight of Carl, baseball bat in hand, was enough to chase off any would-be trouble makers.

Sandra walked down the hall and banged on a door marked 'General Manager'. "Carl! Wake up, damn it!"she shouted. "We got a prowler!"

There was some muttering on the other side and a couple seconds later Carl, dressed in a pair of grungy blue jeans and a smelly Harley Davidson t-shirt, opened the door, revealing the General Manager's office to be a mess of stale beer cans, empty fast food wrappers, and dog-eared paperbacks. "Wuzzit?"

"Gloria told me to tell you to check the perimeter. Someone's sneaking around outside."

"Izzit that dumb-ass motherfucker again?" he yawned, showing the gap where his front teeth used to be.

A couple of weeks ago the boyfriend of one of the new girls decided to try and save her from eternal damnation by dragging her, kicking and screaming, out of the house. Carl had been forced to separate the boyfriend's cowboy hat from his skull the hard way.

"I don't think so. Arlene quit a couple of days ago."

"Get back t'work. I'll take care of it." Carl said as he reached behind the door and retrieved a Louisville Slugger with a taped handle.

"Damn it, can't a guy sleep in peace around here?" Carl mused aloud as he unlocked the front door. As if it wasn't bad enough his jerk-wad brothers had him babysitting a gaggle of old biddies, he also had to chase off their dumbfuck boyfriends. He stifled another yawn and scratched himself. Still, it was better than bouncing at the after-hours joint his brothers ran.

He stepped onto the lawn, the dew wet under his feet, squinting into the darkness. A couple hundred yards from the front door was the old highway. The traffic was light and infrequent after ten o'clock.

"Anybody out here?" he bellowed in his best mean-ass redneck voice. "If y'are, ya better git before I find you!" He walked around the corner towards the rear of the house, swinging his Louisville Slugger with each stride. He wasn't really expecting to find anyone in the bushes. Usually one look at him brandishing the bat was all it took to scare off the little rubber-dicks. Most of the time the prowlers turned out to be high school kids who got it into their thick heads the place was some kind of bordello.

There was the sound of a heel slipping on gravel behind him. Carl spun in time to see the hunting knife. Then it was too late to see anything else.

Gloria took the call.

"Hi, I'm Easy!" she said, trying to make the prepared speech as suggestive as possible. She'd recited the same damn spiel so many times since she'd come to work for the Gazzola Brothers that it had become a mantra. She often went to bed with those three words looped through her thoughts.

"Hello, Easy. It's me. I've been waiting to talk to you for a *long* time."

There was something about the caller's voice that made her pause.

"Is that so? Well, I want to talk to you *too*. 'If you're interested in women who know what men want …'"

"Cut the sales pitch, bitch." The voice on the other end of the phone grew hard, sharp thorns. "I'm wise to the game you're playing."

Uh-oh, Gloria thought. *Yet another dissatisfied customer …*

"You thought I was stupid, didn't you? Thought I wouldn't catch on to the shit you were trying to pull, huh? I bet you don't even *remember* me, do you? You don't even remember me asking you if I'd get to talk to you or some fucking machine. You said I'd get to talk to *you*. You said I could talk to someone real. You *lied* to me, bitch!" The voice grew shriller, biting her ear with needle-sharp teeth. "You're a slut, just like the others!" The caller's voice suddenly went as cold and flat as a metal wall. "So be it. But you should have known I don't scare *that* easy." He then chuckled, as if amused by some private joke.

"What do you mean?" Gloria asked sharply, allowing her sugar-and-spice coating to slip from her voice.

"Who was he? Your boyfriend? Or was he your pimp?"

"What are you talking about?" she demanded, her heart beginning to race.

"Look on the back porch," the caller replied and quickly hung up, leaving her with nothing but dead air in her ears.

Gloria slipped her head-set off. She could tell Sandra and Doris were staring at her.

"What's the matter, Gloria?" Doris asked without a pause in her knitting.

"Just a crank call, that's all," she replied carefully.

"Oh. I *hate* those." Doris clucked as she continued her knitting. "People can be so rude sometimes."

"Sandy, where's Carl?" Gloria asked, trying to sound casual.

"He went to check out the prowler, just like you asked."

"Excuse me a minute, ladies. Nature calls." Gloria said as she heaved herself out of her chairs and waddled out of the phone room. She tried not to move any faster than usual. It wouldn't do to call attention to herself by attempting to run.

But instead of heading toward the bathroom, Gloria dog-legged into the kitchen. A coffee maker and microwave oven sat on the counter, alongside mail tubs full of plain brown envelopes stuffed with Xeroxed nude photos and boxes full of French ticklers, love-dolls and garishly colored rubber dildos. The Gazzola Brothers made most of their money in the mail-order sex-aid business, as well as selling their ever-growing mailing lists to fellow entrepreneurs for a dime an address.

"You're a slut, just like all the others."

There was probably nothing to the call; nothing to worry about. Easy got her fair share of threats and weird calls – at least two or three a week – but so far it had been nothing but a lot of hot air. Still, it wouldn't hurt to double check the porch, just to be sure.

Gloria prided herself on being tough-minded. By the time she graduated from high school she knew a woman of her size didn't stand a chance in a society that valued physical beauty above all else. She'd been denied scores of jobs, even though her credentials were impeccable, simply because she didn't fit in with the company's "look". Her diplomas and degrees from business school didn't amount to shit, as far as employers were concerned. She tried dieting, even going so far at one point to see about getting her jaw wired shut, but nothing did any good.

Working for the Gazzolas was the closest she'd ever come to a real job. The Brothers treated their employees indifferently, but Gloria had managed to impress them enough with her managerial skills that they let her run the show as she saw fit.

"Just like all the others."

Gloria was wheezing, sweat plastering her bangs to her forehead, by the time she reached the back door. Her ankles and knees ached from walking the hundred or so feet from the call-room. She fumbled with the deadbolts and tried not to think about what the mystery caller meant by "the others".

The porch smelled like a butcher shop. Carl lay sprawled across the bare planks, a sticky blackness radiating from his mangled body like a reverse-negative halo. She slammed the door shut, leaning against it as she fumbled with the deadbolts and burglar chains. The newspaper headlines swam behind her eyelids, taunting her.

They called him Butcher John because his victims were prostitutes. He'd claimed six victims in the last fourteen months, carving them up like sides of beef. It had to be him. No one else could have done that to Carl.

I won't scream, she told herself. *I won't scream.*

"Gloria? What's the matter?"

She looked up to see Sandra standing in the kitchen doorway, watching her with a quizzical expression.

"What are you doing away from your station?" Gloria snapped, hoping to shift the younger woman's attention away from her own nervousness.

"It's the phone line ..."

"What about it?"

"It's gone dead."

And that's when the lights went out.

"What th' fuck's goin on here?" ZuZu said, pulling off her head-set and tossing it onto the conference table. The other women in the room were talking all at once, like a bunch of hens clucking away in the dark. "First th' phones go dead, now the electricity cuts out! Where's Big G?"

"She said something about going to the john just before the lights went out," Muriel explained. "Geez, I wish Albert was here. He was my third husband. Wasn't much in bed, but he sure was handy 'round the house! That man could change a fuse faster'n you could say 'Jack Robinson'!"

ZuZu rolled her eyes. She could imagine Gloria falling down in the confusion of the black-out and not being able to get back up again, like one of those giant turtles. No doubt Muriel could find a corresponding anecdote from one of her disastrous marriages for *that*, too.

"Maybe there's a tornado in the area?" Doris mused aloud in her patented June Cleaver voice. "It's that time of year, you know."

"It's more likely some drunk bozo piled his car into a transformer somewhere up the line," ZuZu said as she stood up from her station. "I don't know about you, but I'm gonna go get my lunch outta th' fridge before it starts to defrost. Anybody else want something outta th' kitchen?"

"Stay put, ZuZu! I don't want any of you ladies wandering around in the dark!" Suddenly Gloria filled the doorway, a plastic flashlight gripped in one hand. She shifted to one side to allow Sandra to squeeze into the room.

"What th' hell's goin on here?" drawled Nora, her mouth still working the ever-present cud of Dentine.

"We got us a problem, ladies," Gloria replied sternly.

"No shit, Sherlock," ZuZu snorted, only to fall silent after Gloria shot her a look that would freeze a clock.

"She's not kidding, Zu," Sandra said, her face made wan by the glow from the flashlight. "Carl's been murdered."

There was a moment of silence, and then everybody started talking at the same time.

"That can't be true!" Muriel exclaimed nervously. "You're just tryin' to scare us!"

Gloria snapped her fingers, commanding silence. "It's the truth, alright; some sicko laid him open like a catfish on the back porch!"

"But who'd do a thing like that?"

"I think it's Butcher John," Gloria replied grimly.

Doris looked perplexed, her knitting momentarily forgotten. "But I thought he only killed, you know, women of ill repute. Why would he want to hurt *us*?"

"Some guys have a real broad definition of what constitutes bein' a whore, honey," ZuZu sighed.

"I'm afraid Zu's right. Just before the lights went out, I got a call from whoever killed Carl. Anyway, it seems he's got a grudge against Easy."

"What are we gonna do? We can't protect ourselves against a crazy man!" Nora whimpered. "I wish Gus was here! He'd know what to do..."

"Bullshit!" ZuZu spat in disgust. "If Gus was here he'd be passed out under the table by now!"

"How *dare* you talk about Gus that way!" Nora exclaimed, her bouffant wobbling with rage. "You no-count whore! *You're* the one he oughtta be goin' after! Not us!"

"Ladies – ladies, *please*!" Gloria said, holding up her hands for silence. "Look, I know you're all scared! So am I! But I *did* put a call into the Brothers about the prowler before the phone line was cut. They'll try and call back, sooner or later. You know those guys! But until help arrives, we've got to make sure this loony-toon doesn't hurt anyone else, right?"

"Fuckin' A!" ZuZu agreed.

"That's m'girl," Gloria grinned. "Sandy and I dug around in Carl's office, looking for stuff that could be used as a weapon," she said, gesturing to the meager armload of items Sandra had deposited on the conference table. "See what you can find to protect yourself."

There was barely enough light for everyone to see the half-assed arsenal spread across the tabletop: a field hockey stick with green plastic tape wrapped around the handle, a fishing rod and reel, a badly rusted tire-tool, and an Exxxtra Large fluorescent purple double-dildo eighteen inches long with the circumference of a soda can.

"Don't worry – it's fresh out of the blister pack," Sandra said as ZuZu grimaced and poked at the sex toy with a ballpoint pen.

"I realize this isn't very promising, but anything's better than our bare hands," Gloria said. "Look, I don't know what this crackpot is going to do, but I'm willing to bet he doesn't know how many of us are actually in here."

Nora frowned at the field hockey stick she held in her neatly manicured hands. "But he's already killed Carl. What's to keep him from killing the rest of us one by one?"

Gloria slammed her fist against the table. "Sweet Jesus, woman! Just because he killed Carl doesn't mean we have to stand around and wait for him to slit our throats like a bunch of damn sheep! Yeah, Carl was bigger and stronger than any three of you put together, but Carl was also *stupid*, Nora! That's how Butcher John got the drop on him! Besides, if you don't want to be found stark naked with your guts hanging around your knees and the word 'slut' carved on your backside for the whole world to see, you've got to accept that nobody's going to save us but ourselves."

Butcher John wormed his way through the attic, searching for what he knew must be there. In the dim light spilling past the ventilation grid he had forced open, he could just make out the collapsible stairway that opened onto the house beneath him. He grinned, ignoring the dust swirling in his nostrils. He would not sneeze or cough. Those were affectations for mere mortals, not avenging angels of the Lord. Or was he working for Satan? He occasionally forgot exactly whose greater glory he was striving to promote. It was probably the Lord's this time out, so that meant he was an avenging angel.

He was forty-seven years old. He'd been many things during his adult life: part-time real estate agent; part-time postal employee; part-time clerk in the family business. He'd even been married for a few months, before his grandmother had the union annulled. But what he really excelled at was being a full-time psychotic. He was *very* good at that.

He was born illegitimate back before being a "single parent" was considered a viable lifestyle. His mother worked at the U.S.O. and deeply believed in doing her bit to make sure America's brave lads wanted for nothing. She dumped her unwanted child on her own mother's doorstep and was never seen again, although his grandmother delighted in reporting all kinds of mischief her prodigal daughter was involved in.

She once told him that she'd received "irrefutable proof" that his mother had been tied into the Rosenberg spy scandal from a special radio she kept hidden under her pillow. He believed everything his grandmother said, of course. After all, she was a saint. And his mother was a slut, therefore, capable of any treachery imaginable.

Sluts were not to be trusted. Sluts betray without a moment's thought. Sluts grow bored and ruin your life just to keep themselves amused. Sluts want nothing but money. Sluts will take all you have and laugh in your face. They think they are so smart. Like that slut-of-sluts, Easy.

He pictured her lolling about on a pile of red satin pillows, dressed in a filmy peignoir, stuffing her cherry-red mouth full of chocolate bon-bons as she bilked foolish, lust-crazed men of their credit card numbers. The vision was so sharp, so real, he could smell the scent of masticated chocolate on her breath as he plowed between her quivering thighs.

He closed his eyes and punched his crotch, rebuking his traitorous flesh. But even the memory of his grandmother grabbing his tumescent penis in her dry, wrinkled hands and screaming *"What's this? What's this!!??!"* could not banish the longings inside him. Only the smell of blood and the sensation of flesh parting beneath his knife would douse the fire in his veins.

There was no way around it.

Easy must die.

He came in through the attic trap-door, riding the collapsible stairway like a magic carpet. It was dark, but there was no way anyone living could ignore the squeal of rusty springs and the slam of the stairwell folding back on itself. Not that it mattered. He *wanted* Easy to hear. Wanted her to know that he had penetrated, in the first of many senses, her inner sanctum. He wanted her to know that he had come to collect the wages of sin, and that he expected her to pay all that was due him.

He wrinkled his nose, sniffing the air. The place reeked of sweat, cigarette smoke and old coffee grounds. He had never been inside a whore house before, but he'd always imagined they smelled more of sex and cheap French perfume. This place was more like a secretarial pool.

Moving into a darkened doorway, he brushed against a kitchen counter-top, knocking a cardboard box onto the floor. He stared down at the material spread across the warped linoleum: blurry Xeroxes of naked young girls, their ill-defined labia spread in an approximation of wanton invitation, leered up at him.

"What's this?!? What's this?!?" His grandmother's voice vibrated against his inner ear like a dentist's drill.

Shadows moved in the darkness, jerking his attention from the filth spread at his feet. He pounced and pulled the whore from her hiding place. Stupid! Stupid slut! Didn't she know it was useless to hide from the All-Seeing Eyes of The Lord's Divine Punisher? He held the struggling strumpet by her hair. She stopped trying to free herself when he showed her the knife.

"Repent, slut!" he snarled

"I am *not* a slut, young man!"

He frowned and stared harder at his captive. She was in her sixties and dressed conservatively. She looked a lot like his grandmother. The kill-lust within him abruptly dimmed.

"Let go of me!" Doris snapped. To her surprise, the huge knife held inches from her nose wavered, then disappeared.

"Granny?" he whispered in a hoarse, confused voice, like a sleepwalker woken from a dream.

In reply, Doris drove one of her knitting needles into his right arm.

Butcher John shrieked, nearly dropping his knife, as he clawed at the needle piercing his shoulder.

"Sluts cannot be trusted! Sluts betray!" His grandmother shrieked inside his head. *"Remember that, boy! Have I ever lied to you?"*

Tears of anger and shame spilled down his twisted face. The false-grandmother was trying to make her escape through the back

156

door, clawing frantically at the locks. He would not be fooled again! Ignoring the pain shooting through his shoulder, he steadily advanced on the panicked old woman.

Suddenly there was a high-pitched whirring sound, like the drone of a mosquito, followed by a sharp pain in his left ear.

"Doris! Run for it!" Muriel shouted as she cranked the reel on the fishing pole. The man with the knife on the other end of the line twirled about like a top, slapping at his bleeding ear like a flea-ridden hound. All those fishing trips she took with her second husband, Ray, had finally paid off. Back then she never caught anything more exotic than crappie or bluegill, but now she had a real-live psycho-killer on the hook.

Butcher John shrieked in pain, flailing at the taut fishing line with his knife in an attempt to free himself before the hook completely bisected his ear. The fact that he was shedding his own blood enraged him all the more.

Once Doris darted past the distracted murderer, Muriel dropped the rod and reel and hurried after her, leaving Butcher John to claw at the hook buried in his ear. He didn't know who these women were, but they certainly weren't Easy. He had expected there to be one, maybe two, women in the house, but he never imagined that they would be waiting in ambush. And the two women – he shook his head; no, not women, *sluts* – he'd seen were hardly the big-titted, mush-brained whores he'd fantasized about.

Ignoring the throbbing pain in his mangled ear, he edged his way back into the hall. He stared at the three doors, two on the left, one on the right. Wary of another surprise attack, he tested the knob on the right-hand door. It was unlocked.

"*Psst!* Buddy!" a feminine voice called out. "Why don't you try Door Number Two?"

Butcher John turned in the direction of the voice, only to see a grinning savage with a ring in her nose swing something purple at his head.

"Take *that*, you sexist motherfucker!"

Although blinded by the fireworks going off inside his head, Butcher John still managed to strike out at the crazed she-demon. He grinned in triumph as he heard her cry out and felt the warmth of her blood on his fingers. After a bad start, things were finally turning out the way they should. Upon regaining his sight, he found himself standing alone in the hallway. He looked down at his feet and was startled to see what looked like a purple snake laying on the floor. His fear quickly turned to disgust as he realized he was not looking at a snake, but at a rubber penis the length and width of a man's forehead, with a second head when the balls should have been. The bathroom door stood open, revealing its empty interior. So *that's* where the she-demon had been hiding...

He touched his forehead gingerly. The pain from the rapidly swelling lump fed his righteous anger. He would cut the ring from the scheming hell-slut's nose and skin the tattoos from her supple flesh. They would make wonderful souvenirs. He grimaced as blood and sweat trickled into his eyes. Fuck stalking. They knew he was here. He knew they knew he was here. It was time to announce his intentions.

"*Easy!*"

Silence.

"I know you can hear me, bitch! I *know* you're here!" he bellowed. "I've come for you, like I said I would! I'm going to make you a deal, Easy! I'm not interested in the others! *You're* the one I want! If you surrender to me, I'll leave the others alone!"

It was a lie, of course. He had no intention of letting any of them go, especially the slut with the ring in her nose. But everyone knows how stupid sluts are. There would be much blood tonight. Blood enough to wash himself clean of sin in the eyes of both the Lord and his grandmother.

"*Answer me*, Easy!"

The third door on the left slowly swung open, revealing a shadow lurking in the darkened room just beyond the threshold.

"Hi, I'm Easy," the shadow said.

It was *her.* There was no mistaking that voice: smooth as fine brandy; smoky as a late-night cabaret; sleek as a silk kimono. Before him stood the Whore of Babylon who had lured him into sullying his soul with her promises of carnal gratification. She was the reason his blood burned, his flesh ached, and his phone bill averaged four hundred dollars a month. His knife was hard and ready to taste her blood; ready to fuck her the only way he knew how.

"Easy." He breathed her name as if it was both a benediction and curse.

"Yeah, that's right," Gloria said, stepping into the hall to confront the intruder. She towered over his five foot-eight frame.

Butcher John stared in horror at the massive woman blocking the door. Hearing Easy's voice come out of her mouth was disconcerting. Rolls of flab hung from her upper arms, chin, waist and hips. Her face was slick with sweat and flushed beet red. Her breathing was ragged, as if she'd just climbed a flight of stairs, causing her neolithic breasts to strain against the fabric of her blouse. The knife between his legs shriveled.

"You *can't* be Easy!" he protested in confusion. He shook his head, trying to clear the buzzing from his ears. "Easy's beautiful, but you're fat and ugly!"

"That's all I'm gonna take from you, asshole!" Gloria growled as she lunged forward, grabbing for his knife-hand.

He struck out instinctively, sinking his knife into her flesh all the way to the hilt. He heard the giant slut grunt in surprise and pain, and saw her piggy eyes fly open in shock and surprise. He pulled on the knife, so he could stab her again and again, in a blind fury, as was his fashion, but it wouldn't come free. The giantess rolled her eyes to the back of her head, as if in pleasure, and clasped him to her ample bosom, bearing him to the floor.

Butcher John's last thought, before Gloria fell on him, was that it wasn't supposed to end like this.

The first thing Gloria saw when she regained consciousness was ZuZu, her right arm in a sling, grinning down at her.

"Hey! Big G! You feelin' okay?"

"Not really," she grunted.

"Me and Sandy got the nurses to push two hospital beds together so you'd feel at home," ZuZu proclaimed proudly.

Suddenly Sandra bobbed into view. "You're a hero, Gloria! You killed Butcher John!"

"He's dead ...?" she frowned. "How'd I kill him?"

"You squashed him like a bug!" ZuZu exclaimed excitedly,

elaborating with a ripe raspberry. "Guy was a real nutcase! They went to his house and found his granny's corpse rotting in his bed! Just like Psycho! I'm writing a song about it!"

"That's nice ... I think ..." Gloria replied. "I'm glad you weren't seriously hurt, Zu. That was a damn foolish – and brave – stunt you pulled, young lady."

ZuZu blushed and shrugged her unharmed shoulder. "Look who's talking! I won't be able to play the guitar for a week or two, but the docs here say I should have a nice scar!"

"The last thing I remember, that bastard stuck a knife into my chest. I was sure I'd had it," Gloria marveled in disbelief.

"The doctors said your fat kept the knife from getting anywhere near your heart," Sandra explained with a crooked smile. "If you were built like Easy, you'd be dead by now."

"What about the others?" Gloria asked anxiously.

"Everybody's okay," Sandra assured her. "After you got stabbed, Doris ran all the way to the juke joint down the highway and called the cops. Did you know she competes in the Senior Olympics? That old girl's really something! Oh, and Muriel's got herself all hot and bothered over one of the paramedics who showed up. She says it's the Real Thing Part Five. And Nora's no-good live-in, Gus, finally found out that she was working as a Hot Talker and blacked her eye, so he's sitting in jail. Turns out she was telling him she cleaned offices at night."

"What about the Gazzola Brothers?"

"They say they're not talking to the papers because the family is in mourning. But they sent you flowers." Sandra explained, hoisting a small pot of African violets up so Gloria could see it.

Gloria rolled her eyes. "I'm more interested in finding out whether we still have jobs," she sighed.

"Why wouldn't we?" ZuZu asked.

"Because when it gets out that the Hot Talkers are just a bunch of housewives and Easy is a refugee from a sideshow, you can kiss your Stratocaster goodbye." Gloria looked away, trying to control the emotion in her voice. "Easy's dead. That bastard killed her just as sure as if he really did stick a knife in her!" She eyed the I.V. drip running into her arm with a mixture of distaste and dismay. "And here I am, flat on my back without health insurance!"

"You're taking this too hard, Gloria!" Sandra said. "So what if Easy's dead? So what if you're out of a job? It sucked to begin with!"

"It's okay for *you* to talk like that, Sand," Gloria grumbled. "You're young – and *thin*."

"And you're rich. At least you're going to be."

"What do you mean?"

Sandra held up a thick sheaf of official-looking papers stapled in one corner. "See this? It's a contract, Gloria! A movie contract! This guy from Universal Pictures was in here earlier, while you were still out of it. They want to make a *movie* about what happened to us!" She handed the contract to Gloria, who squinted at it suspiciously.

"Zu, tell me she's kidding!"

ZuZu grinned even wider than before. "It's true, Big G! We've *all* got contracts!"

Gloria stared at the paperwork, but she was no longer hearing what her friends were saying. From what little she was able to scan from the contract, it was obvious the studio sharpies thought they could get the rights to Easy's last stand on the cheap.

"Has anyone signed anything yet?" she asked sternly.

"No – I don't think so," Sandy replied.

"Good!" Gloria said sharply. "We'll have to show a unified front, if we want to get the best deal possible from the studio! Sandy, get on the phone to Doris, Nora and Muriel. Tell 'em to hold off signing anything until I've had time to go over the contract!"

"Aye-aye!" Sandy grinned as she hurried out of the hospital room.

"Zu, be a dear and see if you can't hunt me down a little something to eat. I think better when I'm eating."

ZuZu tilted her head to one side. With her colorful mohawk, she looked like a quizzical cockatoo. "So what's the game plan, Big G?"

Gloria smiled, visions of an office on the Universal Studios lot with her name on the door and a handsome male secretary answering the phone taking form behind her eyes. "Hollywood producers aren't the only ones who know a thing or two about exploitation."

PREGNANT WITH PIGGYBANKS
by Sarah A. D. Shaw

EDITOR'S NOTE

Sarah A. Shaw lives in the middle of Alaska where she thinks up stuff and writes it down. Her work has appeared on The Strange Edge *flash fiction website.*

"After two extremely difficult and high-risk pregnancies, it was pretty clear to me that my body and pregnancy just didn't get along. I had my tubes tied immediately after my second c-section," says Sarah. "'Pregnant with Piggybanks' came into existence after contemplating just how shocked I would be if I suddenly found myself pregnant again."

With that kind of lead in, you might expect a long, sad story about loss and emptiness, but Sarah turns the subject into a weird delight of a tale. I think I contacted Sarah within fifteen minutes of reading her submission, asking if we could have it for the anthology. Hold onto your hats and pass the epidural!

Soon after the birth of my only child, Charlie, the doctor found mold growing all over my ovaries so he scooped out all of my womanly insides with a melon baller and banished them to wherever rancid organs are banished to. Sex without the possibility of pregnancy isn't really that exciting and feels downright pointless ... especially when you're having it with an unimaginative dullard such as Ronald, my husband. So when I discovered that I was pregnant with a litter of piggy banks, a tsunami of emotions battered me: fear, confusion, anxiety, worry ... but mostly I was extremely pissed because if I had known that the possibility of getting pregnant with a bunch of piggy banks existed, I would have made it a point to enjoy the sex more.

"Looks like five ... no, six ... it's difficult to tell," mutters Dr. Doctor as he squints at the monitor and glides the ultrasound wand over my jellied-up abdomen.

"It feels like a sack of rocks," I reply, uncomfortable at the weight of my rapidly growing belly pressing down into my spine, through the exam table and into nothingness.

"They don't seem to be moving," says Dr. Doctor, still glued to the monitor. "They may not be alive."

"Oh, they're alive."

"There's no movement, heartbeat, or any signs of life. The best course of action may be to surgically remove them now to avoid any complications." Dr. Doctor rises and begins to pile his arms full of sharp, stabby, cutty instruments from a nearby cabinet.

" No!" I struggle to sit up on the examination table. "They're ALIVE. Keep that shit away from me, you fucking butcher!"

At this point, my intention is to hop off of the table and stomp indignantly out the door and slam it with a satisfying *boom!* The hugeness of my belly, however, requires me to accept the assistance of Dr. Doctor to help me down and escort me to the exit. I do glare laser beams at him that singe his eyebrows, though.

Back at home, my three-year-old son Charlie is using a jigsaw to cut large pieces of corrugated metal from the tool shed. He's building a spaceship-toaster-world peace machine. It's important to encourage the creativity of children, so I hand him a large pair of metal cutters and take the safety goggles off of his head so he can see better.

Inside our one-story house, Ronald looks up from some god-awful project he's working on at the kitchen counter. He fancies himself an inventor/artist/chef. Today's project includes a shoehorn and grass clippings from the neighbor's lawn which Ronald must have fished out of the bag on the sidewalk since he would NEVER demean himself and mow a lawn himself. Also on the counter sits a small pile of guts. Probably from a vole. We have voles behind the tool shed. Ronald thinks that they're plotting some non-specific evil so he occasionally traps one, guts it and nails the disemboweled carcass to the shed as a warning. It doesn't seem to be working. As I mentioned previously, Ronald is dull, so his plans and schemes are equally dull. And ineffective.

"What's the word from Dr. Doctor, dear?"

"Dear" is the only term of endearment that Ronald ever calls me. He also uses it for waitstaff, parking attendants and the voles behind the shed. It's nothing personal.

"We're having a litter of piggybanks, dear." If Ronald can dish it, I can serve it back.

"Oh." Ronald wipes a bit of grass and gut from just beneath his eye. "How many?"

"Five or six. He couldn't tell for sure."

"We should get that taken care of, you think?" Ronald goes back to applying grass to guts and flattening it into a paste with the shoehorn.

"Get WHAT taken care of?"

"We can't very well raise a litter of piggybanks, now, can we? They'll always be meddling and getting underfoot. No, this situation needs to be taken care of right away. He grabs a small sledgehammer from one of the kitchen cabinets and starts around to my side of the counter.

"Ronald, wait ..." I stammer as I back up away from the counter and into the backside of the couch that divides the living area from the kitchen.

"Dear, listen to me ... this has to be done. Think of the COST!" Ronald raises the hammer to tummy-height and swings it back like a baseball bat.

Adrenaline and maternal instinct flood into my brain and body. "IT'S NOT YOUR CHOICE!!!!" I scream. I grab the couch behind me, lift it off of the floor and swing it smack into Ronald's dumbass face. His head flies off of his unmanly shoulders and bounces off the refrigerator and onto the counter with the grass and guts concoction.

Ronald's body is still standing, swaying on its feet, but there's no blood spraying from his headless neck, like it does in the movies. Instead, sparks fly every which way from jagged wires and I can see the top of a mechanical spine peeking out. He's a motherfucking cyborg.

"Whhhyyyyyy ..." Ronald's head hisses on the counter, half covered in grass and yuck. Its mouth moves up and down in a chomping motion. He's a motherfucking zombie cyborg.

I lean in closer to Zombie Cyborg Ronald's head. The chomping is slowing down and his eyes fix on me.

"WHY, Ronald?" I wrench the small sledgehammer out of the still-standing body's hand. "Because you tried to kill my piggybanks,

DEAR." I bring the hammer down on the head, which crumples into a dented mass of flesh and metal, sending more sparks into the room. One catches a curtain in the kitchen and sets it ablaze.

Before a thought can blink itself into my brain, one whole side of the kitchen is engulfed in flames. I turn to run out through the front door, but I tumble over the couch that I had cast aside after decapitating Zombie Cyborg Ronald and hear an awful "SNAP" from my left ankle and the sound of shattering porcelain from my belly. Pain floods my body and I'm starting to fade into unconsciousness when I hear a tiny siren, several actually, and turn my head toward the front door.

Two vole-sized fire engines tear into the house, followed by some vole-sized police cars and a couple of vole-sized ambulances. The vehicles brake near the blaze and voles in fireman, police and medic uniforms pour out of them. One stands on its hind legs atop the fire engine, barking high-pitched orders into a megaphone. Two uncoil a hose and aim the little nozzle at the fire covering the entire wall. This would be amusing, were I not in extreme pain and the situation not so dire. Fuck it, who am I kidding? It's hilarious.

Two medic voles clamor over my bulging belly, prodding with their tiny feet. The area just to the left of my navel howls with pain from the depth of my abdomen when it's probed by little feet. I'm sweating from the fire and I feel aggressive shifting in my womb. "Only lost one" I think to myself and then the tears come. And they don't stop.

Tears gush out of my eyes with such intense ferocity that it feels like I'm urinating from my eye sockets. My sorrow joins the fire-fighting voles' water nozzle and drenches the flames covering the kitchen wall. Despite the pain in my abdomen and ankle, I manage to stand and aim my tears at the fire. Within minutes, the chaos is reduced to a few glowing embers and the occasional sizzle and pop. The wall is charred, but it's still intact. The cadre of firefighting voles, satisfied that their efforts are no longer needed, hop into their vehicles and zoom out the front door. I sink back down to the floor, exhausted, and suddenly remember that I have a three-year-old named Charlie messing around with the tool shed out in the yard.

"Charlie!" I shout and after a few beats hear the patter of his feet bounding into the house. Charlie's hands have some bleeding gashes on them from his outdoor creative endeavor and it looks like he may have stabbed himself in the bicep with the metal cutters. He points at the destroyed kitchen area.

"Did Daddy do that?" Charlie asks, brimming with the knowledge that yes, Daddy did indeed do that.

"Yes, Charlie, the current state of the kitchen is a direct result of your father's actions." It's important to speak to children like grown-ups. Formal speech helps to build their vocabulary and prevents them from sounding like drooling rednecks.

"Where did Daddy go?" Charlie looks around the room and cranes his neck to peek down the hallway.

Time stops. This is one of those pivotal moments in a parent-child-relationship. To lie or not to lie? Do I tell Charlie that the thing he's known as "Daddy" for his entire short life was actually a zombie cyborg who needed to be terminated because he was trying to bash my stomach in with a sledgehammer?

"Daddy got a call from work and had to catch a plane to Minneapolis for an important presentation." Yep, I lie. It's for the best, really. Parenting is all about shielding our children from the harsh realities of life. What he doesn't know won't hurt him, right? I don't think so.

"What's wrong with your leg, Mommy?" Charlie points to my left foot, which is now jutting out to the side at a 90 degree angle. In all of the chaos, I've forgotten about it. The adrenaline rush hasn't died down enough yet for me to feel the agonizing pain that lies in wait.

"Mommy tripped and fell." Just then, dozens of voles, all clad in little green scrubs, surgical masks and white lab coats file in through the front door. Three of them are carrying a syringe above their heads and rush forward, jabbing it into my thigh. I don't feel it and wouldn't have even known that it had happened if I hadn't seen it.

"Hi," my son says to the general vole medical population. The little emergency staff ignore him and busy themselves with my foot, a few of them bracing their backs against it, pushing it back into place. Two other voles with tiny stethoscopes climb around on my abdomen, stopping to listen at various locations. A sudden movement from inside my belly throws one of the voles three feet into the air. He lands back on my stomach and resumes the exam. I smile widely.

"I told that fucking quack that they're alive!" I quickly realize my outburst and clap a hand over my mouth, casting my eyes at Charlie, who seems to be so engrossed in the voles that he doesn't appear to have heard my profane exclamation.

There's movement in my belly and I can feel the remaining piggybanks shifting and absorbing the broken shards of their fallen brother or sister. I'm also starting to feel the tight pangs of hunger.

"I'm hungry." I say, to no one in particular. I'm still lying on the floor, listening to the crunch of bone against bone as several voles are maneuvering my foot so it lines up with my ankle bone. A roll of ACE bandage towers over a scrub-clad vole, who leans against it, smoking and waiting. Hearing my announcement of hunger, Charlie reaches into the pocket of his jeans and pulls out a few lint covered Gummi Bears.

"Here, mommy," he pinches one of the candies between his fingers and bends down to hold it in front of my mouth. I ignore the fuzziness and open wide so my son can place it on my tongue. I swallow without chewing and immediately regret it.

When the candy hits my stomach, my abdomen begins to buck, expanding and retracting violently, ejecting the voles and their miniature medical equipment to all corners of the kitchen/living room space.

The green Gummi Bear travels back up my esophagus and shoots out of my mouth, splatting against the charred kitchen wall and remaining there, Jackson Pollock-like. I've been introducing Charlie to various art and artists lately to inspire his blossoming imagination. Pollock was our latest unit study.

A hot sensation rises from the depths of my belly, up through my chest and eventually breaks free from my mouth as a steady, forceful barrage of multicolored vomit. The force of the chunky rainbow stream knocks me on my back, geysering up to the ceiling, then raining back down on me, Charlie, and my rodent saviors.

Voles scramble for purchase on half-digested chunks of whatever, kicking their little legs furiously to avoid drowning in the rising lake of brilliantly bright puke. The gush of vomit abruptly stops and I'm lying on my back in a sticky, warm shallow bath of my own regurgitation. The room is flooded with about four inches of nasty. I'm never going to get this crap out of my hair.

Charlie plucks voles from the vomit sea and places them on my chest and stomach. One of the rodents pounds on the chest of another, administering CPR. A few of them are face down in the barf, lifeless. Charlie picks up the dead ones and sets them on a chair. He's a good boy. It's vital to teach children respect early. After ministering to the dead, Charlie wades into the kitchen area and pulls a plug out of the floor. A loud flushing sound reverberates through the house and the vomit level slowly subsides until there is nothing left but a slimy sheen that covers the floor, furniture and us.

Confident that I have nothing left in me to upchuck, I carefully push myself up to a sit, letting several recovering voles tumble from my chest and stomach into my lap. They curl up there and snooze lightly.

Sharp pangs of hunger attack me again with an unbearable force. I have to eat SOMETHING.

"I'm still hungry, Charlie. My stomach is about to detach itself and search for food on its own."

"Are you going to throw up again, Mommy?"

Pictures of roast beef, oranges and tofu fly through my head, each one triggering my gag reflex.

"Probably," I answer, the piggybanks tumbling around in my abdomen, visibly stretching my belly skin into an undulating ball of lumps. Charlie gets my purse from atop an end table and hands it to me.

"Try a pill," Charlie says. He's such a thoughtful child, due to my constant urging to ALWAYS put others first, even to your own discomfort and detriment.

I open my sticky handbag to retrieve a tummy capsule and I see a smattering of coins that have collected at the bottom. I snatch a penny and swallow it quickly, ignoring its blood taste. I feel it catch momentarily in my throat before continuing its journey to my waiting litter. I sit with my mouth clamped tightly shut, willing the copper to stay down. It feels like just the right thing. Pregnancy books scare the shit out of you with everything that can go wrong and that's why I've never followed their instruction.

The movement in my belly increases as my embryonic charges scramble for the penny. I hear the muffled clinking of porcelain on porcelain and the fighting inside me is jerking me back and forth. I brace my hands on the floor behind me and stare at my contorted, bubbling womb.

"Charlie! Coins! I need coins!"

My son dumps the contents of my purse on the filthy floor next to me and quickly picks out the spare change, wiping the vomit residue off of them with his shirt. Since Charlie is also disgustingly sticky, his efforts are fruitless, but I appreciate them anyway. I'm a good mother that way.

A few of our vole friends hop onto the floor to aid in the search, but their paws keep sticking to the carpet.

I open wide and Charlie inserts a dime into my mouth, which I swallow quickly. The force of the fighting piggybanks threatens to throw me onto my back and I fear that they may destroy themselves in their battle for sustenance. The howl of hunger hurts me everywhere.

"More, Charlie! Quick!" I grab a few coins from his hand, including a Sacajawea dollar. Why the fuck was THAT in my purse? Oh, yeah ... for Charlie's history lesson. I'll have to find another one, because using visual aids helps children learn and retain the information effectively. I shove the handful of coins into my mouth and swallow as quickly as I can without choking.

The mass of coins makes its way slowly and painfully down to my stomach and the brawl inside my belly stops. I see and feel the movement of the piggybanks as they mill around the confines of my abdomen, grazing on spare change. The urgency has passed and I relax as much as I can while lounging on the living room floor in my own barf residue. I look up at my son who is surveying the room with a calculating expression. I'm proud of his observational skills.

"You need to go to the hospital, Mommy," Charlie says and a few of the scrub-wearing voles frown up at him indignantly. One of them crosses his arms with a squeaky huff.

"I don't think so, sweetie," I say, recalling the incident just hours before with Dr. Doctor. My blind trust of medical authorities met its extinction when I waddled out of the clinic door that morning. Nope, it was just going to be us. Forever, probably.

I rub my tummy in a circular fashion. I thoroughly feel the contentment and satisfaction of my babies.

"I'd like to lie down on my bed." I say and hold out my hand to Charlie, who takes it and starts to pull. Since he only stands three-and-a-half feet high and has virtually no body weight, he only succeeds in stretching my arm like taffy. Crap, now my right arm is 2 inches longer than my left. Our housemates, the voles, gather en masse at my back and start to push while Charlie continues to pull on my hand and arm. I have never felt heavier in my life. After a little over an hour and with the aid of a chair that Charlie moved to my side, I am standing. The piggybanks have dropped low inside me and it takes immense effort to fight gravity and remain vertical. Charlie and the voles flank me as I shuffle tentatively down the hall on my broken ankle to the bedroom that I share with Ronald. I guess it's all mine now.

Our bedroom is as dull as Ronald was, since he had always insisted that he was allergic to color and that anything blue gave him nasty rashes on his liver. The only furniture is a queen-size bed and a dresser. The closet had long been filled with cement and sealed with wax as an attempt by Ronald to keep the voles at bay as well as anyone who might try to use our closet as a time portal.

I waddle to the bed and allow the weight of my enormous belly to pull me down backwards and pin me to the mattress. My litter tinkles loudly when I hit the mattress and awkwardly adjust my position. I'm not really any more comfortable here than I was on the living room floor, but at least it's cleaner and I'm in a bed, which I think is the proper place for me to be.

My babies start to agitate and I momentarily panic, until I remember the change jar that Charlie keeps in his room.

"Charlie, can you please go get your change jar?"

"Ok, Mommy." Charlie dashes out the door and returns less than a minute later hugging an old pickle jar to his chest with his thin arms. The jar is about halfway full of coins. He hefts it onto the bed and unscrews the lid. He pulls out a small handful of coins and holds it under my chin. I lift my head up off of the pillow and lap a few coins from his hand with my tongue. They taste clean. Charlie must have washed them thoroughly before storing them in the jar. He must have been paying attention when I taught him about money and how many hands it passes through.

I take in a few more coins with my tongue and settle my head back down, expecting the chaotic rumbling in my womb to abate. But it doesn't. The piggybanks are their rowdiest yet, clinking against one another and bouncing off of the walls of my womb. I stare as individual lumps begin pushing hard against the inside of my abdomen and I realize that they're trying to burrow out through my belly. They desperately want out.

"That's the wrong way!" I start breathing quickly and try to push them out the way that babies are generally born. "Down! Go down! Through the tunnel!"

"What's wrong, Mommy?" I can't see Charlie over my towering tummy.

"They're trying to get out! Fuck, this fucking hurts!" Some occasions call for expletives, even in the presence of children. Several piggybanks trying to burst through your stomach is one of those occasions.

Charlie stands next to me and puts a hand on my stomach while three voles jab another syringe into me. This time in my shoulder. I feel the numbing effects immediately and relax as my belly continues to expand and squirm.

"I can help you, mommy," Charlie says calmly. He's always been steady under pressure. When he gave a presentation to a committee of university professors detailing the ways in which humanity can achieve world peace, he only displayed a tiny bit of discomfort. That was when he filled his diaper a quarter of the way through his meticulously prepared speech.

"Ok, Charlie," I whimper through the haze of medication. At some point, children start taking care of their parents instead of the other way around.

Charlie's left eyeball retracts into his head and a long metal probe extends from his eye socket. The probe is tipped with a tiny laser emitter. This is a trait that he must have inherited from his father, since there are no zombie cyborgs on my side of the family. At least not to my knowledge.

Doctor voles on both sides of me grasp the hem of my dress and peel it up to my chest, exposing my lumpy, busy belly. They start to work on removing my panties, but I bat at them and hiss. A mother should always maintain a level of modesty in front of her children and although Charlie is half cyborg, I intend to raise him with the appropriate shamefulness regarding nudity. The voles concede and only lower the brim of my underwear to the top of my pubic bone.

"Hold still, Mommy," Charlie says and I suck in my breath, willing every muscle into complete submission. Charlie tilts his head down and trains his eye probe at my lower abdomen. A vole in a colorful nurse's smock puts a tiny paw on my hand to comfort me. The other rodents surround me on the bed, watching Charlie anxiously, preparing to assist in the procedure.

"Three ... two ... one ..." Charlie whispers and then a thin red laser of light shoots out from his eye socket and makes contact with my skin inches below my navel, just above my pubic bone. I can't see the procedure due to the massiveness of my belly. I do feel a slight numb pressure that is a tad uncomfortable, but not painful. Whatever those voles keep injecting me with, it's definitely the good shit.

I vaguely wonder if Charlie has performed laser surgery before, since his cool precision and focus are unmatched by anything I've seen. His steady nature must have come from my side of the family tree. My grandmother built the most intricate card houses around.

I don't breathe as Charlie burns a horizontal incision across my lower belly, managing a straight cut despite the desperate melee of piggybanks inside me. The red beam goes dark and the probe retracts back into Charlie's head and his eyeball returns to its socket, rolling around a few times to get settled.

The litter continues to ram my insides and something ejects from my freshly made belly opening with a "SCHLOOP" sound and flies into the air.

"Catch it! Omigod, CATCH IT," I scream with my drug-thickened tongue. Voles scramble every which way with their little arms out, hoping to intercept my newborn. My porcelain, mucus-covered baby arcs through the air and then crashes down on several well-intentioned medic voles, flattening one of them into a smear of gore and rendering the others unconscious. Charlie bends down and picks up my baby, grimacing and holding it with both hands out in front of him.

"It's slimy. Yuck." Charlie hands it to several waiting nurses on the bed, who get to work rubbing off the goo of birth with tiny handkerchiefs. The frantic rumbling continues in my tummy, squashing my desire to grab my newborn piggybank and hold it.

"Another one's coming," I try to reach my hands down to my incision to catch the next baby, but the mountain of quivering belly is too large for my arms to get around. Charlie, noticing my distress, comes to my aid and assumes a catcher's stance next to me, with his hand cupped at the ready.

There's pressure on my tummy opening from the inside. One of the piggybanks is having difficulty extracting itself and pushes harder and harder. Oh God, I hope the incision doesn't tear me in two.

Charlie leans in for a closer look. "It's sideways, Mommy. I can pull it out." He starts to probe with his little boy fingers.

"WAIT!" I reach under my pillow and blindly rummage through the stash of sundries I keep under there. Since the room is devoid of furniture, I hide my nightstand-appropriate items in the most easily accessible place I can think of. There are some ancient condoms under the mattress as well, since Zombie Cyborg Ronald and I didn't think that we needed them anymore.

I pull out a small bottle of hand sanitizer and hold it towards Charlie. I'm never seeing Dr. Doctor, or any medical professional other than my live-in voles again, so a nasty infection wouldn't do anyone a bit of good. Charlie takes the bottle, squeezes out far more of the jelly goop than necessary, and rubs it over his hands and forearms. He makes sure to get the stuff in between each of his fingers just like I taught him.

Charlie reaches his small hands into my belly through the caesarian opening. What I can't see, I vaguely feel as he manipulates the porcelain baby into position and eases it out of me with the familiar "SCHLOOP" sound. Charlie hands the newborn off to the voles and resumes his task of pulling babies out of his mother. The remaining births are problem-free.

After cleaning up me and the litter Charlie closes up my belly with a soldering iron from his arsenal of eye-socket tools. He's an extremely skilled boy, which is good, since his zombie cyborg father is now a mangled, charred mess in the kitchen.

The team of voles hand me my babies, five in all, each wrapped in a hand towel from the bathroom. How did we accumulate so many hand towels? It wasn't like Ronald would ever allow company inside the house. Leaning back on the headboard, I cradle my babies to my chest, three on the left and two on the right.

The first time I held Charlie after he was born, I felt like I had been the first woman to ever give birth. He didn't cry. He snuggled in my arms with a knowing expression on his face. Even though he was only minutes old, I sensed the beauty and pure potential of him. And I had created him with my body. That made me more than just a mother. It made me a fucking goddess. Anyone who creates such perfection with just their body has to be divine.

Now, I look down at my newborn piggybanks, their porcelain faces and black-dot eyes expressionless. Their bodies are hard, smooth, and fragile. So fragile that I fear I'll shift my weight on the bed and crack one of them. I think that they are looking at me, at least I hope that they are, given all of the trouble I went through to ensure their birth.

"Mommy? Can I lie on the bed with you?" Charlie asks. His voice startles me, since I had forgotten that he was in the room. A quick look around confirms that the voles have vacated the bedroom. Probably back to their compound behind the tool shed to do whatever it is they normally do when they aren't fighting fires or assisting in childbirth.

"Sure, sweetie." I want to move over to make more room for him, but I'm afraid that I'll injure the litter in my arms. Charlie climbs on the bed next to me and lies down, resting his head on my thigh, so as not to disturb his new siblings. I don't stroke his hair because my hands are full.

One by one, the little white piggybanks begin to vibrate. First softly, then building to an alarming shudder. I think that they're hungry. Charlie thinks so too. He scoots off of the bed and retrieves the change jar from the floor. He grabs a handful of change and starts to insert coins into the slots on each of the piggybanks backs. The vibration slows a little, but remains, now accompanied with the clinking of coins from within their hollow bodies. Charlie feeds them another round of coins. And then another. I'm proud of his responsible and compassionate nature.

I drift off to sleep, listening to the tinkle of coins being dropped into the bodies of my babies. Charlie is going to be an amazing big brother. Even if he *is* half cyborg.

The Band Plays On
by Lorraine H McGuire

EDITOR'S NOTE:
Lorraine McGuire lives a quiet life in the loud city of Glasgow, Scotland. Her time is eaten up by two children; one husband; one Rocky 2 – The Sequel (feline); and a full time job that prevents her from writing as much as she should, but on the other hand puts food on the table. When she does write, she writes poetry and short stories. She has finished one novel (don't bother looking for it – she's not ready to release it into the world yet!) and has another novel in the prepubescent stage. She has no spare time really but occasionally will steal time from somewhere and listen to music; take photographs; and re-purpose and up-cycle old and unwanted furniture. Her husband (she says) is a very patient man.

And 'The Band Played On' is a delightful warning about pride going before a ... well, you've probably heard that one before, but not Lorraine's take on it, I'm sure. Or her deliciously stubborn main character, who wants to make sure her clients get everything they have coming to them ...

The bus crash had been efficient, with only the relatively innocent driver surviving. He walked away with a deep five-inch scar above his left eye as a reminder never to inhale. The others lay scrambled amidst the mass of mangled steel, purple upholstery and glass, no longer recognisable as humans.

Imagine their surprise at finding themselves in my boss's waiting room in one piece when, moments before, they had witnessed their own demise. Without fail, the first thing everyone does in such situations is to check that the limb they saw wrenched from their body is, in fact, still attached. I have to say the look of relief that floods their faces is one of the reasons I do my job; it's why I love it.

And just what is my job? Well, I suppose I am my boss's version of the sainted Peter; I check the names; I catalog the crimes; I send them packing to the relevant departments. I liaise with the crowd upstairs (and He who must *never* be named) to make sure things run smoothly and mistakes are kept to a minimum. I am the right hand man, if you like.

The crowd from the bus had long been anticipated; their crimes and debauchery had become almost legendary in a place where such things are generally an everyday occurrence. What made these guys different was the joy they took in their work. I had to admire their drive in the pursuit of their pleasure. As they stood before me they looked less impressive; a collection of buffed-to-a-smooth-finish types who looked like they were as innocent as the proverbial cherubs.

They were a boy band by the name of N2RAGE, or Craig, Mick-Z, BillE, and Jay, along with their assorted 'crew'; manager; make-up lady; underage girlfriend; under-age boyfriend; dealer; two Swedish girls they'd picked up at the last petrol stop; cameraman; guy who didn't seem to do anything and the record executive who was living out a rock 'n' roll fantasy.

"Where the Hell are we?" asked the ballsy blonde number. She'd been their manager and was the first to spot me smiling in the corner.

"I believe you have just answered your own question." I looked down at my blue plastic clipboard. I didn't need to see the looks being exchanged between them to know what they were; I'd seen it all a million times before.

"What the fuck's going on, man?" one of the little cherubs piped up. I checked my list, BillE, the youngest, cutest member; crime – rape, attempted murder and defiling a holy relic ... yes, I know, sometimes we get stuck with He-who-must-never-be-named's dirty work ... not that I'm complaining too much!

"I'll deal with this, BillE," the ballsy little blonde said, standing in front of him. "Are you in charge?" she frowned at me.

"Well, strictly speaking, no, I'm not." I looked for her on my list, Mary Summers; department E for habitual offenders, she'd probably do quite well. I was in department E myself, once. I decided to keep her around for a bit.

"I want to speak to your boss," she spoke in a voice used to being obeyed.

"That won't be possible." I smiled pleasantly at her; "he only sees the really important inmates."

"Do you know who we are?" the guy who had no function asked. I checked my list, he had no name either ... oops, a mistake. I quickly wrote down John Smith; crime – child killer, he'd get lost in department G for eternity. *Pop* – he was gone.

"Yeah, man, how do we get out of here?" asked the portly record exec with the bad hair plugs.

"You serve your allotted time and are then reborn" I told him as I marked him off my list. *Pop* – he was gone.

"You're crazy, man, let me out of this room!" the dark haired hunk tried pushing past me. Jay: crime – arson, murder and sex with an underage boy, department C. I was about to send him off when he said: "Hey, there's no door."

This is another treasured part of my job – when they realize that it's not some massive Jeremy Beadle prank, it's real.

"No, you're quite right," I nodded; "there is no door."

"Where are we?" the tubby one asked – Craig, not so good looking but an able songwriter. "Are we dead? I mean, I saw your head on the floor man!" He looked at Jay in horror. I breathed in the panic, I love my job.

"Don't be crazy!" Jay frowned; "how can we be dead if we're standing right here?" He turned his head towards his dealer friend, absently rubbing his neck exactly where it had been detached from his body. "What the Hell did you give us, man?" The dealer shrugged his shoulders and kept his head bowed. There's always one who thinks if they keep quiet, we'll forget them, never works out that way. I checked him off the list and *pop* – he was gone.

"I think you've all gathered where you are by now," I said.

"Why are we here? Is this Hell?" one of the Swedish girls asked. "We don't know these guys; they only picked us up half an hour ago!" I checked my list – Lara Svenson – crime – matricide, department C. "You've made a mistake!" she protested.

"Have I?" I raised an eyebrow. She sunk to the floor weeping – *pop* – she was gone. I love my job, I love my job. Love it, love it.

"How do we get out of here?" Mary Summers asked, ever the negotiator.

"You serve your time ... I believe I already stated this."

"Isn't there another way out?" she moved closer, pushing her bouncy breasts against me. I admit that in my existence on Earth I would have been tempted to give her a pass, with what she was offering. However, since residing in the lower dimensions, the part that gave me certain impulses no longer functions. Shame, she would have made an interesting tit bit.

"The time is preset, I'm afraid." I gave her my most sympathetic smile. She glared at me; I could see her trying to figure a way out. Then I saw it flicker; sooner or later they all come round to it.

"There is a way out!" her eyes blazed.

"You're mistaken," I said.

"If this is really Hell," she looked around at her boys' hopeless faces; "can't we challenge you or something?" They always, always remember the song, or if they've got slightly more going on upstairs, the film. A challenge – I tried to look astounded, though acting was never my strong point.

"It isn't normal procedure," I lied.

"Well, I challenge you!" she said confidently.

"To what?" I asked, ticking the other Swede off my list; department C – *pop* – she was gone.

"A battle of the bands!" she said triumphantly. The boys looked at her with renewed optimism. None of them seemed to notice that the room was emptying around them. Only Mary Summers and the band remained. They never seem to notice when it's a big group, I've pondered it and I think it's because the room shrinks to fit the people in it. That or they just don't want to notice.

"Well," I said, pretending to consider it; "a battle of the bands?"

"You don't have a choice, do you?" she laughed.

"No." I looked at her, smiling. I asked; "tell me, Mary Summers ... what do you play in the band?"

"What do you mean?"

"You're not in the band."

"I'm their manager, they don't move without me!" Her voice was shaky as she watched her boys step away from her.

"Really?"

"Guys," she pleaded.

"It's nothing personal, Mary." Jay shrugged his shoulders.

"Yeah, it's just business," BillE smiled.

"You little turds!" was the last thing she said – *pop* – she was gone.

"Right. Boys, am I correct in thinking you wish to do battle using music as your weapon of choice?" Four perfectly coiffed heads nodded simultaneously. "I have to warn you that if you do not win you will be doomed to stay here, performing forever." I give this warning every time and they never listen. Never. "You could just do your time and leave," I said.

"If we win, do we get to leave now?" Craig asked.

"Yes, but, most don't win!" I told them firmly.

"Yeah, yeah, but if we do, we get to leave, right?" Mick-Z asked. I looked to my list. Mick-Z; crime – unstated, department G … must have been bad. Sometimes they don't tell me what it is. Afraid it might give me ideas. I looked at him with new interest, the last unstated I'd had through had been a Chilean dictator.

"*If* you win." I nodded.

"Right. We'll do it!" Mick-Z nodded his head at the others, who took a step nearer him.

"If you insist." I smiled. I *love* my job. Love, love, love it!

Only one person has ever won against my boss and that was a fluke. I stayed around and watched for a while. They weren't too bad, not my cup of tea. I much preferred Wagner's show. Man, was he angry when it finally dawned on him. It took the boys a couple of hours of singing the same song before they realized that they couldn't stop performing it. I did try to warn them. I suppose I should have told them who was doing the judging. But, they never asked. I popped back a few decades later to enjoy the show. They were no longer the superbly polished product they had been. Their eyes were sunken, desperate; the skin sickly pale; two were bald; two had long tendrils of matted gray hair clinging to their shoulders; flesh hung on their bones; the trendy outfits had long since disintegrated; their once yearned for nakedness would have sent their young fans screaming. Still they had to follow the same routine; slide stepping, back and forth, singing into the mike as though they were in love with it. It was a travesty; every moment was agony for them. I left them with glee in my heart. I LOVE MY JOB.

THE HOT HOUSE
by Nikki Guerlain

EDITOR'S NOTE

Nikki Guerlain lives in Portland, Oregon. She holds a B.S. in Fine Arts and a J.D. in B.S. She shares a birthday with Emily Dickinson and Meg White, which means she rocks through dictionaries like you wouldn't believe. Sitting with the Dead, *a screenplay she co-wrote with actor/comedian Ramsey Moore, is currently being used as a paperweight in various homes and offices across Hollywood and various parts of Texas.* Machine Gun Vacation, *her debut novel, is forthcoming from Thunderdome Press. Her work appears both online and in print. Links to work and more info can be found at radwriter.com.*

The glowing glass of the hot house, the long s-curve of my lover's shadow shooting up against the night, against steamy dripping walls, against another woman bracing herself against the blurred dark form of a potting table. Other small dark forms stick to the glass, airing their wings. Glass panes fogged, the hot house resembles one of those lamps that as soon as you turned it on, the heat from the bulb sends shadow images skittering across space.

Sucking hard on my cigarette, I bite it between my teeth to keep it in place, and throw a handful of sperm-like Whippee Snappies onto the street. Gravel against gunpowder. Pop. Pop. Pop.

Raindrops explode on the pavement. I let my binoculars hang against my chest while I open my umbrella. A wind brings leaves swirling up to my knees and one sticks to my leg like a scab.

I watch the Whippee Snappies wilt, then bloat pregnant with rain.

I bring the binoculars back up to my face. I imagine their grunts of pleasure as they jerk and pound amidst a flurry of swirling butterflies. Butterflies that just weeks ago I'd come across in an ad in the back of a magazine. It said I could order a kit and raise my very own butterfly garden. I'd thought the beautiful insects would enjoy the many exotic flowers my lover bought for this other woman, his frigid wife. I'd told him, "Your wife might like them. They might help her warm to you."

They shift their bodies into another position. In front of a cracked pane of glass. A previous casualty of my anger with him. The wife's back reclines against the broken, dripping pane. Her legs go up, ankles hooking around the back of his neck. A large plant looms behind them, its fronds extending out each side of my lover's torso. In that moment, their combined bodies morph into a hideous giant winged insect in the posture of a cat licking itself.

Obviously, the woman had warmed.

The raindrops grow bigger.

The air thickens.

I lose the umbrella, and the rain pelts me thick and hard.

The man places his palm against the glass by the woman's head to brace himself, as he pounds her harder and deeper.

I put my hand up as if to meet his hand with mine. He is so close.

His spasming wellspring is about to flood his sweet bounty; or at least, that's what he'd say, after all, he is a fucking poet.

Fucking poets.

I withdraw my hand from the air and place it into my pocket full of Whippee Snappies. I pinch them between my fingers. They explode harmlessly. The sky begins to grumble and crack.

Lightning explodes, quick-flashing swirling leaves caught midair. Glass explodes, followed by a scream that is just as quickly cut-off as it is started. The burning ether of the hot house billows into the night.

I lose sight of them in the steam and rain. The ether fog thins but then the lights go out in the hot house.

Irritated, I swipe the scabby leaf off my leg while I try to make out their figures in the darkness.

Another whip of lightning tears through the sky and then another and another, freeze-framing in staccato flesh, blood and bone hanging from the teeth of the glass pane that had given under my lover's rigor. The woman's half-severed head beats against the remaining glass stupidly, her body pushed further onto the glass by

her husband's still-ramming hips.
 He is oblivious to her great wound.

MAMA'S SPECIAL STEW
by Peggy A. Wheeler

EDITOR'S NOTE

Peggy Wheeler is also published under the name Peggy Dembicer. Her non-fiction appears in Colorado Serenity, Mountain Connection *and* Llewellyn's Magical Almanac. *Her poetry has appeared in a number of small press magazines and women's anthologies. Peggy has a B.A. in English Literature from UCLA and an MA in English with a Creative Writing emphasis from California State University at Northridge. While attending UCLA, she was one of only twelve students (and only undergraduate) chosen to study with Robert Pinsky, former Poet Laureate of the United States. She's won first prize awards for her poems from an Evergreen Women's Press nationwide poetry contest. Her poetry received honorable mentions from the judges of a Los Angeles Poetry Festival and The Academy of American Poets. Her poem "Du Fu" was nominated for a Rhysling award for Best Science Fiction Poem. She's led adult poetry and fiction writing critique groups and workshops in both Colorado and California. Currently, Peggy is the editor of the online literary magazine,* Straightjackets.

"Mama's Special Stew" was written by Peggy specifically for this anthology. When I asked her what led inspired her to come up with the tale, she said, "Dreadful Daughters is a fascinating theme. I spent hours mulling over possibilities until I hit on the premise for 'Mama's Special Stew', which tells the tale of the most dreadful of all daughters. What kind of demented offspring, or twisted sister (my apologies to the band of the same name), would do such a thing?" I've got to agree. And hats off to Peggy. Women Writing the Weird and Peggy Wheeler? Here's to the start of a very ... unusual friendship.

Maxine felt as though someone had kicked her in the forehead with a steel-toed boot.

Her eyelids were stuck shut. Opening them was painful. Worse, the second she did, she realized she was not at home. *How in hell did I get here?* Her stomach lurched. Acidic vomit rose in her throat with such combined force, volume and speed, she had only a micro second to turn her head and spew barf on the Pergo floor, missing the mattress she lie on by inches. She retched until nothing but bile and watery spittle splattered the faux red oak. *Jesus.* She attempted to shift her weight but found it almost impossible to move. It was as though her bones were made of granite. Everything in her body hurt. She managed to move her head a little so she could wipe her mouth on the edge of the pillow case. *Goddammit. Oh, Christ, my head hurts.* "Mama! Mama!" But, her words came out in weak croaks.

Thump, thump ... thump, thump ... thump, thump. Downstairs, her mother knocked around the old house. With each step, her prosthetic foot and single crutch bumped against the floor. *Thump, thump.* But the thumps receded rather than advanced.

Can't you hear me, Mama? Dammit. She passed out.

The last thing Maxine recalled was a conversation with her older sister. Kathy was the good girl, the pretty one with the thin thighs and wavy hair that Mama always loved so much. Maxine remembered feeling ... *what?* Put out? Angry? No, irritated. That's it. Irritated. *Damn, my head hurts. What did we talk about ... oh, yeah ... I remember. Mama.*

She'd been headed to bed with a book, when Kathy showed up unannounced and uninvited at the condo door. Maxine padded across the carpet in her bare feet, looked through the peep hole, unlatched the lock, and opened it a crack with one hand, pulling her robe around her with the other. "What are you doing here? Do you have any idea how late it is? Some people have to work, you know."

Kathy, the eldest of the three sisters, had married a man twice her age, Jim, some la-de-da big shot CEO who had done quite well for himself. While Kathy spent her time lunching at high-end bistros with other privileged women, Maxine worked a soul-sucking job, and only had one day off a week. Tomorrow, she had to be in early for a dull staff meeting that would go on for hours. To

186

keep from screaming, she'd have to bite her lips until they almost bled.

"Mind if I come in?"

"Yeah, but just for a minute. I really have to get to bed." She opened the door and stood to one side to permit her sister entrance. "I thought you and Jim were in Peru?" she said to Kathy.

Maxine plopped into an overstuffed rocker, tucking one foot under the other. Her older sister perched like a duchess with a stick up her ass on the edge of the sofa opposite her. "We returned early because Jim's meeting with his Chinese investors got moved up." Kathy took a deep breath, then released it through pursed lips. "Maxine, I have to ask you something. Why didn't you visit mom while we were away? I thought we agreed you would do that?"

Maxine rocked back and forth. "I didn't agree to any such thing, and besides, I had to work."

"You couldn't take an hour out of your day to visit Mama even once in two weeks?"

"Nope. Way too busy. But of course, since you've never worked a day in your life, you wouldn't understand."

Kathy rolled her eyes. "Oh, jeeze. Get over it Maxine, okay? Anyway…I dropped by Mama's place this afternoon. Do you know what I found?"

"Oh please, do tell me."

"Her house was an absolute filthy mess, she hadn't bathed in days, and guess what else?"

"What, Kathy? I'm exhausted and I have to get up early. Just *tell* me, and go, please."

"There was no fresh food in the refrigerator. Absolutely not one morsel. She was eating saltine crackers, for God sake. What if she'd gone into a diabetic coma? She could have died because you don't even give a shit enough to make sure she was okay."

"Sorry, but it's not my job to babysit Mama while you are vacationing at a five-star hotel in Peru. Why should I?"

"Oh, I don't know, Maxine, maybe because I was out of the country for two weeks and couldn't do it myself? Maybe because Mama was alone and needed you? Maybe because I asked you to?"

"She can't be on her own for two fucking weeks? Jesus. She

sees you every goddamn day. She doesn't give a crap about being with anyone but you, anyway." Maxine looked away. "That old bitch never cared about me, never. She loves you, sure. Me? Not so much. I put myself through school without a dime's help from her. I worked my ass off until I made senior manager. I bought this condo on my own, but nothing I do makes her happy. All she does is compare me to you, even though, you've done *what*, exactly? Married a rich guy and got a boob job? At every opportunity, she puts me down, berates me, humiliates me. And … she's gotten worse since Shannon disappeared. I do not want to visit her, and I do not want to take care of her, okay?"

Shannon was the youngest of the three. She'd always been self-centered and more than a little vain, but she was funny, outspoken and feisty. Although Shannon was three years younger than Maxine, with their identical chestnut hair, lucid green eyes, and boney frames, Maxine and Shannon could have been twins. Kathy, however, was taller than either of the other girls by five inches, and was a cat-eyed blonde with legs that went on forever.

Maxine loved Shannon. Five years before, at age twenty, after a screeching match with their mother, (ending when she told Mama she hated her), Shannon disappeared. Maxine grieved. Kathy kept her head about her. Mama devolved into hysterics, and then for reasons unknown, she blamed Maxine. "You and Shannon were the closest, so I would have expected you to be a better role model for your younger sister. If you were more like Kathy, Shannon would never have left, and I would have all three of my girls with me right now."

A few days after Shannon's disappearance, Mama lost feeling in her left foot. Her doctors said there was no way to save it. Kathy and Maxine went by every day to visit, but Mama put all her attention, and every ounce of her gratitude, into Kathy -- especially, after Kathy made a huge pot of what she dubbed, "Mama's Special Stew." She froze three months' worth of the meaty stuff in individual microwave containers, and stored it in their mother's refrigerator. Afterwards, all Mama could talk about was the delicious "special stew" Kathy made for her. "She's a gourmet cook, you know," she'd said to Maxine. "Not like you who can't even fry an egg without ruining it."

Maxine quit visiting because Mama talked so much about Kathy, how wonderful Kathy was, how smart Kathy was, how beautiful Kathy was. Never a kind word to Maxine, not ever.

"You and Jim have money," Maxine said. "Why don't you hire someone to take care of Mama while you gallivant around the world, and leave me out of it?"

Kathy sprung to her feet, and balled her hands into fists. "This is our mom you're talking about, *your* mom. She's sick, Maxine. With her diabetes she could die any second. She's alone. She needs her family, not some stranger. And, even if you don't think so, she needs you."

"And ... whose fault is it that she's alone? She drove Dad out with her constant badgering, bitching and moaning. And ... whose fault is it that she's sick? For decades, she ate nothing but cases of Milk Duds, and sucked down mimosas like tropical punch. She was bound to end up with diabetes, or cancer, or something. That bitch drove everyone away who ever loved her, except for you, of course. I hate her. And, it's her own fault that she ran out of food while you were gone, too. She knew you were leaving ... she could have stocked up beforehand. Did she and you really expect me to feed her every day for two weeks?"

Kathy looked as though she'd been gut shot. "Wait ... did you say you *hate*, Mama?" She looked out a window and whispered, "I guess I'm the only one of us girls who ever loved her. Shannon said she hated Mama, too, and that's why I had to ..."

"Yes, I hate her, and, yes, so did Shannon. But, if you are so fucking worried about Mama not having anything to eat, why don't you make her another twenty gallons of that goddamn 'special stew' she raved about for years?"

Kathy sat still as a rock staring at a wall behind Maxine.

"Hello?" Maxine said, leaning forward waving her hands in front of Kathy's face. "Anyone home? Are you still with me?"

Kathy shook her head as though knocking cobwebs out of her ears. Her face broke into a warm smile. Her voice brightened like a canary's. "You know something? I think I *will* do *just* that ... make 'Mama's Special Stew'." She reached for her purse. "Oh ...

before I forget, I brought you something from Peru." She stuck her manicured hand into the Gucci bag and rifled through the contents. "*There* it is." She extracted a small glass bottle, engraved with rose buds, filled with deep crimson liquid. She held it to the light. "This beautiful stuff is *Aperitif de Las Rosas*, a liquor that Peruvians say is not made from rose petals, but from the 'sweat of angels.' How 'bout we open it, and have a taste, then I'll be on my way."

Maxine wrinkled her brow and cocked her brow. "What the fuck? I don't get you. I thought you were one hundred percent pissed off at me about Mama? Just two seconds ago, you were…"

"…it's late, and you're tired, and I'm tired. We can talk about Mama another day. Go fetch a couple of glasses, while I open the bottle."

In the musky guestroom of her mother's house, although it felt as though her head was filled with razor blades, Maxine struggled to get off the bed and stand. She couldn't. Her legs, rubbery and slack, didn't' work. Her arms stayed loose at her sides, useless. *What the hell?* She opened her mouth, and tried to call out a second time. "Mama. Dammit, Mama!" *Shit* … no sound from her raw throat other than croaks and squeaks. She listened to incessant clanging and banging of pots and pans below. *No way can she hear me, with whatever she's up to in the kitchen. No way.*

The sound of footsteps ascending the stairs filtered to her through the closed door, *Thank God.* But, when the door opened, permitting a rush of blessed light to flood the room, instead of Mama, Kathy entered. "Look at this mess you've made all over the floor." She held her nose. "Christ! It stinks in here." She exited, closing the door behind her leaving Maxine once again in darkness.

"Kathy. Come back." Maxine's voice was nothing more than a pale whisper.

A few minutes later, Kathy returned with a mop and bucket. The sickening smell of Pine Sol caused Maxine to wretch again, but her stomach was empty. "What are you doing here?" She croaked. "What happened? How did I get here? Where's Mama?"

"Shhh … don't try to talk. Mama's sleeping." She shrugged.

"Of course, with that voice of yours, she wouldn't hear you anyway." She clapped her hands together once. "Alright, then, I've got an enormous pot of salted water simmering on the stove, and I've sliced the vegetables, minced the fresh herbs. Everything is ready to go into the stew but the meat."

"What in Christ's name are you doing, Kathy? What's going on?"

"A Peruvian *brujo* blended that lovely red liquor especially for me. I had to pay quite a bit for it, but it's worth every penny." She paused to extract a pair of shears from the armoire. "You know? Shannon was more difficult. I had to subdue her with a brick to the head. This is far easier." She stepped to the closet and retracted a roll of plastic. With the shears, she cut it into large neat pieces. She covered the floor, smoothing the plastic into place with the palms of her hands, then she bounced to her feet. "A bit of vomit is one thing, but we don't want to get Mama's new Pergo all bloody, do we?"

Maxine attempted to thrash and twist, but her arms and legs were waterlogged sticks, clumsy and inoperable. "Kathy, please. What are you going to do?"

"Now, now, Maxine. Lie still. Don't try to move. You can't anyway. The potion is a paralytic. They tell me the way it works is this: take a sip, pass out, wake up with an excruciating headache, nauseated to beat the band, hardly able to talk, and unable to move well or walk at all. The effects last about three hours, but we won't need that long."

"But, why?" Huge tears rolled from Maxine's eyes and down the sides of her cheeks, damping the pillowcase. "Why?"

"You hate Mama. Shannon hated Mama. That's simply not fair, especially since our little mother loved the two of you so very much. Someone has to be a responsible daughter and take care of Mama. So … you should be pleased to know that, per your earlier suggestion, I am making another big batch of 'Mama's Special Stew'."

Kathy moved to the side of the bed, the plastic sheeting crackling beneath her feet. She bent down, squinted, looked into Maxine's eyes, then straightened, and shook her head. "Shame on you for hating Mama." Grasping the handle in her right fist, Kathy raised the scissors above her head.

PENELOPE NAPOLITANO AND THE BUTTERFLIES
by Aliya Whiteley

EDITOR'S NOTE

The stories of Aliya Whiteley have appeared in The Guardian, McSweeney's Internet Tendency, Strange Horizons, Word Riot, Per Contra, The Drabblecast, *and others. Her first collection,* Witchcraft in the Harem, *was published in 2013 by Dog Horn Publishing. World Fantasy Award winner Lavie Tidhar described it as "like being waterboarded by an angel". She has also written two comic novels, both of which were published by Macmillan. Her website can be found at aliyawhiteley.wordpress.com and she tweets most days as @ AliyaWhiteley.*

"Penelope Napolitano started out as a joint project with a friend," says Aliya. "He wrote the story of a boy, adrift on an island, pining for his mother, and it provoked an equal and opposite reaction in me. I didn't want islands and pining. I wanted air travel and the rejection of all that feels familiar. I wrote the first section of Penelope Napolitano, and she was soon refusing to meet up with the boy on the island, so the stories were untangled by mutual agreement. I remember that my daughter was fascinated with butterflies at the time, so when they popped up it wasn't too much of a surprise. The digestive biscuits, though – I have no idea where that came from. But maybe that's a necessary part of storytelling. There are parts that make straightforward sense and parts that take you by surprise, and the strongest images come when you mix them together." I must say, Penelope and her butterflies and her digestive biscuits were an extremely delightful surprise when they fluttered across my inbox, and a reminder that we only ever know about another person what they're willing to let us see.

You can travel the world, you can see Kuala Lumpur and the Cote D'Azur, go everywhere, try anything; but it all comes down to one moment where you realise you're about to get engaged to a deeply lovely man who is undoubtedly going to turn you into your mother.

I'm only against turning into my mother on principle. She's a lovely woman, with a habit of phoning my mobile at inappropriate moments; say, in the middle of my snowboarding session. She likes digestive biscuits and fairy tales. She lives in Berkshire; has done all her life.

"Yes," I shout, over the noise of the burners, "Yes, I'll marry you."

Tim's glorious smile, the one that I fell in love with, spreads to his ears, and over the faces of the other couple and the driver. Is driver the right word? Steerist, then. Airman. The man with his hand on the valve that makes this hot air balloon ascend, that's who I'm looking at, with his amused, patient expression that means *I've seen this all before.* Maybe he doesn't even believe in love any more, with all the upping and downing he's done, and so many popped questions and champagne corks. He's probably thinking, as he bends down to flip open the lid of the coolbox, that he'd never marry a person who asked that kind of death-defyingly important question in public, with onlookers. That's what I always thought, until this moment. I'm having to revise my opinion of myself.

He produces a bottle of Bollinger and four plastic glasses. "Congratulations!" shout the other couple, and the champagne is poured.

I shout, "thanks, wow, thanks, amazing," and I can't take in the view, the soaring, razored peaks of the Rockies, because I have to drink and smile at these total strangers with expensive ski-jackets and messy, hot-air-balloon hair. That's suddenly become more important to me, making a good show. I'm my mother already.

Happy? mouths Tim.

The driver/airman/balloonist guy pulls a cord and turns a knob, and the burners diminish. We hang, for a weightless moment, and then begin to sink.

When I was little, sitting on the number 54 bus to Reading town centre, my mother would tell me stories about far-off places, and I used to ask her if they were real. I couldn't believe that there wasn't a kernel of truth in her tales of magic carpets and pirate galleons. There was one about a boy who lived on an island, a paradise, and he couldn't whistle. All he wanted was to be able to whistle. Such a small thing, and he couldn't do it; why did he make himself so miserable? My seven year old self couldn't understand it. Why reach for that which is beyond you? Why refuse to see the beauty of what is right in front of you?

Tim is gripping his plastic champagne glass in his enormous green ski-gloves. He's wearing a white strip of sunblock on the bridge of his nose, and he hasn't shaved for a few days, giving him a dusting of desirable stubble, and the appearance of a wild adventurer. I've known him for nine months; he's here on secondment from an insurance company in Slough. Nine more months and he expects to return home to England. With me.

Can't real love be unsure? Can't it be delicate, wavering, affected by strong breezes? Must true love be like the mountains, so solid against all doubts?

There's a big orange butterfly sitting on the wicker basket.

With the burners turned down, I can hear the *Oooooh!* sounds of the other couple.

"It's a Monarch," says the driver.

One of my mother's stories comes back to me. We're on the bus, heading back from shopping on a Saturday afternoon.

There's a big orange butterfly, the King of butterflies, she says, *and some tribes believe that if you capture it and whisper a wish to it, it will hold that wish for you because it has no choice but to be silent. But if you then let it go, in gratitude it will grant your wish.*

I ask her, as we pass the trading estate – *is that true?*

No, Penelope, she says. *It's all pretend.*

Back in this new life, I reach out, very slowly, and take the butterfly in my hands. I lift it to my lips and whisper to it. I can feel it listening.

"Look!" says Tim. He's pointing to a squall on the horizon, a twisting orange cloud, moving fast, shimmering, falling over itself to reach us, and then a million Monarch butterflies are in my mouth and hair and hands, and I can hear their wings beating against the balloon, a sudden thunderstorm, deafening. They surround me, raise me up on their wings; I feel them, like a hammock, and then there's no longer a basket, a balloon, a solid fiancé. There's only the air and the butterflies, taking me away, granting a wish for which

I had no hopes.

Some of my mother's stories might be true after all.

I am borne away.

The soft touch of their wings on my skin makes me ticklish at first; in the midst of their silence, I can't help laughing. I don't see much of the view as I giggle my way around the Rockies. Occasionally the ball of orange wings and black legs parts to form a window of sky or a glimpse of a clean white mountain: Grey's Peak, perhaps, or Mount Evans. I don't know. Colorado is beneath me, spread out like a map with no markers. Time is marked to the beat of insect's wings.

As the minutes pass, the kaleidoscope of their spiralling bodies lulls me. The freezing air that tangles my hair and makes gooseflesh of my skin becomes inconsequential; I am safe in the giant fluttering heart they have made for me. I am, undoubtedly, the luckiest woman alive: blessed, rescued, reborn at the will of the butterflies.

Of course, eventually, I get hungry and thirsty. The fun aspect of the adventure begins to wear off.

"I want to get down," I whisper to the butterflies, and then I amend that sentiment to, "I'd like to be put down safely. Please. If it's not too much trouble." I don't feel a change in their course, and for a minute I have scary thoughts of staying up here in their ball of movement forever until I'm a skeleton, a ghost, only a strange memory in Tim's mind. But then I'm lifted upright on their wings and I feel my hiking shoes touch something solid.

The orange cloud shrinks away from me and disperses. I'm standing on the side of a freeway, next to a turnoff for a diner, the dated neon sign barely blinking in the strong sunlight. The Rockies are only a backdrop; this road is long and straight and without incline. There's nobody in sight. It's open country out here, but not desert – the ground is lush, grassy, and there's a feeling of dampness to the warm air.

It takes a few attempts at walking before my legs start moving properly. I wobble up to the diner. It's one of those flat shiny buildings that Americans seem to like, and when I push open the door I feel I've walked into the set of a movie. There are red leather booths on my right and circular stools, the kind that spin, on my left, in front of a long counter with hot plates and a coffee machine that makes a reassuring plopping sound every now and again. The smell of bacon makes my stomach rumble. I make it to one of the booths.

While waiting for someone to serve me, I try to comb my fingers through my hair, but its one gigantic knot, as if I've just been driven at high speed in an open-top convertible. Which, I suppose, I have.

I hear a door slam, and the sloppy clip-clop of heels on vinyl flooring. A woman walks in from the open doorway behind the counter that I assume leads to the kitchen. She's wearing an orange dress with a black name tag, and a white Alice band in her black hair. She clocks me, and her eyes widen. She clip-clops over, biting her lips, pulling out a small pad and pencil from her breast pocket.

"Hello," I say.

"Hey. What can I get ya?"

"Coffee and a bacon sandwich please. And I'm betting you have pie, right? Lots of pie. Do you have apple pie?"

"Sure thing, hon," she says, with good humour. She is just what every American waitress should be.

"Do you have a map or something I could borrow?"

She tilts her head as she writes on the pad. "Not much call for that around here."

"For maps?"

"It's not like you get to have a say in where you're going, so, why take the time to look it up? I'll bring your coffee right over, just sit tight, hon." She gives me a reassuring smile that has the opposite effect. Why am I getting no say? What kind of a diner is this? And why is the waitress wearing an orange dress in the exact same shade as the wings of a monarch butterfly?

When I begin to actually think about it, it becomes obvious that I've gone crazy and probably jumped out of a hot air balloon in order to escape commitment and this is a moment of death dream type thing, so I hyperventilate for a while, and hit my head on the table a few times in the hope I'll wake up and find myself still alive.

If that makes sense.

When the waitress brings over my coffee, she also brings a brown paper bag. "Breathe into that, hon." She holds it to my lips and eventually I stop trying to suck up all the air in the world all at once. "Don't fight it so hard, okay? You're not crazy and you're not dead. You're flying Monarch, hon. Relax and enjoy it."

"Pardon?"

"The Butterfly Express Route? To Happiness? That's what you wished for, right?"

"Not exactly." I sip the coffee. It's delicious. "I wished for..." What did I wish for? And why would a butterfly take me seriously?

I look around the diner, at the empty booths and the clean shiny floor, and I notice that the pictures spaced evenly along the walls are all framed photographs of butterflies. Orange butterflies. For some reason, they calm me. This experience makes no sense, but at least it's consistent.

"You wished for some kinda answer. To everything. To why you are the way you are, and where you're meant to be," she says, smoothing her wiry black hair from her face.

"This is the weirdest dream ever."

"Hang on in there, hon. I'll get your bacon." She pats me on the arm and clip-clops back to the kitchen.

I hear, from nowhere, the theme tune to *The Muppet Show*.

Wait; it's not from nowhere. It's from the inner pocket of my ski jacket. It's my mobile phone. I unzip the jacket and dig out my phone. The display says –

very important phone call which you should definitely take, Penelope

which is weird. It's never used that tone of text with me before.

"Hello?"

"Hello Pennie, love, have I caught you at a bad moment?"

"No, it's perfect timing," I tell my mother. "Listen, I'm, I'm at this place, this diner, and it's like..."

"Are you having some dinner? What time is it over there? I

198

was worried you'd be in bed."

"Why? What's the time?" It's broad daylight outside, but suddenly I'm suspicious of that, of time and place and the entire universe and my assumptions about it. "Are you okay, mum? Have you seen any butterflies?"

"Butterflies? It's October."

"Listen, don't worry about me, okay? No matter what you hear, I'm okay."

"Okay," she says, her voice peppered with suspicion.

"Some stories are true after all."

"Well," she says. There's a pause. "I would have thought you'd have worked that out by now. And some truths we all rely on have never been true at all."

I can't begin to deal with that concept. "What do you mean?"

"Pennie?"

"Yeah."

"I don't like digestive biscuits."

My bacon sandwich arrives. My waitress puts the orange-rimmed plate down on the table and winks, and the phone goes dead. "Better eat up," she says. "Restroom's out back if you need it. Your ride leaves in five."

They get me down to Mexico in no time at all. Or, at least, with no helpful sign of time passing: no sunrises, no nights, and no desire to be either awake or asleep. I drift along, stopping occasionally for steak and eggs or blueberry pancakes, and my mobile stays surprisingly silent. Why has Tim not phoned me? Does he not love me at all? And what about my mother? I think about phoning her back and continuing our conversation about digestive biscuits but I don't want to find out more. What did she mean, that she never liked them? Then why has she always eaten two of them with a small cup of tea after dinner? Why does she put them in the shopping trolley every week? The thought that she has eaten digestives against her will for decades bothers me more than the fact that I'm being carried to a new country on a cloud of butterflies.

When we arrive at the next diner I take the phone from my pocket and stare at the screen. It's dead.

I know we're in Mexico because there's a sombrero obscuring the neon sign and the waitress in the orange dress has adopted a terrible fake accent.

"Eh, gringo," she says, "You want the tacos?"

"Whatever."

"They are the best in all Mehico."

"I don't doubt it." I plonk myself down in the booth, and she drops the accent.

"What's up?"

"I don't know where we're going. I don't know what I'm doing. It's been one hell of a ride, but, seriously, Mexico? What's in Mexico?"

"The spawning grounds," she says, as if that were painfully obvious. "The Butterfly Biosphere reserve, on the border of Michoacan. Every October the butterflies travel, millions of them, to that one place. And there, everything becomes still. They sit on the trees. Peace reigns. It's a moment of inner contentment that few are blessed with. Trust me, things will become clear to you there. Things that weren't clear before. Like whether you should get married and why your mother never liked digestive biscuits."

"Oh," I say. "Right. In that case, I'll have the tacos."

She nods, puts away her notepad, and clip-clops back to the kitchen.

Given that such an amazing life experience awaits me at The Biosphere, I feel surprisingly calm. I think all emotion is leaving me; I'm emptying out my fear, my pain, my excitement and my happiness. My feelings for Tim no longer seem real. They've been chased away by the flapping of a million orange wings.

When the tacos arrive I can't even appreciate their spiciness. My tongue is as dead as my heart.

It's midnight at The Biosphere. The moon is enormous, full to bursting. The butterflies cling to the black trees, spent, breathless.

I lie in the grass, surrounded by the pillars of their exhaustion, a testament to their journey. Thousands of miles have been traveled.

I take my mobile from my pocket. It's dead.

"Mum," I whisper. "I'm ready." And the phone comes to life, and dials home. My mother answers. I picture her, standing in the hall, next to the phone's cradle even though I bought her a cordless last Christmas. She's never got used to the idea that she's free to move around.

"Digestive biscuits," I say. It's the first thing that I think of.

"Pardon?"

"You don't like them."

"No, not much." She sighs. "Are you sure you're ready for this story, love? Only you've never seemed very ready to hear anything real I had to say before. Particularly about your dad."

"Yes," I say. "Maybe that's true. But I feel ready now. I'm in a different place."

"Yes," she agrees. "You sound different." The butterflies move their trembling wings to my heartbeats. "I moved to Napoli. Three years before you were born. Your dad was homesick, and I said I would try living there. We moved in with his mother. You're very like her. She wasn't good at listening either. That's not always a bad thing, I mean, you know your own mind. I've never been so sure as you. About anything. But I knew I didn't like Napoli."

"Why not?"

"There was nothing for me to hold on to, nothing familiar to anchor me. I felt so... up in the air."

"But that can be a good thing!" I say. "You've never been open to it. But to be free, to be weightless, it can be..."

"Can I tell you the rest?" my mother says. "Please? Right. Your dad knew I was unhappy. He tried so hard to help me settle in. The only English food he could find in the market were packets of digestive biscuits; he brought them home from work with him every day, and I didn't have the heart to tell him I'd never really liked them. His mother called them disgusting. She couldn't see what was wrong with the amaretti she made; she took it as a rejection. Which it was. I did reject her, and everything Italian. I didn't really try very hard. I can admit that now. I cried and cried.

Eventually I persuaded your dad to give up his job and return to England with me. He was never really right, after that. He thought he'd let his mother down, somehow, and I didn't care enough about that to realise it would be the end of us. Just after you were born his mother had a stroke. He went back to Napoli to care for her, and after she died he never came back. I never asked him to come back, I suppose. Yes. I never once asked him to come back, and if you don't chase what you want, it doesn't happen."

"Why didn't you ask him?" I say.

There is a silence. Then she says, "So I keep buying the digestive biscuits because they remind me of him. And because I think I don't deserve to eat amaretti. His mother made the most wonderful amaretti."

"So there was one thing about Napoli you liked."

"Yes, love, I suppose there was."

I say goodbye and put away my phone. I think about what she has told me, and why I would never have understood it before this moment. But I have been weightless, babied, on the wings of a dream. I know that it is not enough to be carried away to a new place.

You have to know what to do when you get there.

I close my eyes and whistle a nameless tune. I think about the place to which Tim wants to take me. I can picture it clearly. There will not be butterflies, or hot air balloons. But there will be digestive biscuits. My mother is right; I'm not like her. I know my own mind, and I happen to quite like digestive biscuits.

When the butterflies are ready to return to Canada, maybe they will touch down along the way and bring me back to Tim. I'm going to give him a real answer.

TOWER AND THE TURTLE
by Charie D. La Marr

EDITOR'S NOTE

Distantly related to Mary Shelley on her father's side, Charie D. La Marr has created a genre called Circuspunk (listed at Urban Dictionary*) and released a book of short stories in the genre called* Bumping Noses and Cherry Pie. *She also has a dark urban fantasy out called* The Squid Whores of the Fulton Fish Market. *She also has upcoming stories in Alex S. Johnson's* Axes of Evil, *James Ward Kirk's* Bones Ugly Babies 2 *and* Memento Mori, *and many other anthologies. She was September's featured writer at* Solarcide. *She is known for writing in many different genres from crime to bizarro to erotica and even Seussian. Known as a redhead with a redheaded attitude, she lives in NY with her mother and son Travis and three furchildren: Bailey, Ruth and Casey.*

"This is a satirical work," Charie says, "based on a situation that has become very common these days – the single sex family and the adopted child. It is meant to point out the absurdity in people who find this situation unacceptable and wrong. I like to write stories using social situations and take them to the absurd as a way of pointing out how silly such attitudes reallly are by putting them in a humorous light." *While Tower isn't really very dreadful, she certainly gets an answer to that age old question – exactly what does a bear do in the woods?*

Tower Ursidae-Perkins was sixteen years old and deep in the throes of her first love. Her parents were anything but happy and it was easy to see why. The object of Tower's affection was a turtle named Myrtle.

Myrtle originally belonged to Tower's best friends Brendan and Conrad Hastings – twins whose parents were both in the psychiatric field. Sadly, the Hastings twins needed psychiatric care more than any of their parents' patients. Other parents whispered about them and called them "The Crash Dummies" and pretended that their birthday party invitations got lost in the mail. Tower wasn't just their best friend, she was their only friend. Dr. and Dr. Hastings had little time for their boys, and that's where Myrtle came in. The twins were hooked on a cartoon show about turtles and their parents bought them Myrtle as a way to compensate for not spending time with them. The turtle became sort of a substitute parent. But when Mr. Dr. Hastings got an offer to join a celebrity psychiatric office in Beverly Hills, Myrtle had to stay behind. And so the turtle found a new home with Tower.

Myrtle was an ordinary land turtle. About ten pounds of slow moving, slobbering ugliness of indeterminate age that came from a pet shop owner who was more than happy to unload it on the Dr. Hastings family for a hundred bucks, including cage and water bottle. At first, Tower saw Myrtle as nothing more than a pet. She fed it lettuce and an assortment of other crudité, gave it water, cleaned out its cage and stroked its striped head once in a while.

But gradually it became something much more. Maybe it was the way the turtle splayed its feet with those long nails. Or maybe it was the way it opened its mouth when she brought it food. But soon, Tower started having certain impure thoughts about Myrtle. It started when she began to wonder what it would be like to put her little finger in its mouth and have it suck on her. Soon, the idea of using the turtle's tail to give her orgasms started to fill her waking moments. A precocious teenager, Tower began researching turtle sexing on the Internet, learning that they have something called a clocoa – something that serves as a poop chute, pee hole and penis sheath or baby maker – a sort of turtle revolving door. In females, it is near the base of the tail. In males, closer to the tip. Myrtle's was very close to the tip. She also learned that if the turtle's underbelly was concave, it was a male – designed to fit better over top of the female they they mated. Lastly, those front claws that Tower loved so much were very long – designed for courtship. According to all the signs, Myrtle was a male.

The Internet said that a male turtle of Myrtle's size and weight could have schlong as long as 11.8 inches and that turtles do it doggie style. Tower even watched some pretty graphic videos. They made her excited and damp. She imagined Myrtle scratching her naked belly with those long claws. And if a female turtle could take an 11.8 turtle tube, Myrtle could surely take on Tower.

One day, her father Tad caught her with Myrtle on her bed, examining it from the rear. He asked what was going on. Tower said she thought the turtle had something stuck to its tail. However Tad noticed the jar of Vaseline sticking out from under her pillow. Clearly something was happening. A parental talk was in order.

And so, the following day after school, Tower's parents were sitting on the sofa waiting for her.

"Tower," her father Tad said. "I think we need to have a talk about what's going on with you and Myrtle. I may be wrong, but I think I witnessed some inappropriate behavior last night. Honey, Myrtle is a turtle. And playing amateur gynecologist with it is just not what a child your age should be doing with a pet. We're thinking the turtle was a bad idea. It has to go."

"I love Myrtle, Dad. I think I've always loved Myrtle. Even when it belonged to The Crash Dummies, I think we shared something special."

"But it's a turtle."

"Yeah, it's a turtle," Tower said. "And look at you. You're married to a bear."

Tower's other father Hal squirmed nervously on the couch.

"That's true, Tower," Tad said, running his hand through Hal's hairy chest. "Hal is a bear. And when you're older, maybe you'll understand the attraction that some men have for bears."

"Yeah, I get it. Bears who are hairy fat gay guys, but Hal's a Canadian Brown Bear!" Tower said. "He eats salmon whole. He shits in the woods behind our house!"

"Hey there," Hal said. "You know we have a set of rules for our discussions, and that is out of bounds. Yes, I am a brown bear, and yes, salmon is tasty. And I do shit in the woods, but I always bury it. Have you ever noticed how lush and green our woods are compared to everyone else in the neighborhood? That's from my fertilizer, and don't you forget it. Have you ever smelled that turtle's cage? It stinks to high heaven!"

"And have you ever followed Tad into the bathroom after a session with *New Yorker Magazine*?"

"Hey, I use air freshener, young lady," Tad said. "And we have those oily scented sticks, too. The bathroom is not malodorous when I leave it. That's hitting below the belt, Tower. Hate talk! Out of bounds! Out of bounds!"

Tower groaned and kicked the neatly stacked assortment of art coffee table books onto the floor.

"Acting out – another violation, Tower. Acts of violence are forbidden here. This is a peaceful family."

Tad walked over and put his arms around his daughter's shoulders. "Tower, believe me, I understand. Your grandparents had their reservations about Hal at first. They tried to talk me out of it, but the attraction was just too strong. And look at what a great provider he's turned out to be. His Internet leather company is booming. Last month he added dongs and butt plugs to the line and..."

"I don't want to hear it!" Tower said, putting her hands over her ears.

"Tower, we've always been open and honest with you regarding our sexuality. And you help out a lot with filling orders for The Bear's Lair. We've never made it a secret about what all those things were you were packing up for our customers. We've explained it all to you." Hal said. "You know what dongs and butt plugs are for."

"Gee, let's see. I have two fathers. One of them is a bear and sells sex toys online. The other one is a full time housewife who vacuums in shirtwaist dresses, heels and pearls. I'd say he was just like June Cleaver, only there's no beaver involved. They named me Tower, which couldn't be more phallic. And they wonder why I'm fucked up?"

"F-bomb violation! Sarcasm! And defensive attitude! That is out of line! We named you Tower because you were our princess in an ivory tower. It had nothing to do with being phallic. We've told you that. You know the rules of discussions in this family, young lady," Tad said.

"You know, I get it now. You've always told me that you didn't care what direction my sexuality took as long as I was happy. But you didn't really mean that. You wanted a boy! All those birthday parties with superhero themes. Superheroes are nothing but guys who put their underpants on last. Those vacation trips to biker rallies with all those hairy fat guys. Those evenings at the Ballet Trocadero."

"Hey, I happen to think those men do a wonderful job with Swan Lake, Tower. We just wanted you to have some culture in your life. Does it really matter if the part of the Black Swan is danced by a man or a woman? Haven't we told you that approximately one quarter of all black swan pairings are gay?" Tad asked.

"You want me to be just like you!" Tower yelled.

"Well, we did hope that we were setting a very good example for you of a loving, stable same-sex family," Hal said. "Tad and I are very much in love. We've never let the fact that I'm a bear stand in our way."

"And I love Myrtle! And he's a boy, by the way. I've changed his name to Myron."

"But dear, it's still a turtle. It's not even a mammal. So tell us what this is really about. Do you like boys? We know you listen to that Justin Bieber person. Is this your way of rebelling against us and all that we stand for? But you know you can come out if you want to though—if that's what you really feel. A lot of young people are. Ellen Page just did and she is just fine with it. Clay Aiken is running for Congress. You like Glee, and they have at least two. We would be proud to have a gay daughter. But we aren't pushing you, Tower. We just want you to be happy. Tell us what you want us to do. Should we take the rainbow flag down from the flagpole out front? Are you ashamed of us? Do you want to skip the Village People concert next month? Fine. Miss the Pride Parade? Good, we won't go. But we simply cannot allow you to play with a turtle in a sexual manner," Tad said, shaking his head. "Oh my, I wish Dr. and Dr. Hastings were still here. One of them would know what to do."

"They couldn't even handle their own kids! And I don't need a psychiatrist. I need parents who understand me and are willing to let me find my own way in life just the way they found theirs!" Tower stormed into her room and locked the door behind her.

"Locking yourself behind closed doors! That's a discussion

ending violation, young lady. You know that isn't how we solve problems in this house. We work them out and end with hugs." Hal said.

"I don't care anymore!" Tower yelled. "Maybe Myron and I don't want to live in this house anymore!"

She walked over to the turtle's cage and leaned down. Myron poked his nose between the bars and they nuzzled. Tower stuck a finger in the cage and Myron wrapped his claws around it.

"It's okay, Myron. They just don't understand. I'll find a way for us to be together. I promise you."

The following morning, Tower packed a bag, took Myron in his cage and set out for the bus station in search of her birth mother. She had very little to go on. All she knew was that her name was Cindy and she was a dancer from Sin City. Vegas – over two thousand miles away from her New York home. With all the money she had saved up, she bought a bus ticket and sat in the station waiting.

When she got on the bus, she tucked her suitcase in the overhead and pushed Myron underneath the seat. She hated that he had to ride that way, but those were the rules. Every so often, she reached her hand down and lovingly stroked his head.

They had to change buses in Lincoln, Nebraska. It was a long wait and Tower was hungry. So was Myron. She went off in search of a McDonald's and got a couple burgers. She shared the lettuce and tomato with the turtle. Then she fell asleep on the bench. The next thing she knew, she heard the last call for her bus. She grabbed her bag and took off running. The bus was about two states closer to Nevada when she realized her mistake. She'd left Myron under the seat at the bus station in Nebraska. When she arrived in Vegas, the bus company checked the station, but Myron was nowhere to be found. Just about the time that Tower got the bad news, the police showed up and took her to the airport to send her home to her worried fathers.

When she got home, Myron was back in his cage in her bedroom. The bus company had found the turtle, put it on a bus and sent it home in the luggage compartment. Tower was overjoyed to see him.

"Tower," Tad said. "Hal and I have discussed this. We're willing to let you have some time to work this out. I won't deny that we hope you grow out of it, but if Myron is your choice, we'll do our best to be happy about it." They group hugged.

That was all a few years ago. After some sexual exploration that is kind of hard and too disgusting to explain at this time, Tower eventually broke her obsession with Myron and started paying attention to boys, much to her fathers' silent dismay. By her sophomore year in college, she'd met a gender confused boy named Stephanie; son of two hippie parents, and got knocked up. Stephanie, Tower and their daughter Five now live with Ted and Hal and are currently trying to sell a reality show based on their unusual family. Myron still lives with them. Five's first word was "turtle".

Out Now:
Women Writing the Weird
Edited by Deb Hoag

WEIRD
1.   Eldritch: suggesting the operation of supernatural influences; "an eldritch screech"; "the three weird sisters"; "stumps .. . had uncanny shapes as of monstrous creatures" – John Galsworthy; "an unearthly light"; "he could hear the unearthly scream of some curlew piercing the din" – Henry Kingsley
2.   Wyrd: fate personified; any one of the three Weird Sisters
3.   Strikingly odd or unusual; "some trick of the moonlight; some weird effect of shadow" – Bram Stoker

WEIRD FICTION
1.   Stories that delight, surprise, that hang about the dusky edges of 'mainstream' fiction with characters, settings, plots that abandon the normal and mundane and explore new ideas, themes and ways of being. – Deb Hoag

RRP: £14.99 ($28.95).

featuring
Nancy A. Collins, Eugie Foster, Janice Lee, Rachel Kendall,
Candy Caradoc, Mysty Unger, Roberta Lawson, Sara Genge,
Gina Ranalli, Deb Hoag, C. M. Vernon, Aliette de Bodard,
Caroline M. Yoachim, Flavia Testa, Aimee C. Amodio, Ann
Hagman Cardinal, Rachel Turner, Wendy Jane Muzlanova, Katie
Coyle, Helen Burke, Janis Butler Holm, J.S. Breukelaar,
Carol Novack, Tantra Bensko, Nancy DiMauro,
and Moira McPartlin.

ND - #0498 - 270225 - C0 - 229/152/17 - PB - 9781907133442 - Matt Lamination